KEL
Sensations
#2

DATE DUE	1.09	
JAN 2 8 2009		
MAR 0 3 2009		
APR 2 5 2009		
JUN 0 9 2009		
JUN 1 0 2010		
NOV 0 8 2010		
NOV 2 6 2010		
FEB 0 1 2013		
FEB 0 9 2018		
GAYLORD		PRINTED IN U.S.A.

WITHDRAWN OCCTPL

ECHO

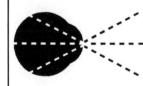 This Large Print Book carries the
Seal of Approval of N.A.V.H.

SENSATIONS, BOOK 2

ECHO

A SILENT PLEA TO BE HEARD, A DESPERATE CRY TO BE FOUND

C. L. KELLY

THORNDIKE PRESS
A part of Gale, Cengage Learning

GALE
CENGAGE Learning

Detroit • New York • San Francisco • New Haven, Conn • Waterville, Maine • London

GALE
CENGAGE Learning

Copyright © 2007 by Clint Kelly.
All Scripture quotations are taken from The New King James Bible Version. Copyright © 1979, 1980, 1982. Thomas Nelson, Inc. Other quotations are the author's paraphrase.
Thorndike Press, a part of Gale, Cengage Learning.

LIBRARY OF CONGRESS CATALOGING-IN-PUBLICATION DATA

Kelly, Clint.
   Echo : a silent plea to be heard, a desperate cry to be found / by C.L. Kelly.
      p. cm. — (Sensations ; bk. 2) (Thorndike Press large print Christian fiction)
   ISBN-13: 978-1-4104-1215-7 (alk. paper)
   ISBN-10: 1-4104-1215-6 (alk. paper)
   1. Campers (Persons)—Fiction. 2. Cascade Range—Fiction. 3. Deaf children—Fiction. 4. Missing children—Fiction. 5. Senses and sensation—Fiction. 6. Large type books. I. Title.
PS3561.E3929E35 2009
813'.54—dc22
                                    2008042578

Published in 2009 by arrangement with The Zondervan Corporation LLC.

Printed in the United States of America
1 2 3 4 5 6 7 12 11 10 09 08

For Shane — my son, my friend,
God's grace.

PREFACE

Starjet Commander Cody Ferguson, six, turned the gears, adjusted the knobs, and jammed the joystick into hyperdrive. Starship *Galaxy* went into a steep climb, super thrusters whining at top speed.

Back on earth, Daddy looked angry. Mommy cried. The doctor rolled his chair over, put his head close to theirs, and smiled the sour little smile that grown-ups smile when there is nothing in the world to smile about.

Commander Cody turned his back to the people and the machines and the charts with arrows pointing to drawings of the insides of sick ears, braced his feet against the big blue plastic box in the middle of the room, and held on to the joystick with both hands. *Galaxy* shook and rolled. Would it fly apart?

In seconds, the starship left earth and grown-ups and doctors' offices far behind.

After clearing the spaceport traffic tower, it blasted out of earth's atmosphere and just clipped the surface of the moon with its starboard tail wing, on the way to Planet Trickster. Trailing crumbs of green cheese, it streaked onward a gabillion light years to a perfect landing on Trickster and a party thrown by clowns and magicians and a pretty teacher in pink named Miss Clark.

He loved pretend.

He sang. He danced. He laughed at the funny clowns in their funny hats. And most of all he smiled, because on Planet Trickster there was everything in the world to smile about.

That picture went away, and God drew another one in his mind. Miss Clark came to the back of the room to see him. He didn't want her to. As long as she stayed up in front of the classroom, she smiled and everything was fine. Her voice was happy and filled with so much he needed to know. Wanted to know.

But the last time when she came down to where he sat with his storybooks and drawing paper, she forgot to bring her happy voice. She told him something he didn't want to know. She told him in a loud voice that scared him. He could barely hear it, but he knew it was loud because she opened her mouth big and leaned close and smelled like toothpaste.

The other kids turned in their seats and stared.

"I'm sorry, Cody. Something is the matter with your hearing. You have to go to another school where they can help you. Don't worry. You'll be fine. I — I will miss you. We will miss you."

She said a bunch of other stuff he couldn't remember — or maybe hadn't heard — but after he saw the tear slide down her cheek, he couldn't hear another thing she said anyway. She took him to the office where his parents waited. She hugged him goodbye and disappeared like the rabbit from the magician's hat.

Poof.

"It's genetic, yes, and irreversible. In a matter of time, he will be totally deaf."

Dr. Haskert handed Cody's parents printed material about sensorineural hearing loss. "But as bright as Cody is, he's an excellent candidate for speech and hearing therapy. He'll get a lot of that at the new school. Despite everyone's best efforts, though, he will be completely deaf. It's a mountain he has to climb, but you are his support team, his base camp. With your love and consistent support, he can live a relatively normal life. There's a vibrant deaf community out there that can give him plenty of reinforcement and enable him to lead a successful life."

Sheila Ferguson sat hard onto an office chair. "He reverses some of his printed letters — *b* and *d* — but he can count to two hundred. I never thought —"

"Mrs. Ferguson, you mustn't confuse Cody's hearing condition with normal cognitive development in a six-year-old. They commonly reverse some letters. That's more a function of not fully developed perceptual motor skills than an —"

"He can be reckless at times and is more finicky in what he eats than when he was two."

"Please, Mrs. Ferguson, I assure you that you're not describing anything out of the ordinary for a child Cody's age."

Andy crouched beside his wife's chair and took her hand. "We'll get through this, honey. We will."

She looked past him at Cody, who made buzzing sounds and squeezed the bulb on a bicycle horn attached to the play console. "My poor baby. Oh, Andrew! What have we done to him?"

Dr. Haskert pulled up a chair and leaned

toward them. "Sheila, Andy. You listen to me. This is a rare condition. There's usually no way to predict these things. What you have to do now is find out all you can about deafness and how best to help Cody cope with this condition. At first, he'll be afraid and bewildered by it, but he's young and will adapt. The question is, will you?"

Sheila began to weep. "Oh, we'll be just fine. Just great. Some day our son will just stop hearing the sound of the ocean or a cat purr or us telling him we love him, but so what? We can always write it down on a slate around his neck!"

She stood and went to Cody. She pulled him to his feet and hurried to the door. "Thank you, Doctor, thank you so much for the worst news of our lives!" With a sob, she was gone.

The hard ball in Cody's stomach seemed to take up all of the room. They went from the doctor's office to the hamburger place with the jungle gym. He didn't want to eat. He didn't want to climb on the monkey bars.

He wanted to hear.

He didn't know if he imagined the roaring between his ears or if it was really there. Who could he ask about the ball? His parents were too sad. Dr. Haskert only knew about ears. Miss Clark had disappeared.

The roaring got worse when Mommy and Daddy fought. They fought a lot more once they found out he couldn't hear much and was going deaf. He didn't like that word. It sounded an awful lot like *death.*

Had he been bad? Was that why they stopped going to church? He was bad and God was mad and the whole thing stank like the dead opossum under Dickie Braden's house.

Mom started to say something, then stopped when she saw him watching her.

"Mom? Tell me the six poem?"

She ran to the ladies' bathroom.

The ball in his belly got harder and bigger.

He took a drink of his pop. Dad ruffled his hair, then took a pen out of his pocket and wrote on a napkin in block letters. When he finished, he held Cody close and read the verse slow and loud, pointing to each word. "But now I am six, I'm as clever as clever. So I think I'll be six now for ever and ever."

He watched Dad's lips and mouth and imagined every word as it had sounded on his sixth birthday when he could still hear it clear as could be. Now Dad pressed his freckled nose flat with his pointer finger, something that usually made Cody giggle.

He didn't want to giggle.

He wanted his mom back.

His stomach hurt.

The server lady brought him crayons and a black-and-white picture of three turtles to color. He stuck a french fry in catsup and made the turtle eyes red. He took the pickle chips out of his hamburger and made the feet of the biggest turtle into wheels. Dad handed him his double hamburger. He took a small bite and handed it back. When he looked away, he tucked the bite under his tongue.

Mom came back, eyes and nose red. He wished someone would laugh. That the big yellow and orange plastic clown would come down off the wall and spray them with a trick flower. That Dad would stuff a whole hamburger in his mouth, bug out his eyes, and stare around like one of the blowfish at the aquarium. They would laugh as hard as that time at the fair and go back to church and pray and God would fix his ears.

But someone else had to be first. He didn't want to laugh, because what if that was the exact second he stopped hearing anything at all?

He might not laugh again.

Ever.

CHAPTER 1

"Cass? *Cass Dixon?* I'll be a monkey's uncle; I thought you were dead!"

Heads turned despite the noisy crowd. Cassie winced as the paunchy, balding insurance agent in white Callaway golf polo, tan cargo shorts, and tanned knobby knees threaded his way through the crowded café to her table. He grinned, leaned down, and planted a neighborly peck on the cheek.

Lowering his voice, he said, "Sorry to be such a mouthy old fool. Occupational hazard."

"No problem, but as a pickup line, your opening needs work. It might have a chance at a convention of mortuary administrators."

"Apologies." The man gave her shoulders a gentle squeeze. "I only meant that you've been less than visible for a while now."

"Please, sit." Cassie motioned to the

bench seat opposite. "How have you been, Andy?"

Andrew Ferguson settled into the chair opposite Cassie and regarded her with sad, searching eyes of amber. She had always thought they were the perfect eyes for comforting grieving widows and skinflints hospitalized in traction. *"No, I'm sorry, Mr. Blatz, that's not covered in the no-frills policy you insisted was adequate, but here, let me plump those pillows for you."*

Andy fiddled with the salt and pepper shakers and caught the eye of the overburdened waitress. "Sheila's well." It was so like him to deflect the question away from himself. "You know Sheila, busy busy with her church committees and the community league. She's a reader, you know, at Cody's old elementary school. No one can do Dr. Seuss justice the way Sheila can."

Ostensibly words of pride, their delivery sounded halfhearted. Andy faltered and fell silent. He looked as if, had he not sat down on the chair Cassie offered, he would have fallen where he stood. The waitress swept by. Andy barely uttered the words "coffee" and "no cream" before she gave a perfunctory nod and accelerated toward several waving hands belonging to a large, noisy party in a window seat.

16

The self-assured Insurance Agent of the Year fumbled with silverware and napkin. He pinched the checked tablecloth into a little peak, then flattened it again with an uncertain palm.

Is that a tremor in his hand? For ten years, Andy had serviced the Azure World employee health plan. Though the Dixons' perfume company was no more, over the past year it had morphed into the smaller, more manageable Choice Brand Beautifiers in partnership with family friend and CB founder, Mags O'Connor. Andy had weathered the inevitable twenty-percent shrinkage in the Azure labor force by creatively restructuring the group plan with minimal loss of benefits. Cassie and Nick and their loyal team owed their friend a great deal.

She suspected a likely source of Andy's skittishness, and it made her sad. The Fergusons were in their late thirties when they brought their newborn son, Cody, home from the hospital. Soon to close in on their fiftieth birthdays, she guessed they were plenty worn down by the double challenge of parenting a child whose budding teenage years could only be made more difficult by the fact of his deafness.

She hoped things weren't as bad as they might be. "And Cody? I'll bet he's turning into a major heartthrob."

Cassie hadn't meant her words to wound, but her friend looked as if she'd shot him at point-blank range. He gave a heavy sigh. "The boy's a handsome one, all right. A regular movie star. But a girl won't ever get within a mile of Cody. He's withdrawn — worse than when you saw him last — moody, sullen, incommunicative. He wouldn't invite anyone to his twelfth birthday party. Just sat around stroking that stupid gecko's head. Wouldn't touch the cake, barely reacted to the presents, wouldn't even play Speed Spell. You know how he loves that game."

She nodded. Back when they made the time to socialize — before their dream perfume, "Cassandra," hijacked their lives, then turned deadly — she, Nick, and their only child, Beth, used to spend many a pleasant evening with the Fergusons. Often the six of them would play board games until midnight. They invented a competitive game using only Scrabble tiles, rapidly building words in crossword fashion until all the tiles were gone and the first person to declare "Done!" won the round.

Cody loved the game and was the player to beat. His deafness couldn't hide the fact that he was exceedingly bright, but according to Cassie's church sources, the boy had become increasingly withdrawn and spent many hours alone with his pets and his thoughts. She'd seen early signs of it when the two families had been closer.

"Sheila's not helping, treating Cody like a rare hothouse plant to be fussed over, protected, and kept from all threats to his safety and well-being."

Andy's comment was a variation of the same thing she told Nick and Beth on every ride home from the Fergusons'. "Sheila thinks deafness means a lengthy list of things Cody cannot, should not, do. The older he gets, the more she adds to the list."

These discussions drew to a temporary close at the driveway entrance of their brick Tudor home overlooking the night sparkle of San Francisco. Allowed the last word — following a knowing look between father and daughter — Cassie minced no words. "I'll tell you this much — Sheila's love is misguided, she smothers him. She needs the counseling, not Cody."

Cassie was startled now to see Andy's eyes mist over. "You remember how bold Cody used to be, always imagining he was Spiderman or some other superhero who leaps tall buildings? Well, that's been all but wiped out. Sheila threatened to put him on medi-

19

cation to make him less . . . I don't know, less reckless! It was just that she worried about him so much. Still does."

"I'm sorry." Cassie knew she should stay out of it, but this had to be said. "It's probably none of my business, Andrew, and I may be guessing here, but wouldn't Cody benefit from spending more time with you? You've always been something of a workaholic. You and he should throw the ball around, go hiking, build a go-cart. You know, guy time. Forgive me for saying so, but sometimes you treat Cody like he's a bleeder or lacks immunity to disease and needs to live in a bubble. He can't hear. That's not a terminal condition and it doesn't mean he can't do just fine by developing his other senses. But to do that, he has to be allowed to live, to taste life."

She thought from Andy's gloomy expression that she might have overstepped her bounds. It had been nearly two years since she'd last seen Cody. *What do I know?*

But when he finally looked at her, a look both penetrating and desperate, she saw that little had changed. In fact, unless she missed her guess, it had worsened.

"I know that, Cassie, and I've thought of doing some of that stuff with him, but Sheila's so afraid he'll get hurt or traumatized

20

or something. So, to keep the peace . . ."

His coffee arrived before he completed the thought. Cassie changed the subject. "How about one of Mae's famous omelets to go with that? I'm buying."

He shook his head and muttered a "No, thanks." For a few minutes, he blew and sipped the dark brew while Cassie stirred the remainder of her hot oatmeal and raisins, which was no longer hot or contained a single raisin.

"Won't Cody be a teenager soon?"

"Thirteen in two weeks."

"Then high school. What happens when he wants to join the wrestling team or get a job? We lost track of Beth's interests in our quest for success, and it hurt her. Hurt us all."

Cassie suspected there was a great deal more going on inside Cody, that he was much more capable than met the eye. His mother, however, was a strong-willed woman of Germanic ancestry who did not invite any conclusion that did not match her own. Poor Andy. It was hard for an acquiescent spirit to assert itself. Ironically, all that repressed angst at home was probably what made him such an effective insurance man on the job. *No wonder Cody stays longer and longer in his internal world. He's only following his dad's example.*

Andy nodded. "Yeah, I worry about that too. Sheila wants to put him in an elite private school for the deaf, but I'm on the fence. He's a good kid, strong, smart as a whip, tests real high, but I'm afraid he's going to shut me out just like he has his mother. He must think I side with her, but I really don't know what to do. If I were to take him fishing or on a business trip, I'm afraid something might happen to him and Sheila would end up hating me for the rest of her life."

Andy looked away before taking a deep breath. "Cass, you're going to think I'm crazy, but it's no coincidence that we've run into each other today. I think God's up to something, don't you?"

"Well, I doubt —"

"No, seriously, I think it's a sign. You always could get through to Cody and Sheila. They listened to you. Sure it's been awhile, but if anyone can bridge the gap here, you can."

"But it's been so long. I've lost track of things, and truthfully, there are issues in my own family I've let slip. We've gotten so wrapped up in Choice Brand and —"

He stopped her with a wave of his napkin. "Truce. Sorry. We haven't been together five minutes and I'm coming on like a TV psychologist. Forgive me. Forget it."

"Oh, Andy, that's not what I meant. It's just that with everything that's happened with Azure World, we'd make poor advisors right now. You should talk to Father B. The church has some excellent trained counselors far better equipped at this sort of thing."

"Strangers?"

"I beg your pardon?"

"It's too personal, Cass. Nor do I have the time to start over with someone who has no history with us."

"But they're professionals who —"

"You don't understand." Andy's eyes glistened in the pool of light cast by an inverted water bucket that served as both decoration and hanging lamp. "I don't need professionals; I need friends who know how to care and to pray. My marriage is teetering. My family is in jeopardy, and I'm afraid I'll lose them."

Cassie shook her head. "God won't let that happen. He loves you too much and wants you to have the desires of your heart. Nick and I are just beginning to get our arms around that truth."

Andy leaned back in the booth and pointed his spoon at Cassie. "You see? He's teaching you lessons similar to what we need to learn. Doesn't God love me enough to send you and Nick just when things look their worst?"

Cassie squirmed and reached for the cell phone in her purse. "Do I have your permission to give the church a call right now and get Father B's input?"

Andy reached across the table and stopped her. "*We* are the church, Cass. I don't care how long we've been out of touch or who's to blame. I've been praying for a solution, for a way to get through to my loved ones. You've always been able to communicate with them. I'm asking for *your* help."

Cassie put the phone back and nodded. "I apologize. Of course Nick and I will talk it over and pray for God's answer."

"Good. And thanks." Andy took a refill on his coffee. "Here I've been blatting away about my troubles and haven't once asked how things are going with you and Nick. Did I hear that Beth's off saving the world in South America somewhere?"

Cassie leaned back while her dishes were cleared away by the efficient, if harried, waitress. "Central America. Honduras. They call themselves 'Teens of Hope.' Beth and two dozen other kids are loving on an orphanage of abandoned children in Teguci-galpa. Can you imagine parents just walking away from their kids? But poverty is rampant, and their moms and dads must figure their children are better off in an orphanage than with what little they can provide."

Cassie pictured Beth with six urchins hanging off her and all of them cackling like hyenas. She smiled. "And Nick's fine. Seems to enjoy managing Choice Brand, and its market share keeps growing. The storm over the 'Cassandra' mess has largely died down, and the asset insurance company for the most part has lived up to its indemnification obligations. They should, considering the size of the premiums we handed over every month. I still grieve for all the families forever changed by the death and injury to loved ones, freakish as the whole thing was. Don't think I'll ever get over the guilt of what happened." She studied the bucket lamp hanging low over the table.

Andy, and everyone else who had a pulse, knew the story. "Cassandra" parfum, touted as "the very breath of beauty," had become the very essence of horror. The pheromones inherent in the fragrance of the rare *celerides* orchid caused temporary insanity in mammals and led to vicious animal attacks in the Golden State. Seven people had died and many more were injured, some critically, before its retail rollout was halted and the entire stock quarantined. Human reaction to the scent, though not as rabid, was decidedly alien, and people reported deeply disturbing Jekyll-and-Hyde transformations. Cassie herself — under the lethal influence of her signature perfume — had nearly thrown herself to the lions at the San Francisco Zoo. In the end, the entire inventory had to be destroyed, and with it, their dreams of a perfume dynasty.

With the help of family friend and spiritual advisor Father Byron Wills at St. John's Cathedral, and a reordering of her life's priorities, Cassie was just beginning to feel whole again.

"Sorry, Cass." Andy's eyes were pained but compassionate. "This is what happens when we forget to call. It all builds up."

She looked at him and saw some of Andy's old fire. *As if by simply staying in touch we could have prevented either what was going on with Cody or what happened to the fortunes of Azure World.* "Remember the time Cody jumped off the roof onto that mattress? He thought he was invincible."

Andy nodded. "A perfect back landing that knocked the wind out of him so bad he couldn't get his breath for what seemed like forever. When he finally did, all he had to say was, 'What's for lunch?' I think it scared him, at least it did until he caught sight of his mother trying to set fire to the old mattress with the charcoal lighter off the barbecue!"

He gave a hesitant laugh, and she joined him. Cassie had been so glad when Sheila had turned the full force of her wrath on the mattress and not on any of them.

She ordered more coffee and the specialty of the house — a plate of café owner Mae Winston's comfort cookies, chocolate chip mouth pleasers fresh from the oven and ready to order any time of the day or night.

"I owed you a call." Cassie leaned forward. "Remember? Nick fixed the motion sensor on your yard lights, and you invited us to stay for a taco feed. I proceeded to beat you senseless at Speed Spell, and Cody showed me the beautiful Swiss army knife you had secretly given him for his tenth birthday without Sheila knowing or agreeing. As we were getting into the car to go home, I promised to call you guys that next week to arrange a bowling party at Sunset Lanes. The very next day we heard about the discovery of the rarest of orchids and that we had a shot at capturing its scent. Nick began preparations to leave, and then all this time speeds by, and here I am utterly

mortified that I have neglected our friendship. I'm so sorry, Andy. I never wanted to
lose you and Sheila. Please tell her that I
will call her tonight and apologize. Has it
truly been that bad between the two of
you?"

Andy bit into a third cookie, smearing his
upper lip with gooey chocolate. "Bad
enough. She does her thing. I do mine.
Cody holes up in his room. But don't beat
yourself up, Cass. We're the ones to blame.
We've been so consumed by Cody's attitude
and needs. It's all Cody all the time. Don't
get me wrong. I love him to death, but the
rift between Sheila and me opened up over
that kid. We both know no cause is ever
found in half the cases of congenital hearing loss. But I'm afraid we want to blame it
on something, you know? And so I wonder
if she's at fault, and she wonders if I am.
One of us gave our son a defective gene.
My great aunt Lillian was deaf as a brick
from childhood, so it was likely me. The
guilt eats away at us, and it's sometimes just
easier to lay it at the other's door. As if any
of that matters or could change anything. It
just is."

He shook his head. "I'm sorry, Cass. This
is all so personal. Forgive me for unloading
on you this way." If misery had a name, it

was Andrew Ferguson. But then, unexpectedly, he brightened. "I believe it was I who beat you senseless at Speed Spell the last time."

Cassie laughed and wagged a finger at him. She laid down sufficient cash to cover the bill and the tip. The waitress materialized, and Cassie asked her to please bag the remaining cookies in two bags.

She handed one to Andy. "If these were magic beans, I'd tell you to go plant them and live happily ever after. But give them to Sheila and Cody so they'll at least know you were thinking of them. I'll give serious thought to what you said, because I know God wants what's best for you. You can take that to the bank!"

Andy hooked his arm through hers and walked her to her car. "You *have* learned a lot since the perfume went south on you. When's the tell-all book coming out?"

She matched his grin with one of her own. "When a certain hot place has a very hard freeze."

It wasn't until Andy's Camry at last exited the parking lot with a farewell honk that Cassie felt the tension leave her neck and shoulders. She started her car and put it in reverse. *What am I thinking? No way can I say yes to Andy. I don't know all that's gone on in the Ferguson household, and besides, I have plenty on my plate. If Andy and Sheila's pride keeps them from seeking professional help, that's their business. And anyway, what would Sheila think of me nosing around in their affairs after all this time?*

He'd asked too much of her. How did that Hank Williams tune go? "If you mind your business, then you won't be mindin' mine."

It was as she paid the three dollars at the Bay Bridge toll plaza that Cassie felt a none-too-subtle nudge in her spirit. *Andy needs your help. When you needed his, he didn't hesitate.*

Cassie hummed something from *Annie* and beat time on the steering wheel.

Instead, he took excellent care of a messy situation . . .

She punched in the smooth jazz station and turned the volume up for the sultry horn of Wynton Marsalis doing "I Got Lost in Her Arms."

. . . was a tower of strength, encouragement, and optimism for Azure World. Don't turn your back on a decent man trying to save his family.

She rolled down the window hoping the tangy wind would take her thoughts elsewhere.

. . . didn't hesitate to meet with each em-
ployee individually, determine their needs, and
spent evenings away from his family to provide
just the right insurance package for you and
your family. The entire Azure family.

"Stop."

When they were at their lowest.

Cassie rubbed the bridge of her nose. God was relentless.

"And when feelings get hurt?"

Don't be anxious. Trust.

"And advice is rejected?"

Persist in a gentle way. Expect me to work.

Cassie sighed, turned the radio off, and hit the button that caused her driver's side window to slide from sight. She drank in the amazing sights of water, bridge, and sky, listening for the voice in the rushing air.

An hour at Pier 39 only delayed the inevitable. Usually, losing herself among the 110 stores, thirteen restaurants, and numerous attractions was a prescription for a return to normalcy. But not today.

The cry of gulls and the toot of ferry horns were welcome sounds, but five minutes with the fire jugglers and stripe-shirted mimes that performed up and down the promenade proved an irritant.

At Charms by the Bay, she spent $57.95

on a ceramic flamingo for Beth's bracelet and then worried whether the expensive water bird should be a welcome-home gift or saved for Christmas.

She argued with herself until she exchanged the flamingo for a cheap laminated bookmark — featuring a photo and facts about Alcatraz Island, an infamous federal penitentiary in San Francisco Bay — and $55 in change.

Charming. Beth would be so thrilled. Why not just get her some black lacquer nail polish and a nose stud?

In a funk, she purchased a waffle cone from the Grand Ice Cream Shop — not deterred in the least by the recent cookie-fest at Mae's — and watched the kids spin on the Italian handcrafted carousel. Their shrill cries of glee were as soothing as a power drill.

The sea lions at the West Marina were their usual amusing selves, though for some reason their billing as "Sea Lebrities" was annoying today. The thought of three hundred blubberous males, each weighing well in excess of a thousand pounds, strutting and barking from a wooden dock, struck her as ridiculous.

The last straw came when she checked the marquee at Theatre 39 and found that the current production was *Menopause the Musical.*

I surrender.

Father B would know what to do. Byron Wills, one of four priests assigned to St. John's Cathedral, had dealt with more than a few sticky situations of his own. They included alcoholism, racial prejudice, and a conservative view of religious piety that ran counter to the liberalization of the Anglican communion in America. The African American priest often found himself a lone voice in the ecclesiastical wilderness, but in his case, it only strengthened his resolve.

"The power of one, dear Cassie. One God, one Lord and Savior Jesus Christ, one Spirit divine. One church universal and triumphant, one saved by faith alone, one hope eternal. The gates of hell shall not prevail against the power of one!"

She found him playing hopscotch with the children from the church school. Coat neatly folded over the crossbar of the swing set, Father B in cleric's collar and blue brocade vest tossed his marker — a small blue beanbag — into square six outlined in pink chalk. He hopped the first three squares without incident, but squares four and five were side-by-side, one occupied by a huge coat button and one by a plastic frog belonging to the priest's two opponents, a small boy and girl, perhaps eight years old. To successfully land in square six, he would have to hop over the occupied squares on one foot. By moving his upper limbs in unison like the arms of an oil derrick, he gathered enough momentum to sail over the other markers and land without falling, but in the process put a hand on the ground to steady himself.

"No hands! No hands!" The boy practically crowed. The girl squealed and clapped her hands.

Father B looked under his arm and saw Cassie. "Good show, Willy and Brenda. You got me. Now I have to talk with this pretty lady. You play it out, and no fighting!"

The priest retrieved his coat and offered Cassie his arm. They walked over to two sculpted cement bulldogs and sat down on their backs.

Cassie pointed to the two remaining hopscotchers. "Nice vertical leap. I'm impressed."

"Don't be. My lower back says I'll be a good week paying the price for such foolishness. Those two come from a home where the adults are at war. They need to be around adults who aren't yelling obscenities. To what do I owe this visit?"

34

"You're not buying that I happened to be in the neighborhood?"

"Not when you've got 'God, please don't make me do this' written all over you."

"That obvious, am I?" She breathed the scent of roses wafting over from a well-tended garden. A bell rang, and when it stopped, a screeching Willy and Brenda were halfway to the schoolhouse door. "Some friends are in trouble. Their home is in turmoil, and I've been asked to intervene. I don't know how or even if I should. We've not seen them for a couple of years, and I don't feel like I'm in much of a place to be giving advice to others. And in the case of the wife, I'm pretty sure it will be resented."

Father B scratched at his goatee. "I see. Were you asked to solve the problem?"

"Well, no, not exactly. Just to help. To get through to a mother and son who aren't communicating well."

"To intervene, take them into your home, loan them money —"

"No, no. Be a kind of sounding board is all."

"A friend?"

"Well, yes, sure, a friend. But it's more complicated than that."

"Who says?"

"It's pretty obvious it will take time, that

35

there's no easy fix, that — that —" She stopped. He waited. She fumbled for words. He said nothing. She tried to read him. "Are you able to help me or not?"

"Pray with me. Our Father . . ."

She waited until the end of the prayer before blurting, "What are you getting at?"

"That it's not rocket science. It is basic. It is humility. It is being there, no more, no less. You were not asked to cure cancer, but to help a family start growing again. You do that by spending time with them, reminding them what it means to be human yet made in God's image, loving them. The rest will take care of itself."

"That's it?"

"No."

"What else?"

"You take them camping."

"Excuse me?"

"Camping. A change of scene is good for all. The city twists us in knots. Jesus got out of the city and into the wilderness or went boating across a lake. He got away. Back to creation, my dear. Out beyond where the asphalt ends, God speaks in mysterious ways."

She stared at him, repelled and fascinated by his answer. Wasn't it insane to even consider packing off to the wild with people

— and issues — so out of whack? Wasn't it?

"I'd go to the Cascades in Washington State. Fly up, rent a van. In two hours you're striding through the firs, packs on your backs, the smell of heaven in your lungs. Camp out a couple of nights, slap a few mosquitoes, sleep under the stars, play. Get back to nature; get back to what really counts — friends and family healing together in God's outdoors."

Cassie let the scent of roses fill her head. "I'm not sure they'd go for it. They've been spending a lot of time in their respective corners avoiding one another lately. The thought of sharing a tent might not appeal to them. Not sure it appeals to me."

"Then sleep in separate tents. Outside on a rock. Up a tree. The key is to get away and purge the senses."

Cassie looked back at the swings and the chalk outline of an old and simple game. "Is camping anything like hopscotch?"

Father B patted her shoulder. "Now that you mention it."

"You've got to be kidding! No way am I going into the mountains with the Fergusons." Nick's hands, clamped to the back of a dining chair, were white at the knuckles.

"Why not? We've all been cooped up with

37

our frustrations way too long." Cassie rinsed the few things in the kitchen sink and placed them in the dishwasher. "I don't know about you, but I need to get out of the city, clear my head and my heart. This will give us all a chance to rethink things and help each other get past this stuff. Andy's at the end of his rope. Both families have been isolating ourselves too much. We're good for them and they're good for us, Nick."

Her husband managed to glower while polishing off the remaining Mae's cookies. "Sheila Ferguson is *not* my idea of a camping buddy. She's wound way too tight and wouldn't know compromise if it jumped up and bit her. How she wants to raise her son is her business. You just focus on Beth."

Cassie reddened. "Me?"

Nick ran an irritated hand through salt-and-pepper hair. "You know I meant us. Cass, honey, from what you just told me, the Fergusons are working with the best counselors and audiologists money can buy. They don't need us butting in where we're not wanted."

"All I'm suggesting is that we take a weekend away together and do something fun. No agenda. Friends is all. Sometimes people just need a burnt marshmallow on the end of a stick."

"What about staying neutral? It's too easy to take sides with those two."

"What about Andy? He's afraid to do anything for fear he'll lose Sheila or Cody or both. He could sure use a guy friend right about now."

"Then I'll take him to a tractor pull. Listen, Cass, if you want to get away, just the two of us, I'm all for it. Royce can watch over the plant for a few days. But if you've got some big notion we're going to head off into the wild to fix the Fergusons, you can just quit thinking it."

A choice retort balanced on the tip of her tongue, but Cassie left it unsaid. She watched Gretchen the Great Dane twitch in her sleep on the dining room floor, waning summer sunbeams streaming through the window making patches of butter yellow out of her tidy coat.

Nick watched her. "Cass, God knows we've been through a lot, and I agree that all that's happened was partly a wake-up call to us to look around. Be more open to others. But the Fergusons! That's a complicated situation that we're not equipped to change. They need professional help, not well-meaning amateurs."

A few minutes passed in silence. Nick fixed himself a cold roast beef and tomato

sandwich. Cassie reached into the refrigera-
tor and handed him the horseradish spread.
"Okay, you're right. This isn't your business. You stay home and I'll take the Fergusons camping. Somewhere up north of
Mount Baker, maybe along the Pacific Crest
Trail. It's mid-August, but we should be
able to find some solitude."

He stopped midchew. "You?" The incredu-
lity in his voice pleased her. After the "Cassandra" mess, there wasn't a lot that could
deter Cassie these days.

"Why not?"

Nick plopped his sandwich back onto the
plate. "I'll tell you why not. I can count on
one hand the number of nights you've spent
in the woods, and two of those were in the
trees back of your grandmother Elise's
house when you were eight."

"Easy there, Jedediah Smith. I seem to
remember you leaping out of the hammock
and making a noisy dash for the van one
night at Big Redwoods State Park."

Nick flashed a mock warning, but she was
unstoppable. "Your story was that a bear
had shuffled into camp and probed with its
nose the bulge made by your backside in
the center of the hammock. Come to find
out, you were goosed by your own dog."

Nick grinned sheepishly over the family

legend, grabbed a dish towel, flipped it tight, and gave her a playful snap. "Thank you, Perry Mason. You're worth every cent of the exorbitant fees you charge. By the way, that bear? I could tell by the sound of its walk that it was missing the third claw on its left hind foot. You find that limp, you've found your bear."

Laughing, Cassie yanked the towel from his grip, threw it around his neck, and pulled him close. "I've found my bear and is he ever grizzly —"

The stove timer buzzed. Cassie removed a blackberry pie from the oven and set it on the wire cooling rack. The kitchen filled with sweet warmth.

"Give it twenty minutes to cool, then it's all yours, as if the cookies weren't enough. I picked up milk, so you're set." She washed and dried her hands at the sink.

"Where are you off to?" Nick eyed the pie.

She kissed his cheek. "To check airline prices online. I think there's lower fares to Seattle right now. Then I'm going to call Sheila Ferguson and convince her to get out of that house for a change. Her family's a ticking time bomb."

Nick followed her into the study. "You need to reconsider, Cass." When she sat at the computer and didn't respond, he sighed.

"Look, you're right, it has been too long since we got together with the Fergusons. Let's have them over. We'll barbecue, have a Speed Spell tournament, whatever you want. But hopping a plane to go camping? That's just crazy."

Cassie waited for the Internet connection. "I want a few days away, Nick. Away from the phones. Away from the routine. Away from California. The Cascades are wonderful this time of year. My friend Joanie — you know Joanie, from college? — lives up there and has all the gear. She's said I can borrow it anytime I want. All we need to take are our sleeping bags and a credit card."

She could see Nick's resistance waver ever so slightly. She whispered, "Babbling brooks, whispering firs, alpine vistas, all the beef jerky you can eat . . ."

"Sheila whining, Cody growling, Sheila bossing, Andy sulking . . ."

Cassie turned and took Nick's hands in her own. "Believe me, I thought of all the reasons why we shouldn't get involved: We've got plenty to do. The Fergusons are their own worst enemies. They'll end up resenting us.

"But it's not about us; it's about our friends in trouble. We left them to their own

42

devices when they needed us most, and we came close to losing everything of our own in the bargain. Maybe it's too late for us to make much of an impact in their lives, but if we don't try and something bad were to happen, we'd never forgive ourselves. We've got to do this, Nick, don't we?" She hugged him tight.

"I still think this is a bad idea — right up there with liverwurst and bell bottoms — but I'll go along." Before she could jump up and kiss him, he held up a warning hand. "But if Sheila grates on my nerves, I may have to maintain my own camp separate from the rest of you."

Cassie kissed him. "As you wish, Jedediah. But should you feel a cold, bear-sized nose in your nether regions, don't come running to me!"

CHAPTER 2

Nick wanted to get away, all right, but with Cassie, just the two of them. Didn't she know how long it had been?

One of his best memories was of the weekend he and Cass went from Portland to the Oregon Coast to conceive Beth. They were eager to have a child, and he wanted everything to be perfect even if money was in short supply. One night with the trimmings was all they could afford.

They whale-watched in a Zodiak boat that skimmed the water and leapt over the waves like a flying fish. A mammoth gray whale did a slow roll past them and showed its great tail before submerging like King Neptune gone to check on the state of his kingdom beneath the waves.

They visited the aquarium and fed the comical seals, whose bulging bellies belied the pathetic, half-starved expressions they presented to the paying public. Everyone had been in on the scam, of course. The herring concession inside the aquarium entrance did business at least as brisk as the saltwater taffy vendor outside the aquarium exit.

Beneath a sign declaring "Amazing Wonders of the Deep," Nick grabbed Cassie around her slender waist and she saw that he held a wad of orange and yellow taffy in his teeth. Laughing, she leaned in and took the exposed end of the offered taffy in her teeth. Together they closed their eyes and bit it in two.

"I hope you thought to make a wish." He nuzzled her neck. "I did."

"A wish? You said nothing about a wish."

"Oh, did I neglect to mention that? Just as well. Only one of the wishes can come true."

"How convenient."

He kissed her nose. "Never mind. My wish involves you and a romantic dinner for two followed by a little trip up the stairs, if you get my meaning."

She swatted his arm. "A Tibetan herdsman couldn't miss your meaning!"

The calamari appetizers in a sweet honey drizzle were perfect. The tender halibut and buttery sea scallops in a rich cream sauce were perfect. The dark chocolate mousse with miniature French vanilla wafers was perfect. Her eyes glistening with candlelight, the soft scent of heat-activated jasmine and iris, and the daring, strapless sea green dress with its glovelike embrace, were perfect.

Nick took the desk clerk's advice and hired a passable tenor, a college student in need of tuition money, to stop by their table and sing "Because of You." Cassie swooned to hear:

> You are the warm in my winter
> The soft breath of coming spring
> To hold you is to know the life
> That gave new life to me
> Because of you I found my voice, because
>   of you I sing.

Their room at the Chart House Inn at Depot Bay was named the Surfrider. The third-floor view of the ocean and "the World's Smallest Harbor" offered stunning sunset scenes from their private hot tub set into a polished mahogany deck.

Perfect.

They slid beneath the ninety-degree water just as the last of a saffron sun slid into the sea. They toasted one another with crystal goblets of sparkling Perrier and felt the lasting reassurance of their "I do's" spoken ten months earlier.

"To us." Nick raised his glass. "Paupers now, but future players without peer."

"To us." They clinked glasses, sipped the Perrier, and in a swirl of heated bubbles, slipped into each other's arms.

"And just what sort of child shall we have?" Cassie murmured against his chest. "Genius? Explorer? Statesman? Jock?"

He kissed her forehead. "You sound as if you may be leaning toward a boy."

"Not at all. I might have been thinking Madame Curie, Sally Ride, Margaret Thatcher, or Jackie Joyner-Kersee."

"Touché." He stroked her neck and kissed her cheek. "To settle it, though, actions always speak louder than words."

She threw her arms around his neck and gave him a deep, urgent kiss.

Alarms sounded. Bells clanged. A Klaxon ripped the night. Lights flashed.

Nick snaked an arm around her back and drew her to him with seductive whispers. "Baby, we've got us a four-alarm blaze!"

She smacked him away.

Pounding on the door. Shouts.

"Nick! It *is* a fire!" Cassie half stumbled out of the tub and had just closed her terry-cloth robe when the door to their room flew open.

In the weird sci-fi glare of emergency strobe lighting spilling in from the hall stood the short, balding desk clerk who had checked them in. "Sorry, folks, but there's smoke pouring from the day room. Everybody down the stairs and onto the street! No dawdling!"

Nick left the tub, hastily toweled off, and tugged on pants and flannel shirt while Cassie threw on slacks and sweatshirt. They jammed their feet into plastic flip-flops, cast a last longing look at the hot tub, and rushed for the stairs right behind the next-door couple who, judging by their bare feet and mismatched attire, were in a similar state of disruption.

Across the street on the ocean side, Nick wrapped Cassie in a warming hug. In a hotel blanket thrown about her shoulders, hair damp and stringy, she watched the volunteer fire crew carry a smoldering leather couch onto the sidewalk. She shivered and buried herself deeper in Nick's embrace.

By the time the all clear was given, it was two a.m., they were tired and grouchy, their room smelled of smoke, and the mood had long passed. Five hours later, they had a quiet breakfast compliments of the management, packed up the rental car, and started for home.

As it turned out, Beth was two months and four days younger than she would have been had someone not dozed off and dropped a lit cigar between the sofa cushions at the Chart House Inn. By their modest second attempt on a Friday night, the mood was set with dinner at Denny's, then back to their first apartment and a two-liter bottle of chilled diet soda with which to toast the occasion.

The sixty-five day delay taught them a lot about expectations and reality. As much as they might wish upon a piece of saltwater taffy, human beings had little control over actual events. The grace of God and his timing, however, now there were things to bank on. Beth was the child every parent dreamed of. Why she had to put off her debut, Nick couldn't say.

The Chart House had been nicely remodeled after the fire. Maybe he could get their same room.

Cassie gripped the phone and swallowed hard. "Sheila, I've not been a good friend to you. Will you forgive me for dropping out of sight like that? I've thought of you and your family many times, but pretty soon I let myself get caught up in everything else

49

going on and neglected the ones who mean the most. By then, so much time had gone by, I was too embarrassed to call."

"It happens, I know. No apology required."

"Yes, it is, Sheila. It wasn't until I bumped into Andy today that it hit me how long it had been and how much I missed you guys. But that's no excuse and I'm sorry."

"Oh, I understand, Cassandra. I'm guilty of it myself. You get so caught up in the day-to-day and before you know it, there are only twenty shopping days until Christmas. How's the family?"

They spent the next ten minutes catching up on each other's lives. When they had run out of things to say, Cassie proposed the camping trip.

At Sheila's sharp intake of breath, Cassie rushed on. "Sheila, this place is perfect. Dodge Creek Campground is privately owned, and my friend Joanie says we can use it anytime. It has easy access to the highway over just a mile of graded gravel road. The campsite sits right on a creek where it tumbles into the Baker River. Rustic, well-maintained bathroom facilities, sweet well water from a pump, and just a short hike to mountain meadow flowers and a set of crags where mountain goats have been spotted."

"Goats? I've never been fond of goats."

"Forget the goats. We'll just stick to the lovely scenery. The guys can backpack up to High Bay Lake if they want a challenge, and we gals can take it easy back at camp and get some reading done. I've got a new Carla Blackstone novel I want to dive into, and did you hear there's a new Robin Cook thriller out? He still your favorite?"

The polite wait on the other end of the line ended. "Thank you for thinking of us, Cassie, but we really can't take time away right now to go camping. Andrew has a six-month review coming up and sales have been slow. He needs to focus on several leads that he so colorfully notes have been 'composting' for several months. Nor can we really afford a costly trip right now. Our son's medical bills are never-ending."

"Oh, it won't be expensive, not really. We'll put the plane tickets on our credit card, and you can pay us back when and as you're able, no rush. As for lodging, Joanie owes me for past favors. The outdoor Ritz won't cost us a cent for a camp member-ship weekend that she can't use. And she's loaning us her camping gear, free of charge. Just some food and the rental car, that's it. Couldn't be any cheaper."

"Cody consults with his speech reading therapist that weekend. We'd like not to interrupt the flow."

Cassie knew a royal *we* when she heard one. "Sheila, please level with me. I don't blame you if you're angry with the way we dropped you when we got on the trail of the new perfume. We were wrong to neglect the people who mean the most to us. It was our one sure shot at making it big in the business, and we gambled everything on it. It was a mistake. Please forgive us. Forgive me for treating our friendship so lightly. I want that to change. I want us to get back what we had and to make it stronger than it was before. Please, let's try."

Sheila let it go for half a minute, then hit back hard. "Our son is not in a place right now that is conducive to vacation rewards. He is sullen, uncooperative, and at odds with reality. I found him building a birdcage the other day — hammer and nails, for the love of heaven! Lucky I discovered it when I did. He'd already mashed one thumb, all purple and black, and was crying and had this idiot smile on his lips. I made him hand over the hammer and I told Andrew to keep his nails locked up. Men! I sometimes wonder what they're thinking."

And I wonder, Cassie thought, biting her

tongue, *why you can't let boys be boys.*

At first, resentment and frustration were all he felt. From his seat at the table where he worked on the plastic model of the Space Shuttle *Discovery,* Cody focused hard on his mother's lips.

Is Mom saying what I think she's saying?

She had no idea how much he wanted to rough it. What he wouldn't give for a weekend of hiking, climbing, escaping the small world she had made for him. He wanted to jump rock to rock like a mountain lion. Fly high above jagged cliffs on invisible gusts of air. Twist and plunge through churning rapids, muscles popping in a fight to the death.

He wanted to spit. Blow his nose on his sleeve. Scratch where the sun had never been.

Some days it felt like he could no longer breathe inside these walls. He choked on the restrictions, the endless precautions, the needless protections. His mom was blind to the man inside the boy and dismissed his attempts to tell her about the thrilling tales of survival he devoured like candy.

"Two of them went nuts and had to be shot. The rest were found sucking on the sails to quench their thirst!"

"That's nice, dear."

"The sun fried their skin so bad their skulls were exposed!"

"I see."

"The wound in his leg squirmed with flesh-eating maggots!"

"Too graphic for me."

He was the boy in her bubble.

Because it was a cell phone and his mother's mouth was clearly visible, he knew she was talking to Cass Dixon. He knew Mrs. Dixon had invited the Fergusons to go camping, that Cody was costing his family a bundle, that he was incapable of handling anything so dangerous as a hammer and nails.

And that he wore a fool's expression after hitting himself with the hammer. *If she only knew.*

Despite the tears, the throbbing pain in his thumb had made him happy. Happy to feel. Happy to build a home for birds whose songs he imagined and only vaguely recalled. Happy to *do.*

It was hard to get dirty in the safe house. "No go-carts. They crash. No snakes. They bite. No hunting knives. They cut." On and on. Not that those cautions weren't true. What angered Cody was that those things were denied him not so much because they

54

crashed, bit, or cut, but because he was deaf.

One hot summer day, he arm wrestled his dad at the patio table. They had their shirts off, sweaty guys grunting, trash-talking, competing.

Cody, face red, teeth clenched, suddenly strained for the advantage. The shock of surprise on his dad's face was worth a month of desserts. He had his dad's arm halfway to the mat before Andy recovered and won the match. Didn't matter. Cody flexed like a strong man and earned himself a noogie.

Mom frowned and told him to wash up for dinner.

Those guy times were rare. Dad worked a lot. When he wasn't working, he gave in a lot, going along with Mom to keep the peace. If Mom had her way, Cody never would feed a dog, mow a lawn, or shoot a single hoop. Shop class was the other side of the moon. He had a doctor's note excusing him. *How dumb is that?*

For the hundredth time, he stared at his black-and-blue thumb. Swollen, purplish, gross. He smiled. *A man's thumb!*

He flexed the stringy muscles that he'd been building secretly under her nose. The dumbbells borrowed from Dickie Braden added definition to the flesh hardened by pushups and stomach crunches. He could feel a bit of muscle mass that was a tall step up from the flabby nerd physique a new growth spurt had left behind. He still dressed preppy to please, but underneath he felt a growing, agile body.

Some days he read from sunup to sundown. IQ of 120. High for anyone, let alone a "dumb" special needs kid. His library card was his passport out. In the past year, he had devoured the complete Conan Doyle series on the master detective, Sherlock Holmes. His mother encouraged reading and never monitored what he read or how much, including a stack of well-worn Incredible Hulk comics. She did not know that along with a four-hundred-page study on the life of Abraham Lincoln, he also devoured the six-hundred-page *Boy Scout Fieldbook.* And the three-hundred-fifty-page *Wilderness Survival Guide,* followed by the five-volume set of *Living Outside: Successfully Roughing It Anytime, Anywhere.*

He would get up from a long stretch of reading and look out the window across the bay and toward the hills to the east. It was like a movie in his mind. Fur trappers. Explorers. Pony Express riders. Frontiersmen, rough and fearless. He wanted to go where they had gone. Go for months without taking a bath. Test his smarts, his wilderness know-how. He wanted to live outside and never come in.

Limited edition genuine Buck hunting knife. Five-inch fixed, mirror-polished blade signed by Chuck Buck and C. J. Buck. Walnut handle. English bridle sheath. Only a thousand made. Certificate of authenticity. $170. Cody returned to the website again and again, dreaming of that knife strapped to his waist. He saved his allowance and birthday money and was less than fifty dollars away from placing the order. His dad knew and told him to have the knife mailed to his work address. His mom wouldn't find out until at least after he had skinned his first rabbit.

If he could find one.

Every smart discoverer he knew about was also well-educated. So Cody read the newspaper every day and timed himself at what he called Speed Spell Solitaire. He could solve crossword puzzles in half the time it took his peers. He was crowned King Freak as soon as word got out that he loved doing story problems in math class. Though he never remembered saying it, when he won the Math Olympiad in record time, he was quoted in the school paper: "Work the mind. Work the body. Live long and prosper." *They can't make that stuff up.* He liked it. It had a nice ring.

Lipreading kept him better informed than the average twelve-going-on-thirteen-year-old. People assumed that because "the deaf boy" could not hear, he must be slow and unaware in other areas. In truth, because even his mother forgot how great his progress, he "overheard" much because they failed to guard their speech. He was gaining proficiency in understanding conversation in context; he could watch lip, jaw, tongue movements, and facial expressions to pick up the gist of what was being said.

People who mumbled, people with no teeth, and people with beards were the toughest to read. He liked it that Mr. Dixon shaved all facial hair whenever they came over to play Speed Spell. They hadn't come by in a very long time and Cody wondered why.

He missed Beth the most. She was so clean and smooth-skinned and friendly. Of all the lips he had ever read, he liked hers best. They glistened with lip gloss and were so pink and pretty. If he could have a sister, he would choose her. If he could have a girlfriend, he'd want it to be Beth. Sometimes how he felt about her got all confused, and he thought of her as sister and girlfriend at the same time. Which bothered him. The

58

older he got, the more his mind and body tangled, and he had to work on model planes to gain any peace.

I love Mom. I do. But why does she have to spend so much time being my guardian? Why can't she just be my mom? He missed the "hot chocolate and encouragement," hearing her say she was proud of him and that he was God's gift, special and unique, never to be duplicated. Stuff like that.

Instead, according to her, his smile was an idiot smile and hitting his thumb was dumb and a sign that he had to be kept out of sight in a safe box.

Dad buckled under to Mom, but at least there were times he felt Dad's hand on his shoulder and saw how often he bit his tongue.

"Sheila, give Code a break! I know, let's go bowling, just the three of us."

"Tonight? Oh, Andrew, none of us needs all that smoke and noise. You know that Biggs boy who plays on the high school bowling team? Dislocated his thumb in a tournament last week."

"Right. Code-man, I say we pop some corn and play a little *Aggravation*." He stressed the last word and gave Cody a secret wink. "That is, if you're not too sad from the last time I beat your sorry rear."

Dad tried.

And now, there they were. Words of hope, even if wrapped in a refusal. "Thank you for thinking of us, Cassie, but we really can't take time away right now to go camping. You understand."

Cody sat up. His mother *had* said "camping"! *Camping! Beth! What I would give to be in the woods, to make camp, to throw rocks in a river, to race Beth down the shoreline, to climb and jump and sleep in the open!*

Holey moley, this was getting good.

Cassie needed to somehow penetrate Sheila's barriers, but with caution. "Andy asked for help and God seconded the motion" would not gain a warm reception.

"Sheila, put yourself in Cody's shoes. Might the source of his sullenness and lack of communication be that he's bored and underchallenged? Look at how many of America's heroic men took the reins of life in their teeth and bit down hard! George Washington, Daniel Boone, Lewis and Clark, John Brown, Mark Twain, Teddy Roosevelt, Walt Disney —"

"Walt Disney?" No one did sarcasm like Sheila. "Now there's a strapping, two-fisted legend if ever I heard one!"

"I see your point." Cassie forced a laugh.

"But you get my drift. They made their mark by throwing caution to the wind and taking risks."

"And how many of them could hear, Cass? As far as I know, every one of them."

There was the slightest lift in Sheila's tone, cold mist giving way to dry overcast. Cassie hoped. "We're not planning an assault on Kilimanjaro, just a quiet few days in God's country. Cody will be with four fully functioning adults. Nothing will go wrong. And you watch. Cody's countenance will improve overnight. I know mine will."

This time the silence drew out until Cassie considered screaming.

"You and Nick enjoy your time out." Sheila was as infuriating as they came. "We'll get together in a week or two and you can tell us all about it." There was a stoic finality in it, a martyr clutching to a shred of dignity under the conquering force of Cody's deafness.

"Sheila —"

"Thank you for calling, Cassandra. I appreciate your concern, you know I do. But we're at a critical stage with Cody and not in any position to place him at risk. Please give my regards to Nick. We'll be sure to keep Beth in our prayers. Have fun."

At first, Cody's heart fell. Then he saw his father standing in the doorway from the living room into the kitchen, his face stormy. Clearly, he had overheard the conclusion to the conversation between Sheila and Cassie.

But there was something else. His dad stood straighter, purpose in his stance. Though it wasn't exactly a showdown at high noon, Cody's heartbeat quickened.

His mom set the phone down and looked at his father. Cody saw her stiffen. He locked on their mouths.

"I think we should go." Cody thought his dad looked a little like the color engravings of Patrick Henry in his American history book. "I think we should climb out of this hole we've dug for ourselves and go. What are we afraid of, Sheila? That Cody might get stung by a bee? Fall off a stump? Bang his head on a rock? All parents watch for that stuff. So what if he burns his mouth on a hot dog or gets whacked in the face with a tree branch? Good! He's got to learn to fend for himself, to suck it up, to know that a good time has its risks. You broke your arm riding your bike when you were nine.

When we met, my leg was in a cast from playing touch football with the guys in my dorm. Big deal! You fix it and move on."

Cody watched his mother's face harden, the way it did whenever anyone challenged the "program" for her son. "We don't have time to be running off on a prolonged picnic that invites danger and does nothing for our son's development. I'm surprised at you. You need to put your foot down and insist that he put in the time required to make his way in a hearing world."

Cody's dad flushed. "We've been over this time and again. Cody is deaf. That's hard enough. Who can blame him if he doesn't want to *look* deaf?"

His mom rolled her eyes. "Well, one look at you and we can all see where he comes by his obstinacy. He's about to enter high school, Andrew. If he's too vain to pursue total communication skills, he will start to lose ground and become the very object of sympathy and ridicule he so desperately wants to avoid. You're enabling him."

"You don't understand!" Cody almost let the words shout free, but he held back. So far his teachers, a few with reluctance, supported his efforts to be independent of listening devices and sign language. Some kids did well with those things and he was

glad for them. But he was different, and that difference required a different learning style. His teachers positioned his desk and spoke a little slower and with greater precision so that he became proficient in lipreading. What other technology did Helen Keller have? She learned through other means until her whole body became an ear.

Of course Mom doesn't get it. How can she when she can hear and I can't? The hearing lived in a world of sound. What she didn't know, but Cody had discovered, was how unreliable sound could be. For a bicyclist, it could actually be harmful because of a false sense of security. The reliability of the source of sounds outdoors was chancy at best. Which was why right-of-way rules in traffic law were based on the sense of sight, not hearing. The next most important senses were balance and touch. *Heck, hearing's not even in the top three.*

He knew it would be a big battle, but he planned to argue just as hard for a driver's license as any sixteen-year-old. No law prohibited a deaf person from operating either a motor vehicle or a motorcycle. *I'm going to have both.*

And if she said no way, he would run away. Lots of boys had run off, enlisted in the military, or left bad homes to go it alone.

No big deal. Go slow, live off the land, work a little, move on. He could do it and write a book about it.

Bad homes? Plenty of kids would give their right arm for the home he had. Trouble was, they had no clue what he had to put up with. He was like the prisoner of Brinker Circle.

"Andrew, remember that Stanislavski boy who disappeared? Like father, like son. They found him living in Boston. Changed his name but not his stripes. He's wanted for embezzlement and the murder of an attorney. He should be in jail for all the grief he caused the family. The sins of the fathers!"

God . . . please forgive me for what I'm thinking. Still, plenty of holy men — even some holy women — had roamed from home and started new lives. Sometimes he thought he could honor his mother better from a distance.

His dad walked over to his mom and placed his hands lovingly, but firmly, on her upper arms.

Cody scooted to the next chair at the dining table, granting his eyes more direct access to his parents' lips.

"Sheila, honey, we have to face facts. Cody will soon sprout chin hair. And I can tell he likes Beth Dixon, not a little, but a *lot*." His mom started to pull away, but Dad held her firm.

Cody squirmed. Had he really been that obvious about Beth?

"Our son is smart and capable and yes, headstrong, just like someone else I know. And yes, he hasn't been one to follow the program. But Dr. Haskert doesn't think that's such a bad thing. He told us that Cody's sense of self, his *position* in the world as he sees it, is key to how he will manage the rest of life. If we don't loosen the apron strings, I'm afraid he's going to cut them early. Look at the camping trip as a test and a way to allow for some normalcy for each of us. Otherwise, we might all lose our ability to hear one another."

He let her go. She turned from him and met her son's gaze. The slight rock back on her heels told Cody she had momentarily forgotten he was there. Neither blinked for a moment.

Cody wanted to hug her, tell her that his dad was right. *Jesus must love runaways. Understand them. He was one himself that time he ran off to the synagogue and couldn't be found. He was the same age as me.*

"Not now, Andy." With an almost imperceptible movement of the eyes, his mother indicated Cody's presence.

"Yes, now. It's Cody's life that's under discussion."

"Camping is for other children."

"Camping is for our child."

"I think . . . not." And yet, his mom didn't look at all certain.

Cody could not believe it. *Mom's never been this unsure. Come on. Come on.*

"It's best we see the present course through."

"Through to what, Sheila? Dr. Haskert's not going to mind if we take a short family vacation to gain some perspective. We all need to stretch our legs, if not our opinions."

Cody held his breath.

Mom fumbled with a gold-edged address book. "So what are you saying?"

Cody's dad looked at him and winked. "I'm saying that you might want to go shopping for a cute little pair of new hiking shorts."

"And why would I want to do that?"

Dad's broad smile took ten years off his face. "Because, Mrs. Ferguson, we're going camping!"

Cody whooped and earned a startled squawk from the parakeet's cage.

His mother shot him a withering glance. "And if I refuse?"

Cody gritted his teeth. *God, God do something!*

"Then it's just the Code-man and me."

Go, Dad! Cody watched his mom absorb the shock of the unyielding declaration. It took her a couple of seconds more to scan all the possible scenarios before coming up short of any that she liked. Her jaw tightened, her lips pursed, and Cody knew in his gut the goal line was within reach.

"Your mind's made up?"

"Tighter than a 38 suit on a 44 frame."

"Don't do this, Andrew."

"Got to, Sheila. The boy can't breathe."

"And his father?"

"Gasping."

His mom studied the backs of her hands.

Please, please . . . Cody willed her to make the right decision.

When she looked up, her expression was resolute. "I can't allow the two of you to traipse off into the wild blue . . ."

Cody's heart fell. *Oh, no.*

". . . without rules and stability. I'll go along."

What? Did she really say that? They could go? They were *all* going?

"But I'm not baiting any hooks, and there had better be toilet paper."

CHAPTER 3

"Seventy-seven bottles of root beer on the wall, seventy-seven bottles of root beer. Take one down, pass it around, seventy-six bottles of root beer on the wall! Seventy-six . . ."

Cassie couldn't help a small, private grin at the camper's ditty given a G-rated twist. Cody had always loved to sing, and his brain retained the songs and pitch he had learned as a younger child. Cassie had read some of Dr. Haskert's writings. He believed that people heard with their brains. Cody could sing on the key stored in memory, but it was his key and everyone else needed to follow.

With Cassie's college friend Joanie at the wheel of the SUV, Cody riding shotgun, the two of them threw exaggerated gestures and roared the lyrics like inebriated old sea salts newly arrived in port. *If that's a sullen, withdrawn boy, I'll eat my rain poncho. All his attitude needs is to stretch its legs.*

69

Behind them sat Sheila and Andy Ferguson. Andy underscored the front seat alto and tenor with a half-decent bass. Beside him, Sheila sat in inscrutable tight-lipped tolerance betrayed by her left index finger tapping the tempo against one pale knee.

In the rear seat beside Cassie, Nick fumbled for both tune and timing, creating a fusillade of spirited bebops that might as easily have worked with "Flight of the Bumble Bee" or "Peggy Sue." For her part, Cassie contributed a passionate subtext consisting mostly of the repetitious "bottles and bottles and bottles" — with the occasional "pass it, pass it, pass it" for dramatic effect.

It was silly good fun, and from the looks of it, had almost all of them in the mood for letting off steam in the great outdoors. When Cassie first heard that there had been a breakthrough at the Fergusons, she was stunned. Now to see the Ferguson men in matching cargo pants, ratty sneakers, San Francisco Giants baseball caps turned backward, and hunter green sweatshirts with the sleeves ripped off, she was convinced that this idea of hers was inspired.

Not that the launch had been without incident. Sheila insisted on packing for a three-week safari for twelve, then added insult to injury by spraying herself with three layers of insect repellent *before* boarding the plane to Seattle.

Andy wagged his head. "For Pete's sake, Sheila, the mosquitoes aren't going to greet you at the gate, and it's safe to say that you will not be bitten by anyone on this plane."

She folded her arms. "Never mind. If I'm to survive this ordeal, it will be by anticipating everything unpleasant. Trust me, it's a long list." One that included a sublist with enough ointments, sprays, and bandages to equip a small military field hospital. A single overnight bag contained nothing but a pair of tweezers, a pair of travel scissors, and twelve rolls of four-ply toilet tissue. It was all they could do to convince Sheila to check the bag through rather than try to carry it on.

Cassie stared out the window. The cornfields and alfalfa pastures morphed into sporadic forest, increasing elevation, and soon they were in the thick of the Cascade Mountain Range. Clouds churned over the escarpments in a gloomy gray and black swirl, but relinquished no moisture. Occasional sun breaks assured that the implied storm lacked teeth.

When the bottles on the wall were reduced to fewer than thirty, Nick piped up. "Hey,

Sheila, you hiding extra Speed Spell tiles in that Swiss army hat of yours?"

Sheila was dressed head-to-toe in the latest breathable, wrinkle-free, long-sleeved attire for the sensible woods woman. She reached up and patted the tan canvas fisherman's hat equipped with pockets and hidden sleeves for maximum storage. "Everything from Tums to cotton swabs." No missing the hint of pride. "In case I become separated from my main kit."

Nick grinned. "Hey, Andy, I thought *you* were her main kit."

Andy snorted. "You've got it confused, old boy. I'm her main squeeze."

Nick gave the brim of Sheila's hat a smart tug from behind. "How many rolls of TP you got stowed in that thing?"

Sheila sniffed. "Jest all you want, Nicholas. I do hope you've brought sufficient funds to purchase extra sheets from me should you run out. I'll share — for a price."

"No need. Me, I'll be grabbing leaves and bark from nature's well-stocked shelves. Am I right, Cody?" He caught the boy's attention by waving and carefully repeating what they'd said.

Though there were still twenty-four bottles to go, Cody laughed and left Joanie to soldier on alone. "Right, Mr. D. Biodegradable is the only way to go. You dig a cat hole six inches down, do your business, drop in the used leaves, cover it over, and in a few days the microorganisms in the topsoil break down the waste." Though his voice had deepened, Cody still spoke with an individualized inflection that carried a unique pronunciation of words he'd never heard himself say, colored by the tonal sounds he remembered from when he could hear. It was, in some cases, vocalization guesswork, largely shaped by memory.

Cassie chuckled at Cody's woodsman savvy. Sheila scowled. "All right, Andrew, you tell me where he got that from? Is that proper talk for a twelve-year-old in mixed company?"

Andrew took his time, and Cassie saw Cody focus on the outcome of the discussion. "It is, dear, when the company is sharing an outdoor experience. I, for one, plan to bathe in the buff. You ladies can go off daisy picking and allow us men a little privacy."

The look he received could peel paint. He burst out laughing, Nick guffawed, and the others joined in. Sheila glared.

Cody's expression was sheer delight. Cassie could guess why. They were a family again, kidding around, doing normal family stuff. Cassie watched Cody drink it down like rainwater in the desert. The outdoors were good for him. He acted like anything but the Gloomy Gus that Andy told her he'd become.

Much as it warmed her to see everyone relaxed and engaged in friendly banter, Cassie had to wonder what future lay ahead for all of them.

Joanie, her college roommate, had never married and liked the single life. But what about when she grew old and there was no family to care for her and give her grandbabies?

The Fergusons would retire comfortably on Andy's pension. He was one of the company's top salesmen in the region. But what about when they were pushing sixty and Cody was just beginning to explore his future in earnest? They'd be elderly before he produced any progeny, and what were the odds the next Ferguson generation would be deafened by the faulty family gene?

Would Cody survive the teen years in a household as protective as the Fergusons'? Would he go to college? What career paths were open to him? Would he find love? What special woman would marry a man with such a limitation? Or would Cody, in his own way, prove more capable than most hearing males?

Cass watched Nick from the corner of her eye. They had weathered a near catastrophe and landed on their feet, albeit with a significant limp. When one dream died, did another rise up? Was Beth their one real hope of correcting their mistakes? How could they get closer to God and better understand their place in the universe before their years dwindled to only a few? Intellectually, she believed she'd experienced the Almighty's forgiveness. Emotionally, things were not as clear.

She had a wealth of questions and paltry few answers. Father Byron said that as a species, human beings were not so good at abiding in God and allowing their lives to unfold according to divine plan. The animal world was much better at it. He said that was why so many religious folk through the ages had turned to the monastic life. To learn to abide. To shut up, sit down, and hold on.

Will I ever learn? Why am I feeling so maudlin today?

"Thank you, ladies and gentlemen, and welcome to Dodge Creek Campground." Joanie's exaggerated formality as she turned in at a gate marked "Private — No Trespass-

75

ing" was perfect. A winding avenue of old growth cedars lined the way, and Cassie rolled the window down — only partway against the dust — to breath deeply of their heavenly aroma. "We thank you for flying with Air Joan and trust that your stay in the Cascade region will be a pleasant one."

Before long, the trees parted and they bounced over river stones to the bank of an exuberant stream and a bucolic camp-ground, several numbered tent sites with tables and benches carpeted in grass and fir needles. A pair of ubiquitous Sanicans slouched toward each other as if gossiping over the new arrivals.

"Those are your well-maintained bath-room facilities?" Sheila scowled. "I suppose any showers we get will have to come from the sky?"

"Guess you'll have to skinny-dip with the boys." So said, Andy gave Cody a sly poke in the ribs.

"In your dreams, insurance man."

Cassie hid a smile. *Sheila, Sheila . . .*

The clouds parted, the sun streamed down, and diamonds flashed off the surface of the river. Mountains robed in forested splendor rose on three sides. High in the far distance, a set of craggy knuckles clutched several patches of last winter's snow tight to the chin of the soaring ridgeline.

"Tight Grip Ridge." Joanie nodded at the rock formation. "Nice views from there."

Cassie felt the tension evaporate. It had been held in for too long.

No sooner were the doors open and the adults moaning and stretching from the long ride, than Cody was off like a shot. Cassie smiled and watched him race down the creek bed for the river, all long legs and coiled energy. He was like one of those spring-loaded, jack-in-the-box clowns that answered only to "Pop Goes the Weasel."

"Andy! You go grab that boy and bring him back here this instant. He can't just run wild like that. There have got to be a few ground rules around here, or next thing you know, he's going to be at the bottom of the river, and what then?"

The light of shared joys that had lifted Andy like the rising sun, quickly set. Cassie watched him hurry after his son, face snared in a dark net of conflict.

It was difficult for her to witness. Whereas she had so recently congratulated herself for arranging this little adventure, she now questioned if it could work. Sheila was edgier than she remembered. *There is little worse than dangling Cody over a garden of delights only to snatch him back every time he reaches out a hand to experience one.*

Nick and Joanie began unloading the SUV. Sheila stood with hands clenched to hips, lips tight-pressed, watching her husband's slow progress toward their excited son. Cassie slipped an arm around her friend's rigid shoulders. "Come on, hon. Leave the men to conquer the territory while we go cook up a tasty feast to mark the beginning of a great weekend."

At first, Sheila said nothing and stood her ground. Only when Andy overtook a giggling Cody and hoisted him under one arm did she relax a little. She allowed herself to be led to the white gas cookstove Nick was priming for the evening meal.

"Burgers, me hardies?" Cassie unpacked the food box and handed Sheila the tomatoes and onions to slice.

Nick gave his wife's rear a playful swat. "Argh, me kitchen wench! Argh!"

Cass laughed. Sheila watched them, expression revealing nothing. Cass hoped she liked the easy, carefree friendship she saw between them.

The tussling and giggling grew louder as Andy and Cody neared camp. Cassie saw the stern look on Sheila's face and knew that the fun was about to end.

She threw arms wide to draw Cody's attention. "So everybody, how about a rousing game of Speed Spell while we get the burgers going? Cody, there's a brown leather pouch of tiles at the top of my blue backpack. Can you go get it and set up the game down at the far end of the table?"

Eager as a puppy, Cody freed himself from his dad and tore off to the SUV. He loved the game. Sheila had said that it expanded his vocabulary and gave him plenty to talk about — and practice — with his speech therapist.

Whatever she was about to say, Sheila bit down on it and remained silent. She looked at Cassie, who did not look away. "He's got to learn there are boundaries," Sheila said. "You can't know what it's like, Cass. Your child can hear."

"Only what she wants to, like any of us. The physical ability to hear is no guarantee we'll do the right thing, and plenty of hearing people perish from doing the wrong thing. Give him time and space, Sheila, that's all I'm saying."

Without another word, Sheila took a knife and chopped an onion in two. The sharp *thwack* of the knife made Cassie flinch.

She found the frying pan, coated the bottom with vegetable oil, and set it on the stove. She slapped a wad of fresh ground beef into a patty and breathed a silent prayer. *Grant us all time and space, dear Lord, and the grace to survive this weekend!*

CHAPTER 4

Why does Mom have to turn everything into a federal offense?

The shorter the leash, the more Cody wanted to run his legs off. He resisted the temptation to defy her, although on occasion he did so. A lot more lately. Like when he'd gone to Blake Harriman's birthday party and gone swimming in Blake's pool. He knew his mother would not have approved.

The other kids had their suits and Blake had loaned him one of his. And then afterwards, flush with the memory of the glorious water and the feel of freedom, he had arm wrestled all six of the boys there and beat each in turn. Blake, the biggest, was toughest. But muscles popping out, Cody endured after his opponent's face went purple. No, he couldn't technically hear the others shout congratulations, but Cody sure could feel it in the hands that slapped his bare back and the looks of admiration, especially from the girls. For one afternoon, the deaf boy was the star.

Nevertheless, Blake and the others found some excuse not to attend Cody's eleventh birthday party. He didn't blame them. What was there to do at the deaf boy's house? His mother did not permit anything more adventurous than watching videos, and nobody — most especially the birthday boy — wanted to watch *Finding Nemo* again, with or without closed captions.

Cody didn't bother sending invitations to his twelfth.

He fingered the metal whistle that hung from a leather thong around his neck and gave it a bitter yank.

That's it! I'm taking off. If she's going to run this cool place just like home, then I'm out of here. Look around! Plenty of air, plenty of water, plenty of food if you know where to look, and I do. Winter is a problem, but I'll deal with that when it comes.

The skin of the leather Speed Spell pouch felt soft and cool in his other hand. It was a goldmine of infinite vocabulary. *Wanderlust* was one of his favorites. An irresistible impulse to travel. *I've got a sweet case of wanderlust. If she thinks she can lock me in a wooden cage the whole time we're out here,*

I've got to prove what I can do.

He loved words, loved their meanings and shades of meaning. He loved to write, yet kept little personal record of his silent journey. Diaries could be found, read, interpreted, misinterpreted. Better to write on "the tablets of the heart," like the Bible said God did. Better to wait until Cody William Ferguson was fully grown before moving the contents of who he was from the interior to the exterior. For now, he would answer their essay questions, fill in their blanks, and play Speed Spell like a champion. Let people read your actions, eat your dust, try to find meaning in your scores. Let them judge your results, not your confusions.

Time enough to write when he had more answers than questions.

As the sun set and streaks of yellow antiqued the mountain peaks, he stood at the rear bumper of the SUV and watched the adults prepare dinner, unpack boxes, spread tents, and generally make camp inhabitable before Joanie took off in her vehicle. The loss of sun made him shiver and think of putting on his sweats. The smell of frying burgers mixed with those of fir trees, flowing water, and clean mountain air made his stomach growl. He saw his dad and Nick ease into their old friendship as they connected tent rods and pounded stakes past a bed of dry needles into the spongy forest floor.

Besides his mother's tight reins, Beth's absence was the other sour note of the weekend. The Romeo and Juliet thing to do would have been to refuse to come without her, but she would have wanted him to come. Besides, nothing — *nothing* — could have stopped him from making his first prison break in forever.

Sure he wanted her there, pretty hair, smooth skin, cute face he would kiss with just an ounce of encouragement.

Whoa! Where'd that come from? Heat filled his face. *Who am I kidding?* Beth treated him like her kid brother. Okay, so she didn't seem bothered by his deafness, but for his twelve-year-old lips to come anywhere near her more mature ones? She would probably think it was gross or weird. No, she would probably hurl.

But look where he was! What did it matter that Beth's kissable face was thousands of miles away? Maybe he would go find her. Rappel out of a helicopter, snatch her from the ground, and fly her away where they could talk. For now, he was in the mountains, wildness all around. Things he had only read about, fantasized over, itched to experience, surrounded him on all sides. He was out of that narrow, choking world of clinic, school, home, and bedroom. Nothing but nature everywhere. Puberty could shut up!

And when you thought about it, women and woods mostly didn't mix anyway. It was a man's world. In fact, women in the woods just might be as bad an idea as women on board ships was to the ancient mariners. For sure he'd have to remember that *jinx* made an excellent Speed Spell word. Anything to use *x* in a word, without having to spell *sex* in front of grown-ups.

He watched the paring knife slip and nick his mother's finger. Cassie had it cleaned and bandaged in nothing flat, and the tension between the two women eased. It was a long way from sisterhood, but enough for him to see his mom's guard start to slip.

He gave the metal whistle another disgusted yank and pondered the consequences of "losing" it. She made him wear it like some stupid farm animal with a bell around its throat to keep from getting lost. Did she forget that he could yell with the best of them? He was deaf, not mute.

Of course, he knew the real reason for the whistle. It wasn't really so he'd feel safer, but that *she* could. As the smaller apron strings that bound him to her snapped one by one, the more she tightened her grip, from safety whistles to her efforts to get him to wear hearing aids when he was younger. He refused. How could she understand that for him the little plastic amplifiers were like ugly carbuncles on the hull of a sleek and sporty yacht? Plus they didn't work. He had tried them before he went totally deaf and all they produced was a tinny gabble of confusing sounds or the dull muffle of people trying to converse underwater. They were only good for one thing. Whenever he wanted to drive hearing persons to distraction, he knew how to set the aids so that they produced piercing shrieks.

The one apron string between deaf child and hearing mother that he hated most growing up was her insisting on an emergency button at the head of his bed. It made the lamp next to his mother's side of his parents' bed flash on and off should he ever need her. Controlled by a pressure disk at the end of a cord, they pinned it to his bottom sheet like those buttons on hospital beds used to call the nurse. When younger, Cody sometimes punched the button just to make his mom come running. He could tell she slept lightly by the speed with which she materialized at his side — every time, without fail. He would either feign sleep or bat wide eyes and ask if he could have a drink of water.

It made him feel guilty — at first.

But after a while . . . well, it served her right.

What did she think would happen? That whatever monster had stolen her son's hearing would come crawling back for his sight? Or, if it had enough sensory organs, run off with his liver or his kidneys? All the button did was make him feel like a loser.

He shouldn't have treated her like his personal servant. Jerks did that. If only she would stop always looking for a way to replace what was gone! If only she would take the time to listen to his heart and get to know the Cody she had instead of always searching for the Cody who was. That old Cody could hear but was never coming back.

Sometimes he fantasized using the emergency button not because he was in trouble or playing a game, but to announce a miracle. When she arrived breathless and anxious at his side, he would look up at her, smile, and say, "Guess what, Mom? I can hear again!"

But with that sweet dream always came

the fear of what he would see on her face when she heard the good news. What if that joyous expression revealed a dreaded truth: her greater love for the Cody who could hear?

A red rolled sleeping bag soared through the air and caught him square in the chest. He held it tight and looked to the one who'd thrown it. "Nice catch, Pokey. Get your fanny over here and lay out our beds, will ya? Guys in one tent, girls in the other." Nick smiled and faked another shot with a tan bag. Cody wasn't fooled by the fake move and relaxed his grip. Immediately, the tan bag sailed toward his face.

With split-second reflexes, Cody fired the red bag back at Nick and snagged the streaking tan bag. They paused, eyes narrowed, scanning the opposition for telltale signs of movement.

Andy crept up behind Nick and pinned his arms to his side. Swift as a cat, Cody nailed Nick's head with the tan bag — and the three-way fight was on.

Geneva Convention! Geneva Convention!" Cassie shielded the food-prep area from the flying sleeping bags zinging past like a juggling act gone bad. "Subsection nine specifically states the site of battle shall be far removed from the mess hall!"

Sheila stood apart, swatting unseen insects with a spatula.

Ignoring Cassie's rules of engagement, men and boy met in hand-to-hand struggle, sleeping bags transforming into squishy battering rams. All three males fell onto a still-flattened nylon tent in a laughing free-for-all. Cassie danced around the perimeter, at first making small attempts to extricate individual combatants. But with a hearty "Geronimo!" Cassie suddenly collapsed onto the writhing pile.

"The British are coming!"

"The burgers are burning!"

"Cody's nose is bleeding!"

The whirling dervish of bodies froze. Cody leapt to his feet. "Ha! Fooled you! My nose is fine." He ran to the other side of the picnic table and slurped down two pickles before his father caught him and hauled him back. "And what" — Andy cried, tone and expression ominous — "shall we do with the boy who cries wolf?"

"String him up by his chinny-chin-chin." Nick pantomimed a noose. "Grind his bones to make our bread!" He tickled Cody, who shrieked in laughing protest.

"Cease-fire! Cease-fire!" Cassie was breathless. "The burgers are on fire . . ."

Without a word, Sheila arranged hamburgers and buns on paper plates.

Dinner rescued with only minimal charring, the five campers donned fleece vests and jackets against the night chill and sat down to the evening meal with eager outdoor appetites.

"And you thought grace couldn't be bought." Nick gave the air a ketchup-smeared smooch in Cassie's direction. "Burgers, baby, the bribe of choice at every peace accord I care to be a part of!"

Cassie poked Cody to get his attention. "More corn on the cob?"

Cody, mouth smeared with butter and corn bits, handed his plate over.

Soon the dishes were soaking. Eager to be in his element, Cody stirred the Speed Spell tiles, blank sides up, on an oversized bread board. He took great pleasure in beating "the old folks."

When everyone had selected seven tiles at random, they lined them up in one row of four and another of three. Cody drew out the suspense an extra four beats before at last declaring, "Go!"

Fingers and tiles flew, each player combining and recombining the letters to make words. In short order, his mom made *quest* and *net* out of her seven tiles. Amidst the groans and good-natured snipes of her opponents, she commanded "Take one!" and a blur of fingers swiped another tile from the pool in the center of the table.

Cody, cursed with two Gs, quickly made *fling* and *gig* and breathlessly achieved five "Take ones" in a row before the advantage went to Mr. Dixon and then his dad in quick succession.

When his dad drew a *C* that went nowhere, Cody spelled *motley* and resumed control. "I'm the only one in the history of the game who ever spelled *motley!*" He then drew a *P* that went nowhere.

He watched Cassie play her sneaky, "minding my own business" style. She grabbed control with a string of two-letter words. Near the end of the tiles, his mom, who had not been heard from in awhile, surprised them all by spelling *dictator* and held the advantage until with the last tile she spelled *drat* and shouted "Done!"

"Pure luck." Cody wore a cagey grin. "Prepare to die!"

Cody won the next two rounds, and his mother the fourth. Each had two wins. Cody puffed up his chest. "I've toyed with you long enough, Mother. The time has come to put you out of your misery."

"Don't forget, Mr. Greedy, that on average females live longer than males."

"All the more reason to end this, here and now!"

The tiebreaker moved along and as the end neared, Cody started his victory chatter. "Prepare for defeat. I, Ferguson the Fantastic, will now take my last tile and achieve the impossible in a dazzling display of genius. With a wave of the hand, presto change-o, I turn this *rabbi* into a *rabbit!*" He added the *T* to *rabbi* and took a bow.

Cody ducked a punch from Nick, but was caught by the shoulders and his dad pulled him close. "Why, you're no magician. You're just that snot-nosed Cody kid!" He received a grin as sunny as the boy's blond head.

While the men argued over the sleeping arrangements, Cassie and Sheila warmed themselves by the fire.

"Thanks for your help with dinner." The river and the frogs filled the night with song. Cassie followed a spark from the orange embers until it winked out in the darkness. The smell of camp smoke filled her with warm thoughts of campouts with her folks. By now, her father would have broken out the Jew's harp and played "Yankee Doodle Dandy" and "Peace Like a River."

"Did you ever go camping as a kid?"

Sheila shook her head. "No. Mother was strictly a motel camper and Daddy liked his comforts as well. I went with the Girl Scouts a few times. I do remember one time, late at night, when my family was locked out of our house. Rather than wake anyone or jimmy the door, Daddy let us climb the ladder and camp on the roof of the carport. We had some old blankets in the trunk and a dish of cold macaroni and cheese my aunt sent home with us. I was just five or six and thought that my brother and me and our parents all snuggled under those blankets was big adventure."

"Sounds fun."

"I've never had better mac and cheese."

Cassie poked the fire, releasing a swarm of darting sparks. "Is your brother in the San Francisco area?"

Sheila grew quiet. "Fred passed away when he was ten. He caught some kind of lung infection that spread despite the antibiotics. They kept him in the hospital for weeks, and my mother stayed with him as much as she could. One afternoon when she was away at a doctor's appointment for some kind of female problem, Freddy started to cough up blood, and before they could figure out what to do for him, he died.

Mother never forgave herself for being gone when Freddy needed her most. Father wouldn't say more than two words for a year after the funeral." She stopped and pulled both hands inside the sleeves of her jacket. "That won't be my Cody. I don't care how mad he gets, I'm going to be there for him."

Cassie felt for Sheila. Her story explained a lot. "Of course you will. I'm so sorry about your brother. How lonely you must have been after he was gone."

"Still am at times."

They were quiet awhile and then Cassie hugged her. "I'll bet Cody remembers this trip as long as he lives."

It was several more moments before Sheila responded. "I'm sure. But I feel that we're rewarding him for being uncooperative. He doesn't know how hard we've tried to arrange what he needs. He'll pretend to get sick and not want to see the therapist. Or refuse to attend a concert with sign language interpreters. It wasn't always that way. We did have him work with a singing coach before he went completely deaf. She agrees with Dr. Haskert that we actually hear with our brains, so she taught him tonal memory, which helped his singing and speaking skills. But for the last year, he's been a handful."

Cassie stared at the stars. "Ever wonder

how God does it?"

"What do you mean?"

"How he communicates with us. How we hear him?"

"I guess we learn what he expects of us and then listen for that the rest of our lives."

"But listen to the sounds all around us right now. The Psalms say that the sound of creation is the sound of praises to God. Could it also be his voice trying to tell us something?"

"I'm just a lowly reading specialist. I'll leave the theology to you."

"You're not a lowly anything, Sheila. You're a wonderfully gifted person with a terrific husband and son. You and Andy have much to be proud of."

Sheila tossed a twig into the fire. "Then why do I feel like such a failure? Life hasn't followed the script I wrote for it."

"Tell me about it. After the perfume debacle, all I wanted to do was hide under a rock. We put every egg we had in that basket."

Sheila turned from the fire and faced the darkness. "At least you had a supportive husband who backed you up. You and Nick agreed on what needed to be done —"

"Our hearts were broken, but God had our attention. He communicated through a disaster because we were too self-absorbed to pay attention otherwise."

Sheila stood and stuck her hands in her coat pockets. "Fine for you. Andy and I keep missing one another. Coming out here is a perfect example. He doesn't want to refuse Cody anything. If you ask me, he's trying to ease his guilt over our son's deafness by catering to him. You know teenagers, they act on impulse and need a tight rein. That's become my job. So Cody thinks I'm mean and controlling, and Andy takes his side instead of working with me to present a unified front. We are a house divided."

Cassie peered heavenward and closed her eyes. *God, please, a little wisdom here!* "It's always a challenge with teens to know when to loosen up on those reins. I'm guessing Andy needs some guy time with Cody, and this is as good a way as any to get it."

Sheila reached down, lifted a good-sized chunk of firewood, and dumped it onto the fire. It succeeded in knocking the fire apart and sent Cassie stumbling back from a choking cloud of smoke and embers. "*Guessing?* I think it's a good deal more than a guess on your part, Cassandra. Just how long have you and Andrew been conspiring over this camping trip anyway?"

Cassie's stomach churned. "Conspiring?

There's no conspiracy, Sheila. Andy asked me for some input and I thought —"

"*Input?* Input into our private business? What did he tell you about me? That I'm to blame for our son's disability? That I'm so unreasonable he needs you to straighten me out? Well, let me save you the trouble! I just need to be supported or left alone. Do you think you could do one of those two things?"

Then she was gone. Swallowed by the darkness quick as a magician's finale.

Cassie swiped at stinging tears. *What am I doing? I could have made this much of a mess at home and saved us a trip.*

Cody awoke from a fitful sleep and looked around. Where was he?

His heart fell when he finally recognized what he'd been dreaming.

It was the day he went deaf.

Fall was in the air, and Cody's family had just returned from the best trip ever to Sea World. He'd even put his hand and arm inside a whale's mouth! A thrill he placed right up there with a lion tamer sticking his head between a big cat's jaws or the first time Houdini escaped from the water torture chamber.

He'd made eye contact with that amazing orca, and the look he found there could only be described as kindly tolerance. Cody knew in his heart of hearts that the beautiful animal *invited* him to stroke its tongue. Though it could have pulled him underwater or bitten his skinny six-year-old arm in two like a toothpick, it surrendered its power and allowed instead intimate contact between boy and beast.

The night after the encounter, Cody couldn't sleep. He was Adam at the naming of the animals, placing a gentle hand on each untamed head, asking God for wisdom, then marveling at the sound of each name that rippled so naturally from his throat. At the naming of the sea creatures, he knelt in the sand at the edge of the sea and felt the glossy smoothness of the creature. "Whale." The first time ever the word was spoken. As if in reply, the mammoth fish threw back its head and sang its song at a pitch so strange that Cody awoke, the length of his body humming with the music of the spheres.

He must have cried out, because his mother, dressed in blue jeans and a white sweatshirt depicting historic wooden sailing ships, settled onto the mattress beside him and stroked his forehead. He tried to tell her about the whale's song still resonating through his body like a tuning fork, but something was wrong.

He couldn't hear what he said.

Or what she said back.

His mother slapped the clock on his bed stand and moved her lips. The clock must have buzzed, but he heard nothing — not buzz nor slap nor mother. Though sunlight streamed in the windows, he heard no birds. Though the air in his room smelled of eggs and toast, he'd heard none of the sounds of preparation as on every other school day of his short life. And where were the familiar sounds of his father starting the car, the garage door opening and closing, or the toot of the car horn, Dad's last goodbye to the family before his work took his attention?

He lay in the bed and whined, complained, pulled at his unresponsive ears. But it wasn't like when he submerged in the tub and played Navy Seal on the hunt for undersea explosives. When he surfaced, he could get rid of the water in his ears by holding his nose and swallowing. Or by tipping his head to one side and thumping the other side with the heel of his hand.

This time, the water wouldn't leave. Sound wasn't just muffled, but gone.

He watched his mother's lips with mounting panic. Lips moved and made no sound. It was as if he was left behind and any words he missed were gone forever.

Mother felt his head. No fever. No more vacation. No faking. Back to school, Cody William. He guessed at her words. He got *school* from what looked like *cool.* The panic mounted. He couldn't keep up.

She rose and turned to fold his church pants from the chair where he'd flung them the previous Sunday before they left for San Diego. He guessed she was still talking, but he couldn't hear any of it. Worse, it felt like what he imagined an astronaut would feel if he was on a space walk and his tether caught on something and snapped. Lost in space. No way back.

Alone forever.

"Mom!" He wailed her name. The next thing he knew, he couldn't catch a breath and his mother rushed to calm his flailing body. That's when he knew she knew something was not right.

She called his father at work but though Cody could not know the exact conversation, he could imagine. "Kid ailments, Andrew. Lots of drama. Blowing little things up bigger than they are."

When his sobbing reduced to hiccupping, she took him in her arms. "I can't hear!" At last she caved. At the walk-in clinic, he was weighed and his temperature taken. They peered into his ears, down his throat, up his nose. In the end, mother and son left with a cherry Tootsie Pop and a referral to a doctor of pediatric audiology.

It was the first mile of a long and winding road. By the third or fourth hairpin turn, they knew the truth. He wasn't faking it. Little kid with the big problem known as congenital sensorineural hearing loss. In time, he came to learn the term and its consequences. There were many different causes for it — including medications, noise, and genetics — but bottom line, in half the cases a single cause was never named.

Of course, the doctor was not so blunt, and his mother used smaller words Cody could understand when she printed out an explanation. But since then, he rewrote that life-changing consult a dozen times.

He immediately fell into a fog of self-pity and guilt. His parents made the painful decision to not have more children. The risk was just too high. So not only was he deaf, he'd wrecked their hopes for loads of grandchildren. Only recently, he began to wonder what would happen if he married and became a dad. What were the odds that his kids would go deaf?

Though he never said anything about these fears to his parents, they felt his guilt and it increased their own. Early tests showed Cody's IQ was exceptionally high, and what parents could have resisted dreaming of their son the rocket scientist? Could their flaw have doomed the next Einstein?

That's when they started fighting more. Even in silence, Cody understood the hurtful accusations hurled back and forth between them. Why'd they rush into marriage? Why weren't they responsible enough to get tested for genetic problems? In the heat of one fight, they forgot Cody was there.

He still remembered staring straight at his mother when she shouted her disappointment. "No way would I have gotten married if I'd known what I know now!" His father stormed out. They learned later that their son spent the night at the bus depot. At four a.m., he called Father Byron at St. John's Cathedral, who called his parents. With misgivings, they allowed him to find three hours of fitful sleep at the priest's manse in a bean bag chair next to a battered black-and-white TV before going to pick him up.

Over time he beat everyone's expectations for his academic accomplishments. What was harder to rise above were the feelings that he was "special ed." While his few close friends seemed often to forget he was disabled, the majority of his classmates thought of him as different. Weird. Broken.

The school losers called him *retard.* They snuck up and popped paper bags behind his head to see him *not* jump. They drew crude pictures of him as a stooped, balding old man with a hearing aid twice the size of his head.

Dr. Haskert tried his best to make things better. "They have their own insecurities, Cody. They feel threatened by you. You have experienced a profound loss and yet are able to cope with life as well or better than they can with all their senses intact. They resent it and are maybe a little frightened that it could happen to them. Ridiculously, some people worry subconsciously that they might catch someone else's disability."

And over it all hovered his mother, nervous, diligent, on guard, watchful as one who never sleeps. By the age of ten, his most fervent prayer was that his parents would take two weeks in Europe and leave him home with his buddy, Blake. Fourteen glorious days of sleepovers, swimming, video games, and gorging on pizza was Cody's idea of paradise.

But his dreams were the closest he ever came to heaven on earth. One day, Cody understood with cold certainty that his parents did not accept that they had a deaf child. They conceived and gave birth to a hearing child, only to later have the children switched on them, with deafness the booby prize. They understood the mechanics of deafness. But that their once-hearing child was now deaf was unacceptable. It was as if he hid the inner gears of his ears in a box and refused to tell them where he'd put the box. It was like they loved him, but didn't quite "get" him, so chose to bide their time until he pulled out the box and reinstalled the machinery to get his ears working again. Until then, he wasn't normal and there was no sense in pretending that he was. They would simply treat him with their one-size-fits-all approach to deafness.

Except his dad was much better than his mom. He came as close as anyone to treating Cody as a regular kid. "Go bang your knees and scrape your elbows. A lizard? Sure thing. I'll help you catch flies for its dinner."

The trouble with Cody's dad was Cody's mother. Most of the time, his dad didn't want to cross her because her control of a home with a deaf child in it was where the last of her dignity might be found.

When he was ten, Cody explained it to

the doctor. "My parents don't know I know."

"And what do you know, son?"

"That my mom has to make all the decisions about me or she'll go crazy. It's her way of making up for making me deaf. That means keeping me locked inside where she thinks I'm safe. If I never get out, *I'll* go crazy. My dad gets that, but he doesn't want to upset my mom. So he works a lot. If he stayed home more, he could help."

As soon as Cody told the doctor about his suspicions, he would have given anything to stuff them back in his gut where they belonged. It was too late. Though he made Dr. Haskert swear on his PhD that he would say nothing to Mom and Dad, Cody knew that he would. Adults loved analyzing those too young and defenseless to prevent it. No doctor-patient secrets where a minor was concerned. Everything a disabled kid said was seen as a clue to figuring out the disablement and restoring order. Except that Cody knew that in the end the only one who could do the restoring was Cody himself. And God. God alone knew for sure where Cody's box of hearing gears was kept.

Thanks to the Internet, Cody knew that generally a deaf child is better off with deaf parents. Deaf parents slow down, touch more, and use large facial expressions and body language to grab their child's attention. Hearing parents are more self-conscious, make fewer allowances, and plain forget to take the time it takes to understand.

"It takes a deaf person to really know a deaf person and the meaning of deafness." He wasn't sure his buddy Blake understood, but he had to say it. "What if I never meet that person?"

They met at the confluence of the river and the little creek that tried so hard to be a river. Close together, Cassie and Nick sat, fingers entwined.

"Couldn't sleep. You?"

"Not a wink. Now that's a gorgeous moon."

An impressionist moon shimmered in the leaping turbulence of the river, while above, its realistic counterpart burned a bright hole in the heavens.

"Wonder what Beth's doing tonight? Do you think we should have let her go? What if there's a coup?"

Nick hugged her close. "I was thinking more along the lines of a fiesta in the town square, bright skirts flying, music, food, streets filled with folklore and laughter. Beth laughing and swinging little children around and around."

"Ever the romantic."

"We can't stop her, Cass. And think how fortunate the world is to have her."

Cassie snuggled against his arm. "I know. I'm so proud of her good heart. Do you think the Fergusons will ever loosen their grip on Cody?"

"Well, I think we'll know more in a couple of days."

"Do you think Beth's somewhere right now doing the salsa?"

"I hope so."

"What were we thinking letting her go off to a hot Latin location?"

"Honey, she was raised right. You can trust her."

"I know. I just miss her so much and want her safe."

"She's in God's hands. And look on the bright side. Where there's a fiesta in full swing, it's unlikely there'll be a coup."

She pinched him. Twice.

He awoke just as dawn tapped its baton and the brightening river became a misty ballroom.

Cool. Cody poked his head out of the sleeping bag, rubbed the sleep from his eyes, turned on one side, and leaned on a bare elbow. He watched in delight as wisps of curling mist dipped and bowed in a water waltz.

The next dance was his.

The guys had finally opted for an under-the-stars first night, their sleeping bags laid on top of the collapsed tent. The adults were snug in their cocoons with no signs of awakening anytime soon. He looked into his dad's slack-jawed face and knew that he would be roused by little shy of a gallon of caffeine and the smell of frying bacon and eggs. Mr. Dixon, lips puffing in and out like a winded blowfish, was just as out of it.

Beyond, at the women's fully erected small blue nylon tent, what Nick called a "two-seater," not a creature stirred. The outer walls of the tent were shiny with dew, as was the surface of Cody's sleeping bag. No way was he going to sleep away another minute of this adventure, especially when the maternal apron strings were as slack as he'd ever seen them.

Forget the early morning chill — he was going exploring.

He stood in the bag and slid it down like a pair of pants. He wore a red T-shirt and white long johns. His jeans had spent the night stretched under his sleeping bag, and he was grateful for the body warmth as he wriggled into them now.

Cody stepped barefoot into a pair of ratty red Converse sneakers and didn't bother to lace them. They were cold and damp but would soon warm up. A gray fleece vest and the Giants baseball cap turned backwards completed the outfit.

He crept away and skimmed over rock and sand, following the tumbling creek until it splashed into the river. The air was the freshest he had ever breathed. The bite of coming autumn prickled his lungs and made his forearms bumpy. A wide smile spread ear to ear. It was good, good, good to be alive.

Don't look back! Lewis and Clark never checked to see if their moms approved of their sons' wanderings.

Cody hopped from log to stone and rested a cheek against cool granite faintly brushed with the day's first warmth. He knew that by midday the surface would radiate from late-summer direct sun. Out of nowhere, an image jumped into his mind . . . him kissing Beth . . .

He grinned, feeling funny and free, and rolled his eyes, though there was no one to see. Sappy Cody, king of the wild frontier. In fact, he was named for William "Buffalo

Bill" Cody, the army scout and Pony Express rider. It was a fine name, one to grow into. He was grateful not to be Willard or Beaufort.

He lay on his belly and watched the strong current whip the water past his boulder. He slid to the gravel and sand shore and collected pebbles and driftwood in a basket he made from the bottom of his shirt. Slowly, one hand bracing the basket, he one-armed his way back up the boulder. Flesh flattened against stone, he squirmed snakelike to the top, careful not to raise his head and alert the robber barons to the presence of the law.

With a silent "Halt, you scum!" he stood and pelted the murderous outlaws with a rain of death. They scattered in cowardly disarray, those shot through sinking beneath the icy waters and begging for the mercy they themselves had denied the innocent victims of their bloodthirsty raids.

He tossed a fleet of sleek twig ships into the current farther upstream, and then raced to the top of the boulder to watch them slide in secret past the base of his crow's nest and fall upon a rugged brigantine filthy with pirates gloating over their ill-gotten take. The plunderers went to their watery graves while the righteous armada restored the fortunes of many.

The sun grew hotter, and Cody tossed his vest to the shore. He was amazed by a sudden thought. In twelve summers on earth, he had never skipped a rock. The remedy was all around him in both directions. Stones for plunking. Stones for target practice. Stones for skipping until your arm fell off.

Hopping down the boulder, Cody didn't care who heard. "Woo-hoo! Yeah!"

Besides, the river probably made enough noise for the two of them.

He executed a two-footed landing that sprayed pebbles in all directions. He tore off his T-shirt, flung it aside, beat his bare chest, and let loose with a Tarzan yell. He kicked off his shoes, scooped up three flat stones made for skipping, raced to the water's edge, and let fly one after the other.

The first two sank into the depths without a skip. But the aerodynamically perfect third sailed just above the water, then touched down three times with the lightness of balsa wood before slicing beneath the waves, graceful as a mermaid. A thrill went through him.

He ran back to a James Bond arsenal of stone weapons, knowing full well that if he didn't attain the top of Mount Vanquished within the next ten seconds, the world would be destroyed in a blinding flash by Dr. Creeps-Me-Out. On the run, he grabbed up a large black rock with just the heft required. He prayed for flawless aim.

At the top of the boulder, he cocked back an arm, eyes locked on the jagged cowling of Dr. CMO's death-dealing hydrogen bomb launcher. In one arcing movement, he fired the counter weapon. It was a bull's-eye for freedom and democracy.

The rock ricocheted off the side of a submerged tree twenty feet from shore. To his horror, Cody was unable to break his momentum. He flew off the boulder and belly-flopped into the racing current.

The shock of the frigid mountain water led to a moment's paralysis, when Cody couldn't think. He bobbed to the surface, sucked air, shook his head to clear the hair and water from his eyes, and almost fainted from the speed at which the shore slid by. Instinctively, he reached down for the whistle that hung from his neck. It wasn't there. He'd slipped it off in the night and hadn't bothered to look for it this morning.

He lunged for shore, thin arms poor excuses for paddles. He kicked hard, the jeans and long johns a soggy drag, but the realization made him pour more energy into the stroke. With excruciating slowness, he began to make headway, and when at last he hit a stretch of calmer waters, he gained the upper hand and felt knees scrape rock at the water's edge. The jeans tore.

For a few exhausted moments, Cody clung to the rocks to catch his breath before hauling himself the rest of the way out. He sloshed up the bank to level ground, bent over, hands on knees, and coughed up water. On his right hand a small cut and a slow trickle of blood and water stained pink the knee of the thermal bottoms. Though he shivered in earnest, he sat on a downed tree and pulled off the sodden jeans. Carefully, painfully, on tender city feet, he followed the shoreline back to where he'd left his shoes.

He spread out the jeans to dry and lay on his back and allowed sun and boulder to revive him. Despite the panic of falling in, he felt a greater surge of elation at having faced a small crisis and solved it all on his own. When called to action, he stepped up. Hothouse plant that he felt like sometimes, he could do it. He *could* take care of himself.

Thank you, God, for not letting me drown.

Without warning, Cody was lifted from the boulder and encircled by two hairy arms. He knew that Rolex watch. Tribute to

113

twenty-five years of insurance excellence. His dad trembled and smelled like wood smoke and perspiration. For the second time that day, Cody couldn't catch his breath.

Finally, his dad turned him around and held Cody at arm's length. The expression on his face was dark and conflicted. His eyes filled with tears.

"Why are you soaking wet? Did you go swimming in the river? Without permission, without one of us with you? Your hand is bleeding! What in heaven's name were you thinking, Cody William?" His dad's eyes widened at the sight of the sodden, torn pants. "Look at you! Did you fall in?"

The use of his first and middle names was not a good sign. Behind his father, he saw Mr. and Mrs. Dixon standing at the base of the boulder. They looked awkward and concerned, as if trying to fence him off from still more trouble beyond. Behind them stood his mother, holding a neatly folded dry change of clothes. *How did she know?* The pained, terrified look on her face said he was going straight to solitary confinement, never to be heard from again.

Cody knew from what his father said that no one saw him fall into the river. He also knew that his life from this moment on, though it would be difficult enough, would still be much easier by far if he didn't tell them the truth.

"Sorry, Dad. It just felt so good to look around. Discover stuff. I stayed within sight of camp — mostly. You guys were dead to the world. Didn't want to wake you, so I just kind of took a walk."

He looked past his dad and saw disbelief on his mother's face. "Took a walk? *Took a walk?*" She shouldered herself between the Dixons. "You run around in a public place in your soggy underwear, half-naked, like some wild child, and you call that taking a walk?"

At least, he was pretty sure that's what she'd said. "Slow down, Mom, please. I'm having trouble keeping up."

Lips quivering, eyes glaring, she looked him up and down. "Where's the whistle?"

More than anything, Cody knew, the whistle was his mother's last grasp at civilization. She cared more about that whistle than about how shameful he looked or how wet he was or how willfully he failed to ask for the right to take a walk. Chief among sins was the fact that he forgot, dismissed, and ignored his promise to wear the whistle every minute they camped. It was the final and deal-breaking condition upon which she insisted. No whistle, no camping trip. And now, the trip not twenty-four hours old, he broke the sacred agreement. He dissed the whistle and by so doing dissed her place in his life.

He thought of lying. Saying he didn't know where the whistle was. That he wouldn't disturb the camp by looking for it.

"I — I don't have it."

Of course you don't. You're too busy trying to act like a boy who can hear. Why do you tempt fate?

The riverbank swam in her vision. Sheila tried to still the slamming of her heart and shut her eyes tight. As soon as she did, she saw the black hearse driving over the cemetery lawn, men in black suits reaching in for a black coffin, the assembled witnesses — male and female — dressed black as crows.

The black box rested beside the black hole. They said her Freddy was in that box. Her friend and playmate, her protector and calmer of fears. Was he in there, or was only a part of him there, another part in heaven, and a third part in the drawings over her bed of angel armies, swords drawn, beings that he said were the defenders of little sisters?

Freddy too thought he was invincible — until brought down by an enemy even angels couldn't see.

Andy's arms were wet with the shape of his son. Still tingled with the heft of his growing boy. His heart was dented in places where Cody's stubborn struggle to be normal had left its marks. Other gouges were from Sheila. More than a few were his own doing.

God, hear me. Don't let us drag our baggage out here. We've all been scarred — let this be a place of healing.

He regarded his son, wanting to be more, so much more, than the deaf kid from Brinker Circle. Cody was more at peace with his deafness than with the hearing parents who both loved and thwarted him. *"Do not provoke your children."* He was pretty sure that was in the Bible.

Tell me what to do, God, and I'll do it.

In reply, the river hurried past, unable to stop.

His mom reached into the band of her Swiss army hat and extracted the whistle. It dangled by its cord, swaying between them like some venomous, flute-charmed cobra.

Cody yanked his hair with both hands.

She knew all the time I didn't have the whistle. She wanted to catch me in a lie. "I didn't need it! I can take a walk or wipe my own nose — or, or anything *else* for that matter!" His mother's eyes widened, but he thought he saw his father hide a pained smile.

Cody didn't care how it sounded. In two more days, he'd be a teenager. If he didn't get some space pretty soon, he was going to explode. "Stop looking at me, please. I'm sorry I worried you. I'm okay. Really. Is breakfast ready?"

"In a jiff, Daniel Boone —"

His mother planted herself between Cody and his dad until it felt to Cody that all he could see were her accusing lips. "Cody William, you're grounded until further notice!"

Ignoring a flash of warning from his dad, Cody snapped. "Grounded? *Grounded?* My whole *life* is grounded, Mom. What're you going to take away? My hearing? Gone! My freedom? Gone!" He snatched the dry clothes from her arms, rammed feet back into sneakers, and stalked off toward camp.

Chapter 5

Andy watched his son go. "He wants to be treated like any other kid."

"Hush, Andrew!" Sheila kicked the gravel. "He's *not* like any other kid, and it's up to us to see he doesn't get into dangerous situations like this again."

"Sheila, Cody *is* like other kids. He's healthy and strong. Smart as a whip. Great sense of humor. All that despite his hearing loss. Maybe because of it, in some strange way we don't understand."

"Oh, that's just wonderful, Andrew. Thank the Lord our son is deaf. I'm sorry for you that you have to grasp at straws like that."

Cassie cleared her throat. "I'm sure Cody just got up to stretch his legs and lost track of —"

"Cassandra, I'll thank you to stay out of it. Andrew and I will sort this out."

After the Fergusons had gone, the Dixons

remained at the river to allow them their privacy. Cassie braced herself for an I-told-you-so from Nick.

When he took her in his arms, kissed her forehead, and kept a tight hold, she relaxed. Maybe he didn't think she was hopelessly naive after all.

"I told you so." He sang it into her ear. "Sassie Cassie doesn't know everything."

He wouldn't let her pull away, so she leaned closer, her lips in his ear. "To bite one's tongue is virtue."

"So how is Uncle Louie? I thought his job at the fortune cookie factory was about to crumble."

When Cassie said nothing, Nick let her go. "Don't fret it, Cass. You can't fix everybody. I think the Fergusons should adopt so poor ol' Cody can get some peace."

Cassie watched an eagle ride the wind currents overhead. "Good idea. They should get a little girl with two good ears just like Sheila has and who listens every bit as well as Sheila does."

Nick wrapped his arms around her waist from behind. "I don't think sarcasm is your color."

"Oh, Nick, I wanted this weekend to be so perfect! Admit it, last night was a good time, everybody laughing and joshing like before. Why can't she just let Cody be a normal kid?"

Nick dropped his arms and let out an exasperated sigh. "Though it's no longer politically correct to say so, he's not normal, Cass. He's handicapped, diminished at least twenty percent by the loss of hearing."

"So, what, he shouldn't be allowed to try and be normal?"

"All I'm saying is Sheila *should* worry about her son. Why God chose her, I don't know, but she was given not only the responsibility to birth Cody but to protect and shield him from dangers he knows nothing about. You're not doing your friend any favors by making her feel like a bad mother. She's doing the best she can, and just look at the proof. Cody's healthy, smart, fun to be with. You got him out of his shell. That's more than we had a right to expect. Let them be."

Cassie eyed her husband. He knew that look. She wanted to agree to disagree, and to do so loudly. "Is this what Andy thinks, that his son is only eighty percent there? Maybe the greatest good is not protection, Nick, but inspiration. Inspire Cody to reach and exceed his potential. Inspire him to think big, love much, and go far. Be there for him if it becomes too much, but don't bar the door so he can never try. And how much of Sheila does Andy get, the Sheila who's so consumed by cushioning her son against the unknown? Is she disabling the man she married?"

Nick hooked her arm in his and started off in the direction of camp. "I don't know, Dr. Phil. Andy has his own drives. To you, the long hours he puts in at work are a negative. To me, they produced a salesman of the year. There's nothing disabling about his 401k. No man's truly happy unless he can realize his passion, and realize it to the full. Maybe the Fergusons aren't half as messed up as you seem to think. Cody *fell* in the river, Cass. You have to know that. He wants to be Huck Finn, but the reality is that he needs watching or he could really hurt himself."

His wife tightened her grip on his arm. "I suppose. But there's observation and there's surveillance. So what if Cody gets a sliver or a black eye out here? Or breaks a leg, for that matter? Kids test the limits. Why should he be any different?"

"You wouldn't be so blasé if it was your kid. That time Beth took karate, you insisted she wear so much padding she couldn't bend over to bow to the sensei."

"For your information, Nicholas, bruising

is *not* a fashion statement."

He gave her a nudge with his shoulder and laughed.

They continued a minute in silence before Cassie asked, "Would you be opposed if Beth wanted to marry Cody?"

Nick halted and looked at her. "Is that a real possibility?"

"Cody's just a boy still, and Beth has her own growing up to do. Stranger things have happened, though. Right now, it's just a hypothetical. But would you be opposed to Beth marrying anyone with a disability or someone of another race or, I don't know, a Greek Orthodox boy? Would you?"

Nick frowned. "Could we have those Greek lamb and chicken gyros sandwiches with the sour cream at the wedding reception? Oh, and baklava for dessert? I'm all over baklava."

She threw her hands in the air. "All I ask is one serious conversation a week and instead I get baklava!"

Nick pulled her to him and kissed her. "I am serious. As long as Beth doesn't elope with a two-headed Martian, I'm okay with it."

Cassie played with the buttons of his shirt.

"Of course, if one of those heads con- tained the cure for cancer, I might reconsider my position even then."

She made a face. "And you, Nick? Are you happy even though things haven't gone as planned for us?"

"What do you mean?" He sounded surprised at the sudden turn in the conversation. "The Almighty still rules. I have my skin. Business is good, and we're making a quiet comeback. Only one of those civil suits is back on, but we should eventually be able to settle out of court." He sighed. "I can't bring those people back, Cass. But I can thank God that my daughter is a wonder and has all of her senses. Last, and certainly not least, my wife isn't half as loopy as she might be, considering all that has gone on. And miracle of miracles, said wife loves me, warts and all, and worships the very ground I tread."

Cassie put on a brave smile. "Colorful lies make for pretty deceits."

"Is there any money in those fortune cookies of yours and Louie's?"

"There is for fortune cookie writers. Uncle Louie paid me top dollar for that last one."

The tension in camp eased by midafternoon in time for a berry-picking expedition. Joanie had left a Dutch camp oven for them to try, and the guys were eager guinea pigs

124

for whatever the oven produced.

"Blueberries, yum." Andy led the way up a trail deeper into the mountain interior. "Loaded with antioxidants. Our hearts will love us."

"Until we take our hike tomorrow." Nick lowered his voice. "You, my friend, are going to Drunkard's Drop, a narrow ledge along a sheer precipice above a two-thousand-foot vertical drop. One glimpse'll grow hair on the palms of your hands."

"No plotting, you guys." Cassie chided from the rear. "Speak up so we can all hear your nefarious plans."

The entire first hour of picking the low mountain berries consisted of Cody stuffing his mouth until his lips and tongue were a dark blue — and blowing his whistle every ten minutes.

Finally, Andy couldn't take it anymore. Nor, from their expressions, could any of the others. He pulled his son aside.

"Look, Code, I get it. Your mother gets it. We *all* get it. You're ticked right now, but let's get one thing straight. It took a lot for your mother to agree to this trip, and for all your intelligence and abilities, this is a foreign land to you. Shoot, it's foreign to most of us. Except for Nick, we're all city mice. We have to acclimate, be extra careful, and look after one another. Understand?"

"I guess."

"The whistle is a precaution, nothing more. Believe me, buddy, it took all my powers of persuasion to convince your mom not to pack up after that river stunt of yours. If you like it out here as much as I think you do, you've got to fly right and not upset her. Wear the whistle, but don't wear it out. Sound good?"

When Andy finished, Cody focused on the ground, his blue fingers, his nearly full pail of berries . . . and nodded. Then he looked straight into Andy's eyes. "Okay, Dad, but it's probably a good idea to let the bears know we're here."

Andy was shaken by what he saw in his son's eyes. It was part boyish innocence, part latent wisdom from another age when buckskin was in. He shifted, ill at ease. "Yeah, right, Goldilocks. Next thing you'll be telling me is these berries are just right."

Cody didn't smile. "Actually, yes. This is peak season. The berries contain a lot of sugar content. Another couple of months and the bruins hibernate, so this is fattening time. From the looks of the tracks over there in that little wet depression, I'd say this patch is the equivalent of their super-market."

Andy's face darkened. "Bruins? When were you planning to tell us about this?"

Cody said nothing.

The five of them gathered around the muddy ground where a spring bubbled from surrounding rock. A profusion of bear tracks — Cody pointed out the pad depressions and claw marks — trampled the area where the animals licked up the water and washed down the fruit.

Suddenly, the quantity of berries they had gathered was deemed more than adequate. They returned to camp at a brisk pace. The entire way, Sheila kept turning to study the boy who knew bear tracks. A half dozen times she had him blow the whistle and no one objected.

That night, the men secured the foodstuffs in a heavy tarpaulin, roped it tight, and hauled it twenty feet in the air between two trees.

"All I'm saying, my friend, is that the pregnant African fertility goddess is one of the most enduring in all of female imagery." Andy cupped his cards close to his chest. "I call spades." The four adults, fat with fresh blueberry coffee cake only slightly crispier than planned, sat at the picnic table surveying the hands just dealt.

Cassie chuckled under her breath. Bellies full, the fire nearby, the stolen anxious glances into the blackness had almost subsided.

Nick, Andy's pinochle partner, groaned. "Fecundity may be a tribal strong suit, but spades is not ours. Why didn't you call hearts? I kept patting my ticker."

Andy frowned. "I thought it was heartburn."

"All right, you two." Cassie waved a warning. "No cross-table talk."

Nick sneered. "You mean like the ever-so-subtle 'diamonds are a girl's best friend' code you two used the last hand?"

Sheila shook her head. "Clearly, we were discussing Brenda Gelasse's announced engagement to that Count Marcos guy. Can you believe it, after all she's been through, she lands herself a count?"

"Speaking of counts." Andy regarded Nick. "You got any counters?"

When Nick laid down an ace in every suit and followed with four kings likewise suited, Andy breathed easier. "So, Nicky." His eyebrows arched. "What's your favorite symbol of the female ideal?"

Nick smirked. "That would be the Wonder

Woman archetype, Andrew. Ask Mrs. D how she likes the Wonder Woman lunch box I got her for her birthday."

"Mrs. D?" Andy counted up his and Nick's point total.

Cassie laid down two marriages and a nine in suit. "Well, Andrew, I can't speak for the imagery, but it makes a dandy little bathroom accessory for holding the toilet brush. Anybody seen our resident Speed Spell demon?"

From just beyond the reach of lantern light, Cody watched the adults pick up their cards.

He glanced over his shoulder into the dark. He shivered, whether from cold or from nerves, he wasn't sure. The brave plan hatched in daylight showed a lot of holes by nightfall.

I'm going through with this. He made up his mind the night before they left for the airport.

David the shepherd boy's parents didn't hold him back from fighting Goliath. Not all David's decisions later in life were good ones, but God gave him a life of adventure full of battles and danger enough for three guys.

His mom had pretty much kicked him out of the camp to do his thinking: "I want you to take some time to think about how you promised me you would cooperate if I let you come camping." It was a lot like being made to stand in the corner. "You need to know that just because you read it in a book doesn't make you invincible, just well-informed. You know what they say about a little knowledge."

"I know Mom." He tried to keep his voice low and not let his irritation show. "But I'm not a baby. I want to be treated like somebody who has a brain."

Her long-suffering smile reminded him of a principal he never liked. He imagined the sound of a diplomatic laugh. "Of course you have a brain. I want you to learn how to use it responsibly." Did she think he had asked her to let him fly a 747?

My mind is made up. Survivors settle on a course of action and stick with the plan.

What he didn't know was what effect running away would have on his parents. He wanted to bring them closer together, not drive them farther apart. He thought he saw a few signs of change for the better — the fact they were out here at all was a miracle. At least Mom agreed to give it a try. He had to give her credit. *And then she comes down on me like a pile driver because I went for a little swim. No, because I didn't wear the*

130

whistle. Her blasted whistle.

He watched her lay down her remaining card and take the pile. She looked like she could have fun any minute now.

And then he knew the real reason why she had yelled at him and grounded him for eternity. She was afraid.

So was he. Afraid to run away. Afraid not to. Afraid of never finding out what he could do.

Of why he was on earth and why he was deaf. Afraid and excited about what was next.

Afraid of having to lie to make it work.

He wished all those stars above didn't weigh down on him so much. They were like God's many eyes peering down from his throne. He was supposed to honor his dad and mom. He wasn't supposed to make their lives any worse than he had already.

Which was why he had to do this. To show them — to show himself — that he could do more than anyone thought.

His mother, lips pursed, picked up two kings and a nine by trumping them with a jack of spades. The lantern flickered softly.

"Mom?"

They jumped at the voice in the dark.

Cody stepped into the circle of light carrying a second lantern, unlit. "Could I please talk to you for a minute?"

Andy motioned in Cody's direction. "You go on, honey. We'll play three-handed until you get back."

Mr. Dixon lit Cody's lantern.

Cody led his mother out of earshot to several upended chunks of fire log. They sat on two of them and placed the lantern between them on a third. Cody turned up the flame, the better to light his mother's face.

"I've been thinking a lot about what you said earlier today, Mom. First off, I'm sorry for worrying you by breaking the first rule of survival: Don't separate from the group and go solo. I was just so happy to be outside in this great place."

The tops of the trees bent in a light breeze.

Cody took a deep breath. "And, Mom? For one of the only times in my life that I can remember, I was on my own. It felt great. No one to watch my every move. No one to criticize my decisions. No one to tell me no. I know you mean well." He stumbled over the words. "Uh, sooner or later, sooner than we think, we'll have to face it. I'm not your little baby anymore. In some ways, I grew up faster because I'm deaf. Yeah, I'm awhile from being a man, I know that, but you haven't let up on me in six years."

His mom blinked, face set.

Easy, Cody. Don't criticize; don't find fault.

"But six years older is a *lot* in kid time. I'm more than a foot taller, almost thirty pounds bigger, and my clothes are way bigger too."

"Gunboats." His mom looked bent under the weight of the word.

"Yeah, Mom, gunboats." Cody chuckled. "Every time we go shoe shopping you say my feet are big as gunboats. Well, an awful lot of that happened in the last six years. I've grown out of everything, except for one thing." *Easy, easy now.*

He took another deep breath. "You don't treat me much different than you used to. I'm not allowed to grow out of having to be watched and kept away from regular everyday stuff. And that feels real tight. Sometimes it's so tight I can hardly breathe. What happens when I go off to high school and then college?"

At the words *high school* and *college,* his mother scowled. "We've already discussed this, Cody. You'll continue going to the Interbay School for the Deaf until you complete your high school requirements, then to the Langley H. Stafford Deaf Awareness Academy. They've had good success with the hearing impaired."

133

Cody jumped to his feet. "To do what, Mom? To become a deaf interpreter, a circus geek, what? That's not for me. That's what *you* want because it'll keep me close to home and you can keep watching me. But what about what *I* want? I need to be with hearing kids where the possibilities aren't limited to repetitive assembly-line jobs. What about psychology, sociology, anthropology, journalism?" He looked up at the night sky and the rank upon rank of trees marching to the ridge. "Shoot, why not a forest ranger? I'm not incapable of great things, Mom, but to have the chance for greatness means you've got to believe in me and let me try."

He sat down. At first, she wouldn't look at him, but when she finally did, tears spilled down her narrow cheeks. Cody's own face was wet. He gave a crooked smile. "What I think I want is to go to a public high school, then get a bachelor of arts in deaf studies at California State University Northridge, where again I'll be surrounded by hearing students. With my grades, I should have a good shot at an Alexander Graham Bell Scholarship." His voice cracked. "I want to perform in deaf theatre and be a guest speaker at assemblies in public schools for the hearing. People need to understand deafness better, and I can help them do that. Please, Mom, don't hold me back."

Cody looked away. A harvest-moon glow backlit the river like a flashlight from space. What he wouldn't give to have air this fresh piped into his bedroom at home.

When her next words came, his mother's face hardened, the lines of burden and worry deeper in the lantern's glare. "You're too young to understand that what I do for you is to give you the best possible chance in this world despite your limitations." She grabbed his arm until he looked at her. "Don't turn away from me. You don't want to admit this, I know, but my job — mine and your father's — is to prepare you for the reality of living in a hearing world. Interbay and Langley understand the limitations. They're realists, not a bunch of starry-eyed idealists at some state school spreading false hopes. They're like me, Cody. They're like you, when it comes down to it. They'll teach you a skill that will help you along in life."

"Yeah. Attach hex nut *D* to bolt *E* and place on conveyor belt *F.* Return to hex nut bin, begin again. Busywork, Mom, and nothing like what I *know* I can do."

His mother worked a twist tie back and forth in slender fingers. "Honest labor may not be all that glamorous, but it puts food on the table."

Cody buried his head in his hands. "It can also kill you off if it's not what you think you're meant to do." He looked up. "I'm meant for bigger things, Mom, I can feel it!"

His mother stared into the lantern light until he again raised his head and looked at her. "Disabled isn't defective, Cody, but it is different. The whole person is the one who accepts what is and doesn't waste time with what might've been."

Cody coughed. *Is she talking about me or her?*

He fixed her with pleading eyes. "Is that what you would've told Helen Keller?"

Time slowed, the breeze died, and the trees swayed less. "She — she was the exception."

Cody felt pierced through. So that was it. That was the real reason she put him in a box and kept him stored away. He was nothing special. She saw no more potential in him than in a thousand others who couldn't hear. Keep the poor deaf kid from hurting himself. Keep him busy; keep him quiet. Oh, and make him wear a helmet to protect his dead ears.

He fought to control a rage of emotions.

"And you don't think I'm exceptional? You don't think even though Helen Keller was deaf *and* blind that I can't do what she did and more?" He was slipping into forbidden territory, but his hurt couldn't be contained. "Or is it that you're afraid I might do something that you can't do with both your ears? That without me in the house, you might not have anything to do or anyone to feel sorry for you? Dad has already proven himself, but what can *you* do except take care of me?"

The slap snapped his head to one side, like an electric jolt. The lunging force of it knocked the lantern to the ground and shattered the glass housing.

Cody and his mom stood but inches apart, sides heaving, hot breath streaming in the sunless cold, two rival elk locking antlers in the dark.

CHAPTER 6

Andy tried to sleep with one arm around his son, while feeding the fire with the other, but Cody tossed and turned the night away. The mosquitoes weren't that bad so late in the season, but the few that lingered persisted late into the night. Surrendering sometime after one a.m., the boy finally slept with only the occasional twitch and moan.

Andy awoke with a ferocious headache. *Deal with reality or reality will deal with you.*

He checked his cell phone, amazed it indicated service this close to the mountains. Good to know.

Even though at present he was drooling on Andy's arm, Cody looked every inch a handsome, healthy young man on the verge of an active, fulfilling adult life. It was only when he was cornered, usually by Sheila, that he flattened his nonfunctioning ears and the snarling began. Andy couldn't blame him.

He'd read the research. Every day in the US, thirty-three babies were born profoundly deaf and twice or three times that number were born partially deaf. That made hearing loss the number one birth defect in America, not even counting those children like Cody who became deaf later in life. Somebody estimated that without early intervention, over a deaf person's lifetime it could cost them, their parents, and society about a million dollars in special education.

Andy didn't know how much to tell Cody about his condition or future prospects. He was always telling other people about their chances based on age, health conditions, and government statistics in the hope they'd see the wisdom in being adequately insured. It was a whole lot different when it was your kid.

Generally, he believed in the whole truth. The more facts a person had, the better able they were to cope and make plans. His mother had tiptoed around his dad's cancer and even in its advanced stages had assured him with false hopes for a miracle recovery. It was cruel.

One time he and Cody had crossed paths outside the bathroom during a particularly competitive night of Speed Spell in the Ferguson dining room. Andy was coming out; Cody was going in. From the distressed look in his son's eyes, Andy knew there had been words while he was out of earshot.

"She treats me like a lab rat!" Cody slammed the bathroom door.

Several times Andy flipped the light switch on the outside of the bathroom, a special feature that signaled Cody he was wanted.

"Go 'way, please," Cody had yelled."

Back in the present, Andy looked over at his still slumbering son and brushed the hair off his face. *How much he wants to exceed what people think he can do, yet blend in with everyone else.* Cody often said he didn't want to experience the indignities suffered by a couple dozen deaf teens from Britain who were detained on their way to vacation. According to news reports, when the airline discovered the teens were without hearing escorts, the airline kicked them off their flight and embarrassed them in front of an entire terminal full of passengers.

Racial and cultural prejudice weren't the only kinds of discrimination out there.

After being able to hear well the first six years of his life, Cody wanted a minimum of accommodation for his increasing lack of hearing. "All I ask is a clear and unblocked view of your mouth or for you to use pen

140

and pad, and I'll take care of the rest." Credit him for his intelligence, eager personality, and zest for life. Medical experts noted in his charts that he possessed "well above normal cognition."

Through lipreading, facial expression, body language, and conversational context, he was exceedingly bright enough to capture most, if not all of a discussion. He had the patience and understanding for rapid speech, verbal asides, and changed topics that sometimes proved troublesome. They could be written out. And he could follow most of a feature-length movie, which unfolded more deliberately than shorter TV shows. Regardless, that was Cody's deal, and he would handle it as long as someone who could hear didn't lose patience or put him down. That was, in fact, Cody's definition of an arrogant person: someone more interested in the sound of his own voice than in the person on the listening end.

It was as ridiculous to say that all deaf persons were incapable of traveling on their own as it was to say that all Mexicans play maracas.

God, please help me get through to Sheila. Early teen rebellion was bad enough. Early teen rejection of your carefully constructed plan to cushion that teen's fall and live an okay life could prove devastating. Sheila's plan was beginning to crack.

When Cody first started talking about more mainstream schools than his mother had in mind, Sheila had complained to Andy. "Someone's planting these crazy notions in his head. Are you?"

"He knows his way around computers, hon. Any college recruiter worth his salt will start cultivating Cody while he's in middle school. You need to show an interest in his choices at the same time you let him know about the schools you think are good. Otherwise, he'll resent it, and that resentment will push him to thoughts of living on his own and going to that 'hippie school in Northridge,' as you call it."

Without telling Sheila, Andy had interviewed admissions counselors from both of Cody's top-choice schools. Their programs sounded interesting and challenging. Society never used to offer kids like Cody the hope of an advanced degree, but now, in the company of his peers, all things were possible.

"He tells me there are more than two hundred kids enrolled in Cal State's deaf studies program. Think of it, Sheila, the deaf achievers in that one school outnumber all of the students in my high school graduating class."

"Two hundred deaf hippies."

He tried to kid her out of it. "Didn't you get the memo? The last real hippie died somewhere around the end of the Reagan era."

The look she gave him would have soured milk.

And now the slapping incident. What was Sheila thinking?

"I never meant to hit him! I smacked him right in the ear. What kind of mother am I?"

Andy held her after the incident, liking how she settled in the shelter of his arms. He'd missed this. "You're right, you shouldn't have done it. You're both frustrated. He mouthed off, you overreacted. So go to him, maybe in the morning when you've both gotten some rest, and tell him how bad you feel, ask his forgiveness, then tell him you'd like to hear more about his college plans. There's lots of time yet to decide, but he needs to know you're interested in what he thinks. That's all he wants — to know you're behind him and you'll be okay wherever he goes because he can succeed wherever."

"And if I'm not happy with his choices?" She was rapidly returning to the old, composed, iron-willed Sheila.

"Then join the club of parents whose kids didn't go with the program. But we've got to make the effort. Try to see what he sees in those other schools. Were your parents okay with all of your choices?"

Sheila shrugged. "Mother was glad for the discount insurance premiums that you arranged for them. Daddy was just glad I found any man at all. He thought you were decent enough."

"Wow, thanks."

"You know what I mean. He wasn't the most demonstrative man alive. He always called me his little 'sour sides' for my critical approach to life and secretly predicted I'd be a spinster justice on the Supreme Court. Mother let that gem of info slip after Daddy died of cancer." She dried her eyes. "I proved to him I was marriageable. Now all I have to do is avoid passing the bar."

Andy put extra effort into a laugh at her little attempt at a joke. "A good night's sleep, my dear. Beats all for putting a brighter stamp on things." He hoped she would bed right down beside him and they'd fall asleep together.

Instead, she said good-night with the formality passed on from her father.

He caught her hand. "Sleep tight. I love you."

She nodded and was gone.

Dawn's early light wrapped the camp in a blanket of thick, drippy fog. It cloaked the camp in beads of damp and plastered tousled heads with what Andy joshed was "frog spit."

"The little cretins!" Andy mumbled to himself, unsuccessful in an attempt to coax Cody into a tickling match. "They hop and spit, hop and spit, until the whole world's soaking wet. Mountains, trees, rivers, my son — all covered in a nasty film of gray frog spit!" He raised his voice. "Too bad the women are dry and warm and un-spit-upon." He grabbed a fir cone and lobbed it at the tent, but it didn't go far in the moisture-laden air. "A great day for a hike!"

He poked the sleeping bag next to him one more time. Cody groaned, turned away, and burrowed deeper into the moisture-coated cocoon.

"Pipe down, Ferguson!" The gravelly command came from deep within Nick Dixon's sleeping bag. He poked his head out and swiped a hand across a grizzled two-day growth of stubble. "It's Sunday, man, and in keeping with civilized Sabbath law, I tell you to put a cork in it."

Andy stretched. "Technically, putting a cork in anything requires the lifting of a finger and that, Mordecai, is unlawful on the Sabbath. Not a lick of work, my friend, not a lick —" It was necessary to duck a ball of yesterday's socks hurled from close range.

Andy whacked Cody's backside. "Now if I could just get this lump up, I'd have someone to fetch my morning coffee!"

Not yet.

Cody had lain awake for hours, tense, desperately wanting out of the bag. But for his plan to work, he had to be patient and outwait the others. He had invested hours alone in his room learning the ways of the woods, biding his time, being as still as a fawn in a thicket. He had to appear co-operative. Anything else could ruin everything.

"The devil is the father of lies."

That was the other thing that kept him awake. Honest people didn't break the trust others placed in them. Liars in the Bible did not prosper.

God, let me prove myself this once. I have to prove I can do it.

He gripped the hated whistle on its leather

thong about his neck. *Don't I have a voice of my own?* He dreamed of swallowing the hated thing. It would stick in his throat and every time he breathed, it would warble like a songbird and his mother would know that yes, thank God, he had successfully drawn another breath.

What was he, some freak of nature? Hearing devices, whistles, sign language — why not hang a big yellow sign around his neck that read, "Slow — Deaf Child — Beware!"

Another whack. He knew his father was saying something. He could feel the vocal vibrations through arm and hand. It was for Mr. Dixon's benefit or their wives', of course, although his father liked to occasionally pretend his son was not deaf as a rock. *Mom never forgets. Ever.*

Cody moaned by way of answer and pressed the hard metal of the whistle into the thin skin of his chest. Harder he pressed, until the flesh over the bone became deeply indented. He could take the pain, like the Native Americans of history who cut their flesh and hung themselves by bone hooks in various rites of passage.

Harder. It didn't hurt — never hurt — unlike the thought of not being taken seriously.

Father Byron took him seriously. Once after catechism class when both his parents had to stay late at an employees' banquet for his dad's work, the priest let him hang out for a couple of hours to watch an old black-and-white film — Sidney Poitier in *Lilies of the Field* — and eat cheese pizza with him and Father Chris.

The movie was a good one, and with Father B's help, he figured it out. An unemployed construction worker stops at a remote farm run by some nuns to get water for his overheated car. The mother superior believes that Homer, the construction guy, was sent by God to build a church in the desert. It was really good how everyone learned from each other and the church got built. The pizza wasn't half bad either. He finished off three slices and a tall glass of cola with ease.

"Father B? Do you think I was sent by God for any particular reason?"

"Without question."

Cody pointed to his chin and Father B wiped pizza grease from his goatee. "How come you're so sure?"

"So many reasons, Mr. Ferguson. It was our Savior who said that he came that we might have abundant life. The only real question is what will we do with the life we've been given?"

"How do I find out what God has for me to do?"

Father B shoveled another generous slice of pizza onto Cody's plate. "Excellent question. The answer is that you set about doing anything that you know pleases him — feeding the poor, finding homes for orphans, praying for the lost, watching sappy old movies with your pastor — and one day when you least expect it, when you're already busy doing kingdom work, zap! It will be like the handwriting on the wall, and you'll know what you are perfectly equipped to do."

"How did that happen for you?"

"I was inside painting a windowsill for an old lady who'd displaced a hip, when what through her window did I spy but a man in clerical robes twirling down the sidewalk with a little girl in his arms. They were dancing and laughing and the rest of the world beyond the two of them did not exist. I decided right then that I wanted to be that for the church. A priest at play. Showing how to cast one's burdens on the Lord and forever after feeling the lightness of walking with him."

Cody left the fresh slice of pizza untouched. "Did it work out that way?"

"Some days, yes, some days, no. Today,

yes. How's that pizza?"

Cody smiled big and took another bite. "The fourth piece is the best yet!"

"So —" Cassie rubbed her hands — "a little oatmeal in the belly and then we're off to Sky King Meadows. Hopefully the fog will burn off. Joanie said the late season wildflowers are spectacular."

Cody, having shed the damp sleeping bag, jumped as if stung. "What? We're going up on the ridge, right, Dad? I want to see Drunkard's Drop."

Sheila shot Andy a "thanks a lot" look.

"Yeah, hon." Andy waved caution in Cody's direction. "We plan on wetting a line in High Bay Lake and frying up the catch over propane on Tight Grip Ridge. Why don't you girls pack a lunch and go gather daisies and let us do our manly men stuff? We'll meet back here at dusk for a killer round of Speed Spell."

His wife eyed him. "I don't like exposing our son to that much stimulation his first time camping." She looked about the area as if searching for cord with which to lash Cody to the picnic table. "We agreed to take it slower this trip and not try too many things or anything too adventuresome. It's four miles roundtrip to the Meadows, and no narrow ledges, sheer precipices, or two-thousand-foot vertical drops."

Cassie winced. Poor Andy looked exposed.

Nick was no help. He examined a burn hole in his jacket sleeve from last night's fire.

"I overheard you two plotting." Sheila's disapproval may as well have been a billboard. "You think now that I'm out here I'll drop my guard. Not on your life. Cody doesn't need that foolishness. It won't kill you males to bond over a few buttercups with us girls."

Cody's hands balled into fists.

Cassie forced a laugh. "I'm sure it'll be okay, Sheila. Let's go on up with the guys and we'll be there before you know it. Once this fog wears off, what a view!"

Andy pointed at Cody. "What do *you* want, Code-man?"

To Cassie's surprise, Cody went to his mother and threw an arm companionably across her shoulders. "I want us all to go together, up there." He pointed through the fog in the general direction of the mountains. "I want us to hike and fish and eat together. That way, some day when we're all sitting around telling my kids about this weekend, it'll be a memory we share. Besides —" he gave a loose tug on the ever-present whistle — "I've got my trusty tooter and it's only, what, Dad? Maybe five miles round-trip?"

Andy went with his son's confident argument. "Closer to six, but you've seen that it stays light fairly late this time of year. And it's downhill all the way back. We'll skirt the blueberry patch, for sure, and keep to the main trail. We should be fine. Let's load up the packs and get going!"

Sheila tried puffing up to twice her size, but soon gave up. She was outnumbered. "If I so much as hear a bear, we turn right around and head for a hotel in Seattle. And you be prepared to carry that boy back to camp, mister. Cody wouldn't know three miles from thirty. He's untested."

Cody threw his hands in the air. "I'm right here, everybody. This is me, Cody. Please talk *to* me, not *about* me. Criminy, Mom, no wheelchair here. Two good legs." He gave them a slap. "I've read a lot about hiking, pacing yourself, all that. I'm strong, and the difference between three miles and thirty is 142,560 feet."

Cassie stifled a smile. Then Cody seemed to think better of smarting off and went for disarming instead. "Besides —" he was all grins — "I've got to make up for lost time." He looked at his dad and earned a wink.

Cassie watched Sheila let go. It was a reluctant surrender, but when Cody had referred to "my trusty tooter" with all the charm of a man twice his age, you could see her start to melt. Not, of course, without the last word. "I'm holding you personally responsible, Andrew. This was your call."

Andy's face broke into a "don't look at me" smile. He smacked Cody's chest with the flat of his hand. "Sheila, old girl, this was Cody's call."

The boy stood taller. "Off to the tent to change. Wait up, Mom." Cassie couldn't resist sneaking him a thumbs-up.

He passed by and whispered, "Boys rule."

Andy nodded at his wife. "Good one, babe, you'll see."

Sheila's thin lips remained shut. Cassie knew that look.

The US Forest Service ranger entered the camp as they made ready to depart.

"Good day, folks." The ranger wore the ubiquitous olive green uniform complete with government-issue shorts and Smokey Bear hat. A neat brown nametag read "Dick Duarte." "Headed out on a hike?"

"Yes, sir!" Cody's enthusiasm brought a smile to the man's face. "Are you an honest-to-gosh forester?"

"One hundred percent. Summer hire from Oregon State University. Forestry major, junior year. You're sharp. How long have you been deaf?"

"Since I was six. How'd you know?"

"Subtle voice inflections. The way you focus on people's lips. I have a kid sister who's deaf. You folks headed to the ridge?"

Andy nodded. "Yep. Some climbing and fishing. Nothing too ambitious."

"You from these parts?"

"No, we're up from San Francisco."

"Taking the cure, eh?"

"Beg pardon?"

"You know. Here to soak up the healing power of God's country? We get a lot of folks from the Golden State. Well, I won't hold you up any longer, but I do want to warn you that the bears are pretty active right now. They've started storing up for a long sleep and the eating's good — mostly grasses, berries, and small animals rich in protein and fat. Shoot, maybe I should be talking to the mice, gophers, and ground squirrels, you think?"

His broad grin said that he had committed a little ranger humor. He became serious soon enough. "No need for alarm, but you should stay together. Somebody said they've got deer and elk on the run. That's unusual for black bear, but if you do see one of those larger prey run past you, I'd turn around and follow them out. If you encounter a bear, don't run. Don't make eye contact, just make yourselves as big as you can by waving your arms and making lots of noise. Clap your hands, sing, knock rocks together. That's usually enough to scare 'em off. Glad to see you've got your food hung high. And that whistle of yours —" he ruffled Cody's hair — "is the perfect noisemaker. You folks have any questions for me?"

"How fast can bears run?" Cody wore his fascination all over his face.

"Well, black bears, which are mostly what we have around here, have been clocked at thirty miles per hour."

"Cool! How strong are they?"

"Heh. Occasionally those babies can grow to five hundred pounds. They have immense strength, claws long as barbecue forks, and teeth up to three inches long. I once watched one tear a log to shreds in twenty seconds. Can't say how true it is, but the story goes that one bruin closer to six hundred pounds came down into North Bend last fall and ripped its way through some guy's garage wall and ate his dog. I saw the gaping hole in the wall but I didn't see no dog. Never come between a bear and his meal!"

Sheila gasped.

"Okay! Thank you, Ranger Duarte, for a most enlightening talk." Andy signaled Nick to get ready to roll. "We need to be sure we have plenty of daylight, so if you'll excuse us?"

"Sure thing, folks. One more caution. These bears are notorious tree climbers. You'll want to stay on the ground."

"Right." Andy ushered the ranger to the edge of camp. "Don't run. No eye contact. Make big. Stay on the ground. Got it."

"Oh, and I don't want to forget the most important thing of all." The ranger, wearing a double-wide grin, tipped his hat in the direction of the ladies. "You nice folks have yourselves a beautiful day!"

Cody zipped the tent closed and changed into a pair of clean red briefs. He knew the long johns he slept in would be too hot for the hike, but he stowed them in the bottom of the pack for later. He pulled on a clean pair of tan cargo pants, sniffed his pits, and although he'd smelled worse, decided on two quick blasts of Right Guard. He slid into a long-sleeved, blue-and-white checked wool shirt with breast pockets; cotton socks;

a second pair of wool socks; and a pair of new low-top alpine hikers. He hoped the two pairs of socks would prevent blisters. He'd also taken the precaution of trimming his toenails extra close to prevent losing any.

The picnic table and all its supplies ended just outside the entrance to the tent, half hidden from the rest of the camp. He snaked an arm out of the tent flap, and into the day pack's pockets and pouches went a half dozen granola bars, a package of red licorice, one chocolate bar, a small bag of peanuts in the shell, two oranges, some cheese, and a bottle of Gatorade. The adults carried the food for the day's hike and these were items he thought they weren't as likely to miss.

He'd just inserted the Gatorade into a side pocket of the pack when the tent shook hard. He jumped. Hastily, he pulled the tent zipper down enough to stick his head out.

His father, pack on back and walking stick poised in one hand, carried two fishing poles in the other. A faded yellow thrift store rain hat slouched between his bald spot and the sun. "What are you doing in there, making a soufflé? We're waiting for you to take the lead!"

Cody felt his guts tighten. He forced a calm reply. "Yikes, Dad. I thought it was an earthquake. Or a bear. I'll be out in, um, a sec."

His dad beamed. "No problemo, Code-man, no problemo. And don't let that ranger spook ya. I think he was having a little fun with the crazy Californians."

Cody watched his father trundle off in the direction of the others. *Think, Code. Think.* He threw a flashlight and small box of stick matches in on top of the other items. He patted his pockets for the Swiss army knife and felt its reassuring contours. That covered the essentials. He didn't want to raise suspicions with more delay.

Then came the familiar boil of anger. If his mother were a professional wrestler, she'd have him in a constant choke hold. He closed the pack and scrambled from the tent, her cutting words ringing around him as if he could hear just fine.

"But we've got to get you straightened away first . . ." Was he crooked and all wrong, in need of fixing?

"They know all about what you need." Why, had he come from a cookie cutter?

"It's not wise to expose our son to that much stimulation . . ." Was he some pale sickling?

"We agreed to . . . not try anything too adventurous." Why? Was there danger in enjoying himself too much?

And the clincher: *"Cody wouldn't know three miles from thirty. He's untested."* We'll see who's untested.

A smile plastered firmly in place, Cody scrambled to join the waiting hikers. He turned up the trail marked "Tight Grip Ridge. 3.0 mi." The others followed.

He couldn't resist raising a hand and throwing it forward in the best "Westward Ho!" tradition. He was in the lead for the first time in his life, and it felt good.

CHAPTER 7

Andy loved the fresh tingle of Northwest mountain air. He decided then and there that any expedition he took in the future must include an air-conditioned mountain range, preferably in North America.

The subalpine stillness was broken only by the thump of their boots navigating over rocks, the occasional windfall, and the soft huffing of air as they and their city lungs strained upward in faith that the ridge was actually there, behind the fog. Soaring western red cedar and Douglas fir stepped aside for mystical glades of alder and vine maple. Deep in the shadowy recesses of lowland woods, dark and ghostly as galleons in the ocean mist, the hulking stumps of once-proud giants marked the tombs of a lost armada.

Sweaty and winded after a couple of miles, they stopped by an icy spring spurting from a rift in solid rock. They siphoned great draughts of sweet water that slaked their thirst and cooled their faces, then leaned back a moment and listened to the faint hiss of the creeping fog.

Cody sat on a small rock outcrop near the spring and faced the others.

Gazing upon a riot of golden toadstools, Nick spoke in awe. "It's like we've stumbled upon a fairy church."

"Yeah." Cody twisted around to take in a thick red fungus dotted with white specks perched high atop a tall, thick, snow-white base. "And that bad boy is the pulpit."

They all grinned at the colorful image, except for Sheila, who had pulled a small mirror from her hat and was inspecting a bug bite on the side of her nose.

Andy scratched at a fresh mosquito bite of his own. *You tell 'em, Cody. You are so quick.*

He watched Sheila rummage about in the lining of her Swiss army hat. "Hey, hon, doesn't that thing weigh you down? You carry any shoe inserts in there? My feet could use some help."

"Then, Andrew, I suggest you make an appointment with your podiatrist."

Cassie started singing "Amazing Grace" and was soon joined by the others, including Sheila eventually. When the last syllable faded, it felt to Andy as if the words continued to echo in another place. Cody watched and nodded along but did not join in.

They'd been sitting long enough. Nick got to his feet and rubbed hands briskly together. "Well, friends, in the immortal words of Mark Twain, 'the coldest winter I ever spent was a summer in San Francisco.' Cody, lead on before my teeth start to rattle."

Cody nestled further into the hillside. "I should answer a quick call of nature first."

Andy stood. "Nick can have the lead. Cody and I'll catch up."

Is it my imagination or does Cody look annoyed? Andy caught Nick's attention and motioned up the trail with his chin. His friend nodded.

The others resettled their packs and started off, Nick in front, Cassie next, and Sheila trailing with an anxious look at her son. As soon as the two stragglers stepped into the woods and unzipped, however, she hurried off to catch Cassie.

When they'd finished and were back in the clearing, Andy squeezed his son's arm. Cody looked up and there was that incandescent light that was uncannily man and unflinching boy. Blue-green with minute flecks of gold, the eyes held the openness of youth and the veiled knowledge of maturity. *What we have here, doctor, is a superior intelligence.*

"So, pal, what's up with you these days?"

Cody didn't answer. He stared wide-eyed past Andy, a finger to his lips. "Eagle." He infused the word with reverence.

Andy turned. High on the branch of a bleached, lightning-split snag, a bald eagle perched enthroned in aloof majesty. The immense dark body, starched-white head and tail, and hooked yellow beak accentuated both its regality and its endangered vulnerability. Between its shoulders was an unusual blaze of white as if a paint brush had been dropped on its back.

"The lord of the wilderness." Cody acted as if he didn't dare breathe. *"Haliacetus ieucocephalus."*

"No kidding." Andy kept his voice hushed. "I seriously doubt I could pick a tanager out of a lineup, but there's no mistaking that fine fellow. What a bird!" Cody wasn't watching his dad's mouth, which meant he also wasn't "listening." Andy couldn't blame him. The impressive bird mesmerized.

As if on cue, the eagle fanned its great feathers, leaned forward, and took flight. With a half dozen powerful wing beats, it soared toward an opening in the fog where the sun was at last beginning to penetrate, and disappeared.

"Wow." Andy and Cody breathed the word as one.

They stood a minute longer staring up into the void, remembering every detail.

Andy broke the spell with a clap on Cody's shoulder. "How's everything?"

Again that piercing look. As if the man part wanted to say something. Maybe a whole lot.

The boy toed the ground.

Silence.

Andy tried again. "Nice boots. You know how to pick them."

"What? Sorry, I didn't see what you said."

Andy repeated it.

"It was $59.99 of your money well spent."

"How do you know how to pick them? I'm curious how you seem to know what works in the woods."

"Farther. Faster. Safer." Cody lifted one foot and displayed the boot tread. "That design grips but doesn't collect as much mud and gunk as some. Doesn't weigh you down. I just study online catalogs and stuff. Blake Grantham has a great site and he's hiked on every continent."

"No kidding."

"Nope. Once he climbed Mount Silverthrone in Alaska wearing nothing but shorts and a pair of these same hikers. Over thirteen thousand feet."

"Pretty good." Andy took a deep breath. "So you just study up on this stuff? See, son, I think that's pretty incredible, never mind Blake Grantham. You've had an awful big peak of your own to climb with your hearing and all, and I don't tell you enough how much I admire that. Admire *you*. I'm too much the salesman, always poring over actuarial tables —"

"Actual what?"

"Sorry. They're also called life tables or tables that show life expectancy. Helps us price the insurance I sell. It's all based on probability theory, survival rates, that kind of thing. Listen to me. Here we are in paradise, and could I be talking about anything more boring?"

Cody put a hand on his arm. "No, Dad, I want to know. Really. I always used to wonder what you did every day." He dropped his hand and his eyes. "I knew what my friends meant when they said their dads were firemen or chefs or car mechanics. But you . . . I couldn't explain what you did."

The words jabbed. *My own fault.* He put a finger under Cody's chin and lifted his head. "Sorry, chum, I was too busy trying to build my business to pay attention to details —" He saw the distress on his son's face. "Oh no, Cody, I didn't mean that you were just another detail. I mean that before I knew it you were another foot taller and into reading and video games and I sort of gave up. By then, Mom and I weren't going so smooth —"

"Because of me."

"Because of *us*. Somewhere along the way, we took a time-out. A marriage takes a lot of work and constant attention. And for a family to work, its members can't take each other for granted. But like two boxers, tired after twelve rounds, we went to our respective corners and never came out."

Cody stared at his boots. "I don't think Mom likes these."

"She doesn't like the price tag. She thinks you'll wear them once or twice and that's it."

"If she had her way, I'd wear corrective shoes from the medical supply store."

Andy grimaced. "Is it all that bad? She's just looking out for you."

Cody shook his head. "She's looking for Charles Dickens's Tiny Tim. I'm nothing like that, but she doesn't know that. And that makes me mad. She should know what

I'm like." He paused as if considering, then released a rush of thoughts. "I don't have to be carried. I can feed myself *and* do early calculus. Let me dig a hole, climb a tree, hunt ducks, play soccer. Right now, I'm not allowed to do any of that or use sharp objects, fire, or power tools of any kind. Can't even fry myself some bacon because I can't hear the grease spattering and might burn myself. Dad, I swear to you, you don't have to *hear* grease to know it spatters. That it's hot. I get *hot,* okay? I understand more than she knows."

"And that scares her." Andy pulled Cody to his chest, hugged him, and kissed the top of his head. Then he held him at arm's length. "Most mothers are overprotective, more or less. Mine wouldn't allow me to collect coins. She thought I'd swallow them because when I was two, I did swallow three marbles, two buttons, and the spare wheel off a toy car all in one sitting. I had a twenty-four hour bellyache and cried to wake the dead. Of course, the trouble passed — literally. My mom never forgot and I took up baseball cards instead. She still jumps if I flip a coin." He grinned.

Cody didn't smile. "Not fair, Dad. I got over being deaf a long time ago. Why can't she?"

"I hear you, but if you think parent-kid relations is a lot of work, you should try husband-wife politics." Andy waved a mosquito from Cody's neck. "She may be a bit hard on you, but she cares. What do you say when we get back to civilization we thank her for going on this trip and show her how much she means to us? It's going to take some patience, but we'll win her over."

Cody thought about it. "Okay, Dad."

Andy nodded. "Now we'd better catch up with the rest."

Cody's eyes clouded. "Dad, uh, I . . ."

"What, pal? Say it."

"You don't get it all the time either. Sometimes you take Mom's side because it's the easiest thing to do. You both say you'd do anything for me, but you won't even consider the thing I want most. Let me be normal!"

Andy watched the sun poke through the fog to reveal increasingly more of the earth beneath. The rapidly dissipating fog pulled back the curtain on the lichen-pinked knuckles of Tight Grip Ridge, much closer now, where ragged, discolored patches of last winter's snow lay like crusted scabs.

"I can't promise how this will turn out, Son. But I can promise that I will try harder, talk to your mother, and when we have time, tell you the fascinating truth about life tables, mortality, and other creepy tales of the undead."

"Cool!" Cody started off in the footsteps of the others. "And, Dad? That eagle was awesome!"

Andy released the lungful of air he'd been holding in. *He has his mother's toughness.* But was Cody too willful for a deaf kid? What clue did he have of the dangers lurking for someone with all five senses intact, let alone one limited to four?

"Thanks for teaching me to ride a bike." It was as if Cody had so much to say he didn't know what to say next.

Andy grabbed a strap on Cody's day pack and swung him around. "Every boy needs to know how to do that."

A smirk came over his son's handsome features. "Bet you didn't know I ride with my eyes closed. For real. You can't see me from behind."

Andy let out a whistle. "No kidding? Sounds risky." He resisted everything within him that wanted to lecture the adolescent daredevil.

"You egg me on."

"Me?"

"Yes, you. Remember you took me to the kite hill in Oakland once when Mom thought we were at the audiologist's? A quarter mile unobstructed six percent grade, smooth as a baby's behind and a level grass runway at the end. Bet I was doing thirty-five easy. That was the best!"

Blind, deaf, and a six percent grade. Such a good dad.

"Thanks for sticking up for this camping trip. For us. For me."

Andy lifted his rain hat and ran a hand through his hair. *That sounded kind of funny. Almost sad.* "Sure thing. Now get moving, or they'll think we've gone AWOL."

"What's that?"

"A — W — O — L. Absent Without Leave. It's an army term for an enlisted man who takes off without permission. Enough questions, private. March!"

He watched boy and pack shoot up the next rise. *I love you, Code. Sometimes you're man enough for both of us.*

They caught them a little over two miles from the ridgeline, seated on a table of granite admiring the view. The forest had thinned to sparse, stunted trees and low-lying, subalpine shrubs. At tree line, the wide expanse of windswept altitude opened up to reveal inspiring vistas filled with small lakes and peak after jagged peak.

Icy blue wildflowers dotted the thin soil and marmots sounded shrill warning from their rocky dens. The pink lichen that they had spotted from camp was here in every shade from rosy to mauve.

Across the near valley, a thin waterfall laced the rock face with threads of silver.

Sheila sprang to her feet at first sight of Cody. She walked him the last one hundred yards, ignoring strident protests, inspecting him for signs of deterioration.

She hovered over him. "So, what took you two so long?"

Andy waited, not wanting to steal his son's thunder. When he didn't respond, Andy motioned for Cody's attention. "Tell her, Code, tell Mom what we saw."

Cody hesitated. "Oh, yeah, we saw a big bald eagle fly out of a tree and vanish into the fog."

"Big? This thing was huge as a B52 bomber! Tell her, pal."

"Way big, like Dad said."

Andy, brow furrowed, studied his son. "Cody knew the scientific name and everything. It was ready to grab us, but Cody bit it on the foot and called it a scrawny robin."

Cody did laugh at that. The sound rippled in the brisk air and caromed off the rock wall that formed one edge of the "little finger" of the knuckled ridge. "That's baloney, Dad. That eagle wanted nothing to do with us. And it was you who bit it on the foot, not me!"

Andy chased him around the others until he hid behind Cassie, the tense moments in the forest seemingly forgotten. Nick sprang, hoisted the crowing miscreant under one arm, and carried the kicking, wriggling son to his amused father. He hung onto Cody's forearms while Andy secured the flailing legs at the ankles. They swung the boy back and forth and threatened to throw him off the mountain.

"Enough!" Sheila yelled it, visibly shaken by the roughhousing. "He's not some rag doll for you to throw around. Andrew, turn him loose. Cody, sit on that rock and take this multivitamin with some water. Rest up for the last push to the top of the ridge. The sooner we get there, the sooner we can head down. We don't want to be caught in the forest after dark."

Cassie would have laughed had Sheila not been so serious. It wouldn't be dark for another six hours.

"Oh, lighten up, Sheila." Andy put up a hand to stop her response. "A little innocent horseplay was all it was. Testosterone demands it!"

"And if I lighten up, Andrew, who's going to buckle down and teach our son that this is no candy store, but a wild place with real dangers?"

"I think the ranger made that quite clear."

"No, no, the lady has a point, Fergie." Nick reverted to Andy's despised nickname. "Let's get up on top for the photo op, then go relieve High Bay Lake of its trout. How about it, Cody? You ready to pull a whale out of a puddle?"

Cody couldn't get back on the trail soon enough. With the resilience of youth, he looked to be over the most recent skirmish. He shouldered his pack and set off first at a trot, then, as if thinking better of it, looked back at his mother. He slowed to a stroll until the trail went down a steep decline and out of sight. Then he took big strides worthy of a mountain man.

At lunch, they shared six trout, minestrone soup, and peanut butter and jelly squeezed from tubes onto whole-wheat bread. Cody had hooked just one fish — his first — but Andy let him reel in his three, and Nick his two. The look of sheer delight on the boy's face was worth every point-counterpoint that Sheila raised in opposition.

Andy had in the end played one of his

hard-won "Get out of jail free" cards. He raised a hand, palm out. "End of discussion, Sheila. There is no way on God's green earth that you are keeping him back while we go fishing. We promise to watch him like a hawk, if he promises to do the same for us. Code, promise?"

Cassie feared Cody's head might fly off, so vigorously did he nod in agreement.

"And what about this Drunkard's Drop of yours?" Implied was that out of spite, her husband had created the geologic wonder with his own two hands. "What if he gets vertigo or slips on loose shale?"

Andy shook his head. "C'mon, Sheila, Cody could get E. coli from a Burger Baron bacon double cheese next week. Nothing is for sure except 'Jesus loves me, this I know.' Give us all a little credit here, please."

Before Sheila could let loose the words Cassie saw forming, she grabbed her friend and whisked her away to photograph the meadow flowers. Better for them to be out of sight when the men took off on their expedition.

Cody went quiet, concentrating. No way was he blowing this chance to show he could do anything the others could. Tackle boxes and poles in hand, the men tramped single file along the edge of the middle knuckle, made a rough descent above an old rock slide, rounded a corner, and came face-to-face with the awesome plunge to the valley floor known as Drunkard's Drop.

Cody's sharp intake of breath made his companions smile. The trail was well maintained but passed beneath a brooding overhang that clung to the rock face in a slender mascara line. Beneath it, a two-hundred-story free fall into the jaws of death. The trail extended two hundred yards at a gentle slant before it again crossed the timberline and regained the safety of the trees. They overtook a weathered, hand-lettered sign at the beginning of the drop that read: "Do not cross in high winds."

There was no wind. His dad led, then Cody, then Nick. They hugged the rock wall and kept their gaze forward. His dad turned, slow and deliberate, and admonished them. "If there's a slip, do not make any attempt to save the fishing gear, just the fisherman."

Halfway across, Cody looked down and froze. "My legs are like rubber." The fear came in raspy little gasps. "Can't take another step."

His dad took his gear and one hand, while Nick took the other hand. Cody faced the wall, the adults faced outward, and all three inched along sideways moving as one, taking a single synchronized step at a time. On the other side, after catching his breath, Cody whooped and hugged both men. "This is the coolest trip ever. Thanks, Dad! Thanks, Mr. D!"

They resumed their hike down to a pretty basin of dark green water rimmed with big trees and massive boulders. High Bay Lake was a tiny gem of a fishing hole.

"First order of business is a nice swim." His dad made the announcement by yanking off his shirt and unbuckling his belt. "Last one in is an egg-suckin' snake!"

They stripped to their underwear and raced for the water. His dad got his trousers in a twist, tripped twice, and brought up the rear.

Cody couldn't stop laughing when his dad finally climbed a low tree-dotted promontory jutting into the lake and belly-flopped with a resounding smack. "Oh, Dad, the glare! Rub yourself with mud, would ya?"

His dad chased him back onto shore and smeared his head with mud. They both cannonballed off the promontory on either side of Nick, who submerged just before splashdown.

Nick surfaced with a yell. "Alert the authorities! Tidal wave!"

The men watched Cody perform back-flips into the lake before the three ran shivering to stretch out in the warm sun.

Cody, teeth chattering, stared at the perfect blue sky. "Th— that w— water is f— freezing! Must be p— piped in f— from Antarc—ti—ca!"

"You think that's cold, you should go ice swimming in Norway." Nick blew water from his upper lip. "They've got winter swim clubs there that no self-respecting polar bear would touch. I tried it just once and before I could get back from the hole in the ice to the sauna, my lips and eyelids were frozen shut. They worked on me with a blowtorch for a week before I could even say my name."

"You g— guys want to hear the poem I wrote?" He looked shy but willing.

"Sure, Code, bring a little class to our rough-hewn friend here, please."

Nick gave his dad a look of mock warning.

"I wrote it last week. It's called 'That Noble Silence.'

"Can you hear the unheard
Sound without sound left unsaid?
Must we speak? Or hear? Or weep?

Or can we say nothing, hear nothing, and
    know?
Can the nobility in silence speak for us
Eloquent as speech, eloquent more?
Lie against my heart and hear it beat,
Return my soundless love with no sound
    of your own."

His dad cleared his throat. "That's beautiful, Cody."

Nick agreed. "How did it come to you?"

"I was just on my bed staring at the ceiling one day when I thought maybe I was coming at it all wrong. What about monasteries and cemeteries and huge empty places like the moon where nothing, no one, makes a sound? The Einsteins and the great philosophers of the world do their best work when they say nothing or when they go to a mountaintop to think and wait on God. Is there nobility in silence? Can I learn to hear God better because I'm not distracted by sound?"

The silence between the three stretched on. Too long.

"Dad, did you know you can polish your shoes with the inside of a banana peel?"

"No, Code. Did you know that one of the best ways to catch Dungeness crabs is with partly chewed chewing gum?"

For fifteen minutes, they outdid each other with crazy factoids, laughing, trash talking, and being anything but silent.

"What do women talk about on vacations, Dad?"

"Well, men can't say for sure, but I subscribe to the nails, sales, and tales theory. The first ten minutes is all about the latest nail polish, the second ten about what stores are having what sales, followed by forty minutes of tale swapping about who's marrying whom, what celebrities are doing what, and which political candidates have the most supportive spouses."

"Yuck! How boring is that? Can I get a dog for the deaf?"

His dad tossed a pebble at his son's ribcage. "Did you take a breath before that subject change?"

Cody grinned. "It's so cool how they rescue dogs from the shelter and teach them to alert to seven possible sounds: fire/smoke alarms, telephones, door knocks, doorbells, oven timers, alarm clocks, and name calls. I'd name him Farley."

Nick pelted him with a pebble from the other side. Cody flipped over and leaned on that elbow, watching Nick's mouth. "Did you know they sometimes train them for an eighth sound? A crying baby."

"No way! I love it. Dad?" He flipped back over to face his father. "Can I join the US Deaf Ski and Snowboard Association?"

"Don't you have to know how to ski or snowboard?"

"They give lessons. I can learn. How about space camp for the deaf? Can I go?"

"Whoa, whoa! Where's all this coming from?"

Cody arched his eyebrows. "Well, I figure you're in a weak moment, with your pants down, so to speak. I might as well go for it!"

His dad returned his grin. "You might, huh? Can I get a guarantee they'll send you to a galaxy far, far away?"

"This is serious, Dad. They teach you all this incredible stuff like space simulations, rocket building, flight dynamics, robotics. We get to learn about the solar system and the laws of the universe. There's even a mock shuttle mission. How great is that? Bet you wished you'd had space camp back in the Dark Ages."

"Smart guy. Sounds pretty interesting all right."

"No kidding. A whole week of it for only seven hundred bucks."

"Plus airfare, spending money, etcetera."

"Still cheaper than sending me to the moon."

"And was that my other choice?"

"Yep. I just saved you about two million bucks."

"Tell you what, Son. I don't know if we can talk Mom into space camp, but I can maybe swing us a private tour of NASA's Jet Propulsion Lab in Pasadena. A college buddy of mine works in information systems. All the behind-the-scenes stuff. Lunch in the employee cafeteria. What do you say?"

"Are you kidding, Dad? I'd love it! JPL is the leading US center for the robotic exploration of the solar system. Comet chasers. Rovers on Mars. Airships to Europa. Bring it on!"

"No promises, but I'll see what I can do."

Cody grinned. This was going good. It was a real rush to talk with someone about the things he hoped for, someone with the power to actually do something about it.

"You bathing beauties gonna sit around and jaw all day? Those fish won't catch themselves." Nick leaned on an elbow and eyed the other two. "I predict this lake has more than one lunker lurking around that bend." He got to his feet.

They got dressed, grabbed their poles, and headed for a stretch of shoreline where a couple of large firs overhung the water and provided shaded seclusion for "monster fish."

"We should go salmon fishing in Alaska, Dad. How about just us three guys go after some giant kings? I read about a deaf guy who owns one of the largest charter fishing outfits up there."

"Let's see you catch your first one pounder before we talk about going after your first fifty pounder, sound good?" His dad watched Cody lift the lid on a carton of fresh worms. "Here, pal, let me show you how to make the bait dance."

"Hey, Cody, Cody!" Nick thumped him on the back. "When your dad finishes showing you how to make your worm do the old lady waltz, check back with me and I'll show you how to make it do some jumping hip hop."

Cody got the giggles as the two men argued over the right way to bait a hook. After three casts, he got the hang of it and sent his hook with precision to the far edge of the shadows. He hitched up his pants and complained about the grit in his drawers.

"Well, Son, I'd say that's not as high a priority right now as the fish that just took your bait. Look at 'er dip!"

The pole bent and the battle was joined.

Cody hooted and hollered the whole time until a plump bright rainbow trout lay flopping at his feet.

Pure joy spread over Cody, head to toe, and he believed that all things really were possible.

Nick watched Cody hop rock to rock. He was going to fish for "Moby Dick" under the shaded overhang of the next fir down. "Man, is that kid of yours ever full of spunk!"

Andy smiled. "He's something, isn't he? I never knew all the stuff he's been thinking and dreaming about."

Nick cast and tightened the line with a couple of cranks on the reel. "How's Sheila doing?"

Andy's shoulders slumped. "Totally different story. She's just looking for ways to declare this trip a disaster. At least it seems that way, and worst of all, Cody sees it and gets discouraged. But it doesn't matter what I say, she twists it around and it comes out a negative. Why talk when all that results is hurt and frustration and accusation?"

"Exactly. Why talk?" Nick considered where he was going with this, and went anyway. "Look, pal, I'm no expert in the female nuances, but I have to tell ya, I think what Sheila wants is action. Talk is cheap, and apparently misinterpreted, so why not stop talking and start showing? Flowers for no reason. A mushy card expressing the things that brought you two together in the first place. Get her car detailed. Sell your golf clubs at an Internet auction and buy her a gift card for the dress shop. Isn't her birthday around the holidays? Throw her a surprise party. Let the romancing begin!"

Andy ran a hand through his hair. "And Cody? None of those things addresses the core issue. Cody's deaf, Sheila blames herself, and we're doomed to a life filled with her trying to make it up to him. Because she loves him so much, she thinks that by sacrificing herself, us, the penalty will be served. Trouble is, it's a life sentence and exactly what Cody doesn't need or want."

"I can understand that." Nick gave a sharp tug on the pole to set the hook, but whatever was sniffing around the bait swam on. "He doesn't want to be labeled a problem, an issue, a price that must be paid. He wants to be an asset, to be the fruit of your love, to make you proud. I think that with a little family counseling from a Christian professional who cares and understands, you guys could turn this around. But everyone has to agree to it for it to work."

"And there's the rub, my friend. Sheila thinks that would signal a failure on her part. She's convinced that she made Cody disabled and that only by her efforts can he ever get along in life. She'll drive us all crazy before she's done."

They were silent for a time during which they could hear Cody singing "Jeremiah Was a Bullfrog."

"I forgot to tell him about not scaring the fish."

Nick laughed. "Nothing wrong with his volume." He cast again. "Do you know what an echocardiogram is?"

"Sure, it's a test that helps a doctor get an internal picture of how well your heart is doing. My clients have those a lot. I should schedule one myself." He set his rod to twitching. "A little hula action on the worm makes the fish swoon."

"Yeah, right. Anyway, an echocardiogram is an internal picture, sure, but it's more. It sends sound waves into the chambers of the heart and receives echoes back, providing a moving picture of the heart at work. Stay with me here, but I think you need to perform an echocardiogram on your wife's heart."

"Have you been smoking the locoweed?"

"No, smart guy. I'm just saying that a mother is going to feel her child's disability in ways stronger than a father, stronger even than the child feels them. That which is out of her control makes her frantic that she can't do more. You need to listen past the surface stuff and hear the echoes of her heart."

Andy considered Nick's words. "And then what?"

"And then the wining and dining. Meantime, you go to counseling with Cody and tell Sheila that it's for you, to help you get past your guilt and regret. Don't say anything about her going. Just let her see you go and hear you share some selective things you find out. Let Cody share too. Not a lot, nothing that will threaten her. I'd be surprised if she didn't soon get curious enough to go see for herself what goes on with the counselor. It'll help her let go of the reins to hear an objective third party say how healthy a lighter grip would be. Father Byron at St. John's can recommend someone."

"Makes sense." Andy reeled in his worm and a wad of green vegetation. "You know what Cody told me once? He said that a bat's echolocation system — kind of like your echocardiogram — provides a picture of the environment so accurate that the bat can maneuver in the pitch black. That's what I feel we're in sometimes. Complete darkness."

"No kidding. When our perfume company fell apart, it felt like I'd been dropped into a deep well. Zero visibility. When I found out that our product had led to people's death and injury, I wanted to sink into that well and never surface again."

Andy nodded. "How'd you get out?"

"In some respects, I'm still climbing the walls, but at least now I can see that little circle of light above me and know that the way out is almost within reach. Oddly enough, speaking of bats, most of them can produce high intensity sounds that significantly increase their range from the standard fifty feet or less. I've been told that a bat's higher sounds are as loud as if you held a screeching smoke detector four inches from your ear. They call bat species with that ability 'shouting' bats."

"Shouting bats make noisy vampires."

"Groan. Good one. So I started shouting at God. Asking, demanding, pleading, screeching. You name it, I did it. And gradually, with the help of Cass and Father B and the Scriptures, I began to understand the contours of peace. I was able to locate God's grace and experience it. I was no longer paralyzed, and that's when the foundation was formed and we started to take action instead of complaining and lamenting."

"Flowers and mushy cards, right?" Andy gave a rueful grin.

"And fine dining."

Andy slapped Nick on the back. "Don't I have my work cut out for me?"

"That you do, my friend." Nick watched Andy separate worm from foliage. "And you can start as soon as we get back to the campground by opening a fresh package of the biggest, plumpest frankfurters on the planet. Offer to roast Sheila's for her, and roast it to perfection!"

Cody returned to their camp on the ridge with his catch strung on a pole over one shoulder, shirt tied at the waist, chewing on a blade of sweet grass.

Andy wanted to hold that picture in his head forever. "The conquering heroes have returned!"

Cassie snapped seven pictures from every angle before she would allow him to clean the fish. Nick supervised the gutting while Andy prepared a flour coating and heated the pan over a single propane burner.

The aroma of frying fish worked its magic.

They ate with gusto.

"Juicy!"

"Flaky!"

"Finger-lickin' good!"

But it was Cody who took the prize for the most original praise. "Toothsome!"

Nick hooted. "Where did you pull that from?"

Cody sniffed. "You don't remain the grand champ of Speed Spell with baby words. Look it up!"

"I *know* what it means, smart guy. It's just you have to be twenty-one to use words like that."

Cody's derisive "Ha!" could have been heard on both sides of Tight Grip Ridge. He finished off the trout and would have devoured bones and all had not his mother been right there to extract the entire skeleton. She reminded him that "those who live off the land ought not be any less civilized."

Andy stared at her. "Hon, seriously, do grizzly bears remove the bones before dining? Well-chewed, the vertebrae provide a lot of nutrition."

Sheila ignored the question.

"I propose a toast." Nick hoisted his sport bottle, and was quickly joined by three more and one plastic Gatorade bottle. "As me mum used to say, 'May the roof above us never fall in, and may the friends gathered below never fall out!' "

Andy watched his son suck down Gatorade like there was no tomorrow.

CHAPTER 8

They languished in sunny afternoon torpor, letting lunch digest.

Sheila watched Cody fidget, slumped in the shade of a granite outcrop. Now tossing pebbles at the toes of his boots, now flipping twigs into the branches of a nearby sapling, he clearly wanted to be underway. His body language made it plain that with all the world to explore, slothful grown-ups were a drag on the voyage of discovery.

Andy stretched on solid rock — "Good for the spine!" — and the Dixons lay back-to-back, snoozing among a bed of icy blue wildflowers.

Sheila motioned Cody over. "Would you like to take a walk with me, just the two of us? There's something a little ways back called the 'Snow Bowl.' Let's check it out."

Cody hesitated.

"Come on. I promise to be good company."

"I'm pretty tired."

"Tired of sitting around, I think. C'mon. I saw the sign for the Snow Bowl. No mileage given, so probably it's just off the main trail. Who knows what we'll find?"

He looked torn, wary.

She disliked that look. When had he stopped enjoying her company? "I promise not to lecture you."

"Yeah, uh, okay. Should we tell anyone?"

"Your dad knows and his exact words were, 'Knock yourselves out.'"

The short walk brought them into a natural little amphitheater in the rock face on the east side of the ridge. Just from the way their footfalls were amplified entering the bowl, now snow-free, Sheila guessed it was a nature-made echo chamber.

She tested it with a hearty "Hello!" and received a half dozen diminishing echoes in return. "Supercalifragilisticexpialidocious!" She laughed at the tumbled response. It was like a crowd of people trying to sing in a round a song they hadn't fully mastered.

Cody cocked his head, eyebrows raised.

"Echo." She framed her face with open hands. Then she inscribed an arc in the air, indicating the rock formation surrounding them. "Great acoustics."

He made her repeat *acoustics,* then nodded understanding. "Great Speed Spell word. First dibs!"

She shrugged. "Be my guest. I'll be too busy spelling *supernatural.* Indians thought echoes were the communications of supernatural spirits. There are hundreds of sites like this on all the continents, every one of them considered sacred."

She could tell he was fascinated. "And not only that, but some even think the locations of prehistoric rock art were chosen for their acoustics. For instance, when they painted the plains bison, drummers could mimic the sound of hoofbeats. Sometimes people would clap to get the desired effect." She pantomimed a stampede.

"No way." Cody was eager. "You mean like their own little audio-visual display?"

"Sure. Not exactly surround sound, but pretty close to it."

"Cool." Then a cloud came over the fine features. He was starting to get sunburned. She wanted to turn back and get the sunscreen, but resisted the urge.

He went silent and studied his boots.

She sat on a rock and looked up at him. "What Cody? What is it?"

His words were tinged in regret. "I wish I could hear them, Mom. Echoes, I mean. Real ones. Sometimes I hear my own thoughts, loud like, repeating over and over, or a kind of rushing sound that repeats, but . . ."

She smoothed the hair back out of his eyes. "Go on."

His voice caught, but he forced himself to say it. "I can't remember what real echoes sound like. I — I'm forgetting sounds. I think it's because I've lived longer deaf than I lived able to hear." His eyes were bright and wet.

"I'm sorry." Sheila's stomach hurt. She could only imagine what forgetting sounds must be like. She didn't want him to experience hurts she could do nothing about. Still, he had confided something private, and when was the last time that happened?

Motioning him to follow her, she went over to the rock wall of the amphitheater. She touched the rock with the flat of her hand. Cody followed suit.

"Because the echoes came at them from the rock, the Indians believed the spirits lived in the wall. Those surfaces, these echoing rock sites, were considered sacred dwelling places."

He pressed the side of his head against the cool rock and closed his eyes, as if listening for voices in the wall. The sadness appeared to leave him and the worry drained away.

She waited. He looked at peace, neither the Cody eager to seek new experiences nor the Cody dejected and burdened by his condition. Just a boy named Cody. Her boy.

"I make my own music sometimes." He said it shyly and peered at her through half-open eyes as if checking to see if he should be embarrassed to have revealed so much. She smiled encouragement, the pain in her heart a never-healing sore.

"It's hard to explain. I imagine music — the rhythm, the beat — and take the sounds in my head and my heart and set them to that rhythm. Like right now I'm thinking dum-ta-dum-ta-dee-da-dee-da-dum . . ."

He closed his eyes again and as he gained in confidence, the music grew louder and stronger. He took her hand and beat time on the heel of it.

The music bounced and echoed around the bowl in Cody's pure, boyish tenor, always with his unique inflection. Surprisingly pleasant, it made a haunting antiphony between the boy and the echo that in places seemed parts of songs she knew and in others like nothing she had ever heard. She brushed his cheek and when he looked at her she clapped softly in time to Cody's

195

song and to the music of his heart.

Her reward was a golden smile that lit the Snow Bowl.

And then the music stopped, as if the voices in the wall had in unison sucked in their breath.

Cody's chin quivered and he stretched on tiptoes to reach as high as he could. Sheila thought he might want to pull the wall down on top of him to hide the pain made plain in the melody.

"You have a lot to give, Cody William."

Face flushed, he looked away. She supposed that this wasn't at all regular guy talk.

The moment passed. "Mom, did you know that Beethoven kept his deafness a secret until he was thirty-one? I wish I could've kept mine a secret from you and dad until I accomplished something wonderful. Then you wouldn't have to suffer so much."

Sheila sat on a boulder and felt his arm around her neck. "No, Cody. That's not your worry. We should never have put that on you."

"You don't seem happy very often. I think it's a heavy thing for you."

"I know it must seem like I don't have a positive attitude about your condition. I only want you and Dad to face facts and not build on false hope. Try, of course try, but don't put up your house on maybes. That's quicksand."

He gave a guy snort, then looked as if he thought better of it. "When I was little, you used to sing to me and do nursery rhymes and stuff. But it was like you lost interest when I lost my hearing. I was going to ask you if I could join the children's choir at church, but going deaf changed all that. By the time I went to bed, you and Dad were too tired from taking me to doctors and therapy and helping me adjust at school to encourage any singing. You prayed with me before lights out, but the stories and songs got lost. How come?"

Sheila flinched. "Oh, Cody, it — I — I'm not sure. I guess it took too much out of me to see you in your pajamas all fresh from your bath, hair all slicked down, and no longer able to hear the stories you loved. No longer able to hear the sound of my voice. It was like, oh, I don't know."

"Like what, Mom?"

"Like God was cruel to give you something so wonderful as the gift of hearing only to snatch it away again."

"Some music experts think Beethoven's best work was composed because of the deafness and the suffering it caused. Maybe being deaf can be a blessing."

"No, don't say that! *Never* say that!" Her words echoed back, but like the audio illusions of the native storytellers, it was Cody's word *blessing* that rang longest in her ears.

"It's true! His Fifth Symphony was written four or five years after he went deaf. *Bom bom bom bommmm.*"

The famous musical phrase reverberated in the bowl. Sheila shivered. "Three quick Gs and a long E-flat." Where did she remember that from?

"Bom bom bom bommmm." Cody pressed his head against the rock while his mother watched. His brain must be vibrating with remembered joy and the resonance of the stone echoes.

He hopped away, a child lost in a world where he could hear and his mother could not.

They said nothing for a long time. Sheila watched two squirrels quarrel over a lump of something. It was comical how they chittered and fought and she had to stop herself twice from calling them to the boy's attention. He was too old to be distracted from his troubles by a toy car or an ice cream cone. He was technically still a child, but his challenge was fully man-sized.

She was just about to suggest they head

back to the others when Cody gave her a pained expression. His neck and ears turned red. He had remembered something else, and it contained no joy.

"I told you once that when actor Lou Ferrigno — you know, the Incredible Hulk guy — was a teenager, he was teased by kids who could hear. They called him Deaf Louie. So he puts all that anger and hurt into bodybuilding and was Mr. Universe when he was only twenty-one. The next year, he wins again. He was the only person to ever win two consecutive Mr. Universe titles. Do you remember what you said about it?"

"Cody, how can I remember —"

"No! You have to!" He clenched and unclenched his fists, but all there was to punch was hard rock.

Sheila's mouth went dry. "What Cody? What did I say?"

"You said, 'All that muscle stuff is so grotesque. Is that the best he could do?' " His exaggerated, high-pitched impression of her made it clear how long he had harbored this resentment. "Can you *believe* you said that? He overcomes his hearing problem and all the crud being dished out by those idiot kids and puts in hours and hours to become the fittest guy in the world, and that is all you could say!"

"Cody, please, that was a long time ago. I don't think I meant to put down the man's accomplishments. Moms have such high expectations for their kids and don't always think about alternatives to their becoming lawyers or surgeons or foreign diplomats. I didn't want you to think that the answer to your problems was to lift weights."

His irritation showed no signs of lessening. "Give me more credit than that, Mom. I've tried to tell you about Thomas Edison, Alexander Graham Bell, even FBI agent Sue Thomas, but you'd always say, 'Those are the exceptions, Cody. You must be practical about this, Cody. People are not waiting around to offer good jobs to the deaf, Cody. You've got to set your sights lower, Cody. Prepare yourself for the real world, Cody.'

"*That* thinking is bogus. This isn't the Middle Ages, Mom, when the sick got sicker and the crippled had to survive by their wits."

She looked at her trembling hands. *Where is all this coming from?* "Then tell me, please, what is the real world for someone who is deaf?"

"Thank you, Mother. I've waited for that question forever. I know what a battle it is for anybody who's lost one or more of their senses. But there are too many success stories for it to be that much of an exception." He counted off the fingers of one hand with the index finger of the other.

"Sue Thomas was the youngest freestyle ice-skating champion in Ohio before she went to college and graduate school and joined the FBI.

"There are six craters on the moon named for outstanding deaf scientists, including Henrietta Swan Leavitt, who was nominated for a Nobel Prize. Two deaf scientists have won the Nobel. Konstantin somebody of Russia went deaf when he was eleven and still wrote hundreds of scientific studies on rocketry and space travel."

Sheila nodded. "I didn't know that."

"That's not half of it." Cody was on a roll. "You ever heard of Paul Thompson? He's a deaf designer of yachts. He captained a sailboat crewed by two blind guys. Newspapers joked that it was the deaf leading the blind, but Paul didn't care. He was the first deaf person to sail the southern Atlantic Ocean by himself, and he did it in a thirty-two-foot sailboat he built himself!"

Sheila was stunned. "Cody, those are exceptional — no, those are *outstanding* accomplishments. You've been busy. I admit I often think of the deaf as a closed community, shut off from the outside world. You're talking about people in the mainstream."

"Yeah." Cody leaned back against the rock wall and flexed his biceps. "Who knows? Maybe in another eight years, I'll be six-foot-five inches, two-hundred-eighty-five pounds. Then you'll *have* to listen to me."

She waited and was rewarded with a grin. "Just kidding, Mom. Losing one of your senses is not so bad once you understand it. I started to understand one day when I went to the bathroom at the clinic. When I walked in, it was all dark. I flip on the light and there's this man standing at the urinal. It creeped me out until I saw the cane under his arm. What does it matter to a blind person if the light is on or off?"

"I see your point."

"Thanks."

He considered her in a long moment of silence, broken at last by the cracking of his knuckles. "Do I sound stupid? When I talk, I mean. Is my speech funny? The Hulk — Ferrigno — was kept off a TV interview once because his speech was unclear."

"It's a little different, the way you talk, but I think of it as your unique accent. It's pleasant and not at all difficult to understand."

"What if I forget how to talk like I forget the sound of other things? What if in my head, it sounds fine, but what comes out of my mouth is mush? What if —"

"What if, as you are quick to remind me, you stop worrying so much? God gave you plenty of abilities"

From the look he gave her, she knew she had been indicted by her own words. He sat down on a boulder, but even then his feet would not be still. He hugged his knees tight before glancing at her. His look was all boy. "What about Beth?" He said the name softly, reverently. "Do you think she thinks I'm weird?"

Sheila was amazed at the onslaught of questions piled up inside her son. "Not that bright girl. She hasn't seen you in awhile, but if she'd wanted to avoid you, she could have found excuses all those evenings she joined us for Speed Spell. You're good company and a lot of fun."

He looked skeptical. "Mothers get paid to say that about their kids."

She leaned back and locked fingers around one knee. *This is great! It feels so — so normal.* "You know girls — well, maybe you don't, but they mature at a different rate than boys. Right now, my best guess is that she sees you as the very smart little brother she never had."

At the look of horror on Cody's face, she rushed on. "What I mean is, you can't expect — uh, it wouldn't be logical to think that — of course, not everyone shares the same . . . Cody, please don't look like your team just lost the World Cup. Beth is into a million things right now. Cassie says she has a particular interest in humanitarian service and church aid relief. When she returns from Honduras, we'll invite the Dixons over, let her show her pictures, and you can ask her what she's thinking about these days. And, of course, blast her out of the water with a hot round of Speed Spell. Sound good?"

Cody was momentarily unreadable, but at least he didn't look quite as miserable as a moment ago. When he spoke, it was with such earnestness that only at the last second did she keep herself from chuckling aloud at his zeal. "Could it just be me and Beth, no parents?"

"Well, I don't — I mean, *what?*"

"She could give one presentation to you and Dad, and another one to just me. Do you think she would? Will you talk to her mom? Tell her it's for my birthday. Please?"

It was so cute. Cody with a crush. Growing up before her very eyes. A lump formed in her throat. She coughed to hide the well of emotions. "I'll promise this much, Son. Though the decision is hers to make, I'll ask Beth if she might do that. Knowing her, I'm sure she'll be glad for an audience of one or a hundred. Her mother says she was very excited to be chosen to go on the trip. Right now it's time to get everybody up and moving or we won't eat 'til midnight."

Cody stood, hands on hips, and stared up at the rock wall of the amphitheater. "Thanks, Mom, for telling me all that cool stuff about echoes and Indians and rock paintings. I just want the chance to show people what I can do. Some kids think I'm a nerd for all the reading I do, but I like learning about stuff."

She paused to tuck a stray strand of hair back behind an ear. "I'd say you've learned a lot for one so young."

Almost as much as she'd learned in this brief time with him.

"Thanks. Before we go back, tell me one thing about when you were a kid, and make it good."

"Okay, then, Charlie Tates."

"Charlie tastes what? And who's Charlie?"

"No, you joker, Charlie Tates, a boy in fifth grade. He was always hitting me with dirt clods."

"What did you do about it?"

"I'd chant, 'Charlie Tates is full of snakes,' over and over and over until he couldn't stand it and went and told Mrs. Wetzel, who made me stay after and write 'Charlie Tates is *not* full of snakes' until I couldn't stand it. That cooled us off for a few days until the next time he hit me with a dirt clod."

Cody patted her shoulder. "You were a weird kid."

"Tell me about it." She put an arm around him and together they walked out of the bowl and back to the ridge.

Stubborn, like your father, yet sweet. You don't want any props to lean on, and I have to admit you are naturally smart and capable. For all that, you're naïve and innocent about a lot of things. If we let you, you'd do something foolhardy. You still need me, Cody; you still need protecting.

But he'd come a long way . . .

My son is in puppy love with Beth Dixon. How normal is that?

CHAPTER 9

By now, the solid-rock sleeping experience was as comfortable as bunking on the garage floor.

Andy stretched, checked his watch, then spotted Sheila and Cody coming back to camp. They'd been gone some time, yet both looked quite mellow. *Good. No knock-down, drag outs.*

Maybe Sheila found something out here that agreed with her. The old reserve was there, the vigilance, but with a trace of the more relaxed Sheila he'd married. Less camp guard, more doting mother. Those who knew only the hard-shell Sheila might not see it, but he could. The clarity of alpine air, sunlight etching every tree and rock in sharp relief beneath a cloudless dish of blue, was good for everyone's spirits. *Just please, Cody, no more unauthorized swims.* Maybe they could all go down to the sandy stretch of quiet river farther down the bank and splash around before they left for California.

He gave her credit. Handed a life with a deaf child, she stepped up. Her instincts were good. No one could accuse her of neglect, indifference, inattentiveness. With God's help, she marshaled the necessary forces to compensate for a difficult loss.

In the process, they'd suffered their own losses. Loss of joy, loss of intimacy. Their home grew quiet like one of those sterile science fiction environments where the doors seal and unseal with a soft whoosh and everyone floats along on cushions of air. The last time Cody and he wrestled in the middle of the living room floor, Enron filed for bankruptcy.

The lump in Andy's throat swelled. He wanted her back. He wanted them to be in synch again. To collect garden gnomes. To draw straws over whether to plant zucchini or butter squash. To watch old movies, stain the deck, sing in the choir. He wanted to plan and dream for their old age. He wanted to be a family, not three separate armed camps.

Andy could not — *would* not — lose his family. Have them one day walk away from each other as strangers, like some failed social experiment.

Of course Sheila was scared. What mother

didn't want the best for her child? But what good would it do any of them if they were destroyed in the process?

The ache in his chest where his heart should be felt cannonball hard. He was scared too. Scared of taking what God made, crumpling it up, and tossing it away.

"God, help me." He sat up, the decision made. "Sheila, old girl, while you're looking a mite vulnerable, I believe I should act."

He rose and went to take her by an arm. "Come with me." He ignored her wide eyes, marching her to the top of the ridge.

They stood in a patch of old winter, more ice than snow, that gave a loud crunch at their abrupt arrival. Nothing but line after line of mountains and the breathtaking contours of forest and gorge lay at their feet.

Andy released her arm. "Tell me, what do you see?"

Sheila scowled and he took that to mean she didn't want to play his mind games. "Mountains and more mountains."

"And beyond that?"

"More mountains."

"And beyond that?"

She rubbed her face in her hands. "Look, Andrew, I don't have time —"

"*Beyond* that?"

209

She sighed. "I can't see any farther than that."

"Precisely!" She stared at him as if he were melting. "None of us can see farther than that. But eternity's out there somewhere, Sheila. Don't miss it. Don't get so caught up in what didn't pan out that you miss the riches of what's to come."

She rounded on him. "What are you talking about?"

He took her firmly by the shoulders and turned her back to face the view. "Don't take your eyes off that. Every time we do, it's like a mushroom cloud of toxic chemicals descends and we end up choking on our own regrets. Do you know that of the three of us, Cody's the happiest? Or he would be if we'd stop smothering him and let him try his wings."

Sheila went rigid. "You mean if I'd stop smothering him."

Andy stood shoulder-to-shoulder with her and stared at the vista. His voice lowered. "This isn't about placing blame. Honey, this is about recognizing that the longer you tie down a frisky colt, the more likely it is to bolt at the first opportunity. Cody needs us to let him run, to test his legs, to see what he can do. God has great plans for that kid and for us. Let's don't miss them." He reached out a hand and touched her cheek.

She pulled away. "Easy for you to point fingers. You go off for hours to sell insurance, stay away days at conferences, while I'm with Cody every hour. Always having to get his attention, repeat myself, endure his resentment. What do you know of the day-to-day grind of a special needs child who refuses to learn sign language or try new technology? Does he prefer his secret silent world to the hearing world? Seems like he does sometimes!"

Andy's jaw went rigid. "What if he does? He's adjusted and wants to get on with life. But don't forget, *you* decided to shadow Cody, not me. I offered to get him into day care or day camps. It would do him good to meet other people, other gifted kids who share the same challenges."

Her eyes widened and her jaw set. Before she could protest, he rushed on. "Cody could socialize and try different things under trained supervision, perhaps even a personal mentor, but no. No, Sheila, you'd have none of it because you were so blasted afraid he might befriend another adult. Admit it, Sheila. You were jealous."

Why did I push that *button? I always paint her as the problem. It's so simple, isn't it? Fix her emotional inadequacies and you fix*

211

Cody's. She's right. I'm just as bad. An avoider. A runner. I hide out in my actuarial tables because they are hard statistical facts that don't talk back.

"And where have I heard that before?" Sheila's eyes blazed. "Oh, yes, Cody's junior high Sunday school teacher. The class is having a deep discussion of Christ's final hours and Cody wants to contribute. In the process, Mr. Cain laughs at Cody's mispronunciation of the word *Golgotha*."

"Yes, I know. We've been over this a hundred times. Cody gave it a long *O* and the kids laughed along with the teacher. What has this got to do with Cody getting out more?"

"Don't you *dare* do that, Andrew! I'm not one of your insurance clients that you have to steer into a purchase. Don't you shut me down! Cody burst into tears that day — he admired Mr. Cain a great deal. The thing is, I was there and I demanded an apology. Someone had to defend our son and that teacher ate crow. Yes, I yanked Cody out of the class for good measure. He was too vulnerable for that kind of male insensitivity and better off with me — with *us* — in the adult Bible class where he could just listen and draw."

"He doesn't *need* to draw, Sheila. He

doesn't need to be babysat. He needs to learn to take what people dish out and be one of the guys. To laugh it off, not take it personally —"

Sheila wept. "Despite what you think, I wasn't jealous of Mr. Cain that Sunday. For the first time, I saw the panic in our son's eyes when 'the guys' turned on him, stopped listening to the point he was trying to make, and focused on his speech. If you were there, Andrew, you would have witnessed the herd culling the weak. It was horrible."

Andy hugged her to his chest. "Oh, Sheila." She'd handed him something new to chew on. Had she said all this before and he just not heard? Had she seen a struggle within Cody that had escaped him?

In a flash of wings the color of sapphire, a large camp robber landed on a fir branch and favored them with a harsh scolding. Cocking its head as if for an answer, and receiving none, it flew off to another tree farther along the ridge.

Sheila pulled away.

As Andy thought about it, he realized their love life went south about the time of the Sunday school incident. Truth was, their romance department had become a stock room for discontinued items. A coldness crept between them, and he knew she pretended to be asleep when he got home from working late. That way, they could lie to themselves that they hadn't made love because he didn't want to wake her.

Neither needed Scotland Yard to know the actual truth. He didn't make love to her because whatever allure she once exercised over him was annulled by what he believed was her obsession with keeping Cody safe from the outside world. He wanted her powdery, honeymoon soft, and by necessity she had traded the sensual for a defensive armor. For Cody's sake. All for Cody. If people thought that made her a frump, then a frump she was glad to be.

"Remember how happy we were when Cody was conceived?"

His candid words — and the sad regret with which they were spoken — startled her. Andy launched the questions churning within him into the wilderness void. "Remember how, when the pregnancy was official, I brought you Belgian chocolates — the really good, hand-dipped kind — and you thought it such a wonderful extravagance? I fed them to you in bed, and we laughed over how hyper all that sugar would make the tadpole hidden inside you. Then you —"

"— held your hand and asked you if you

could balance an amaretto on your nose. I remember." Sheila gazed into the distance. "You grinned that goofy grin and said, 'An armadillo, ma'am? Being a Texan, of course I can!' That got me to —"

"— giggling so hard that you fell off the bed and —"

"— you were right behind me. We rolled and tussled and kissed. I said maybe you should back off and you said maybe you shouldn't. If memory serves —" her voice quieted — "you didn't."

He chuckled. "Nope, I didn't. Our love was without reservation back then." His smile faded and he turned to her, eyes exploring her face. "Can't we find our way there again, Sheila?"

She shook her head. "We can't go back, Andrew. There's no rewinding the past and giving it a different outcome. We have to come to grips with that."

"With what? You make it sound as if we've been cursed, sentenced to a life of woe. Nothing could be farther from the truth if we recognize it and accept it. Cody's a terrific, warm, wonderful kid. His deafness doesn't make him damaged goods like some floor model appliance. He's our pride and joy, with or without hearing!"

Sheila stared at him. "And when did you

become so eloquent, so accommodating? It wasn't that long ago you told our son he wasn't trying hard enough. That he was deliberately hanging a 'No Trespassing' sign around his neck and keeping the world at bay. Locking us out. I happened to agree with you."

He looked surprised, as if trying to recall if she'd ever said that before and how he could have missed it. "You do?"

"Don't look so amazed. I might even agree with you on another thing or two, but lately each of us has been — you know."

Andy's hopeful expression faded. "I know one thing we don't agree on. It's time to take Cody off the leash. He's nearly thirteen, and if we don't start giving him space to run, he'll grab for it in ways we don't want."

"Leash? Is that what you call my concern for him, a leash?"

"Easy, Sheila, I didn't accuse you of robbing a bank."

"No, just of robbing our son of his independence."

"I never said that."

"You didn't have to. For a minute there, Andrew, I thought we were close to agreeing on something for the first time in eons. But no, then you have to criticize my parenting like you always do. And how is it that you just happened to run into Cassie at the restaurant? Next thing I know we're all cozy in an SUV headed for a campout proposed by somebody we haven't seen in ages!" She turned her back on him. "I don't know, Andrew, I don't know . . ."

He didn't like the way her voice trailed off . . . as though they were out of alternatives.

When she turned back, tears streaked her face. Andy held out his arms, but she folded hers and turned away. "Is that it, Andrew? Is your friend Cassie such a fascinating, tragic figure these days that now you go to her for insight and understanding?"

"My gosh, Sheila, honey, please . . ."

"Don't! Why, Andrew? Why drag us to this insignificant mountain ridge in an endless sea of mountain ridges when all the time there's an Everest at home waiting to be conquered?" She stormed off.

"Sheila, be reasonable! Come back!"

There was no reply other than the screeching of the grouchy jay.

CHAPTER 10

Cody began the hike back to camp in the lead. He sang the bottles of root beer song in a reedy country western twang. Four times he dashed in and out of line to quench his thirst at a spring or to relieve himself behind a bush.

He loved it out here, more than he ever imagined he would. He felt free and strong, and even where he ached, it felt good, like what his body was meant for.

Maybe he could be a wildlife photographer or run backpacking adventures for deaf kids. There was so much he wanted to learn. And so much he had learned that he wanted to put to the test. He imagined himself legendary frontiersman Jim Bridger, beaver trapper, fur trader, Indian interpreter, and guide to the Wild West. He guided more wagon trains than all other scouts put together. His photographic memory took in every shift in terrain and he spoke not only

English, French, and Spanish but six Indian tongues to boot. He knew Kit Carson personally.

Bridger was great company — trusted, respected, and mild-mannered. He'd pull the legs of tenderfeet and uppity easterners by telling tall tales of glass mountains and giant songbirds that sang petrified songs, only he pronounced it "peetrified." Just when he had his audience where he wanted them, he'd let loose with a mighty roar and they would know they'd been had. Once he held a circle of Sioux and Cheyenne mesmerized for more than an hour with a tall tale told completely in sign language. Another time he reported an Indian campfire ahead so faint that it could not be seen through field glasses. Advance scouts rode ahead to confirm that it was there, all right.

One of Bridger's favorite stories, and now Cody's, was a breathless tale about being pursued by one hundred Cheyenne warriors. After being chased for several miles, he got cornered in a box canyon. Dead end ahead, warriors bearing down on him from behind, and such an overwhelming memory that Bridger would go silent. "What happened! What happened!" his awed listeners would beg. Bridger would look them in the eye and reply, "They kilt me."

That was Cody's kind of man.

After the second pit stop, he dropped behind his mother, letting her know that he could easily eat four hot dogs for dinner; after the third pit stop, he fell into step behind Nick, who was just ahead of Cassie at the back of the line.

The breeze died and the sun beat down. The distractions multiplied. Small flies paid unwelcome visits. Andy complained of a heel blister and accompanied it with a limp. Red necks, sweaty backs, and dry mouths kept everyone busy with sunscreen, ventilation, and hydration.

After stepping out of line a fourth time to lap at a small, moss-lined basin of rock and wash his face in the chill subterranean trickle, Cody brought up the rear.

He noted that, immediately ahead of him, Mrs. D's gait had deteriorated from brisk and determined to bent and resigned. Her once sure placement of each boot was now a fatigued plodding that dislodged stones and avoided fewer encounters with fallen branches and other forest debris. His legs hurt from the downhill pounding too, but he welcomed the jarring soreness.

Mrs. D had ceased to observe her surroundings and was head-down, focused on toughing out the remaining distance to camp.

Cody slowed his descent, holding the whistle tight in one fist so it wouldn't flop against him and with every touch telegraph that he was a cow with a bell. He'd considered flinging the hated symbol off the first cliff he came to, but knew that out here one neither littered nor wasted.

The trail steepened, the distance between him and Mrs. D lengthening with every stride. He watched his dad and mom disappear around a weird rock formation that resembled a duck's head. *Their guard is down.* A moment later, Mr. D followed, and soon after, Mrs. D. For one delicious moment, everyone was out of sight.

Cody was alone.

Not yet. The patient woodsman bags the deer, summits the mountain, lives to see another dawn. The impatient woodsman makes unhappy headlines.

He scanned the terrain ahead, mentally ticking off the landmarks he remembered from the hike up. It was somewhere close now, easily missed if he didn't stay sharp.

There!

No, not it.

Two vine maples, their crowns interlaced like slow dancers, marked the place he looked for. The way could easily be missed, but not those twin maples.

It's down there, just past the next hook in the trail. He swiped a sweaty arm across his eyes and saw the feathery green and yellow leaves in the distance. His skin went chilly with goose bumps, heart racing. He flexed the stringy muscles he so recently coaxed to the surface and almost shouted a primitive *"Huh!"* He was like that eagle who answered to no one but God.

Or he wanted to be. Truth was, he had sweaty palms and was jittery with self-doubt. Some eagle. In his teens, David the shepherd boy was out killing lions and a giant. The kid was brash, skilled, bold, but was he disobedient? Later in life, yeah . . . but how far would he have gotten with God if he had disobeyed his family?

His parents and the Dixons wound left past the maples, then shifted right into a stand of firs.

He stayed left, following a fainter trail he'd noticed on the way up, beneath the maples that parted a thicket of tall fiddlehead fern before breaking into a treeless, rocky expanse that was host to a profusion of wild blueberries.

Swiftly moving — not eating the berries and giving himself away, wanting to put as much distance between himself and the others before the first person asked, "Where's Cody?" — he reached the far end of the rocky expanse and stopped before a natural stairs made of rock and root. The terrain dropped away. There were animal tracks in the soft, muddy earth — deer, rabbit — and to go that way would leave telltale Cody signs.

He stood on a dome of granite that took a gentler course in the opposite direction, a gradual descent through a field of boulders that leveled out beyond before disappearing downhill into the forest.

Not wanting to be exposed on open ground for long, he ran. Here all was dry, and he made long leaps from boulder to boulder, soaking up the alternating stretch and shock, the cooperation of nerves and bone and tissue taking him wherever he commanded.

He heard in his mind. The thud of boots. The scrape of rock. The distant cry of a marmot. The soft whoosh his lungs made each time he landed on spring-loaded legs and feet.

Again at the forest's edge, he crouched low and watched, sniffed the air, brushed fingertips over rough, crystalline rock. He was tracker. Explorer. Indian scout. Early man through whom all nature flowed.

He left the trail, worked his way carefully and light-footed over an unmarked floor of fir needles. In those few places where he stepped too hard, he raked the indentations smooth with a fallen bough. The forest floor was dry and less likely to reveal location. By the time he reached the bottom of the slope and regained the hardpan, and given the forward progress of the others, he guessed he put a mile of random wilderness between himself and them.

A wide, uneasy grin split the sweat and grime he suspected streaked his face. He was on his own. In command. Making history. Defiant as Marco Polo. Free as Christopher Columbus. Like the eagle, lord of the forest.

Hurry, knees bent, arms out to side. Decrease profile. Stay low. Cover ground.

Finally. The time had come.

He was free.

Lost deep in thought about Choice Brand Beautifiers and how Mags O'Connor was getting on with the marketing campaign for Georgia Peach skin conditioner, Cassie hadn't realized she was trudging.

A rock flew from beneath her left boot. She stumbled, shot out a stabilizing arm, and sat down heavily on a nearby boulder.

"I'm already numb to my surroundings." She steadied herself against the stone wall next to the stony bench and slowed her breathing. She looked at the tree-studded ridge above her and wiped perspiration from a grimy forehead. *More rock. One o'clock, two o'clock, three o'clock, rock. In every direction, hard, unyielding, except to water and wind, time and erosion. Where's Cody? He can tell me all about geologic deconstruction and if what I'm seeing is igneous or sedimentary, potato or po-tah-to.*

Cass snorted. "I'm losing it." She pulled the nozzle on her water bottle and gave her tongue and gums a blast of tepid water. "Mmmm, good!"

High in the far distance, she saw a scattering of what looked like bits of white cotton against dark granite cliffs. Probably the mountain goats Joanie urged them to watch for. Above it all. Unencumbered.

She looked back up the trail and waited. "C'mon, Cody boy. Quit dinking around. The faster we get down, the sooner we can fall on those franks and show 'em who's boss." *That kid has the smallest bladder in Christendom.* On the contrary, she was a sweater, moist as a marsh, and hadn't had to go yet.

Of course he couldn't hear her anyway. The others would notice them missing soon enough and wait up. There wasn't much risk of getting lost. Just follow the main trail downhill right into camp. *Easy deal.*

Georgia Peach was a wonderful addition to the line. Pale orange in color, creamy with lanolin and real dairy, it also contained a squeeze or two of actual peach juice. Enough for them to advertise, "For your daily fruit and dairy, rub it in!" They secured the rights to use the old jazz standard "Georgia on My Mind" in electronic and print media, and planned a major Halloween launch and a co-op promo with one of the nation's largest maker of candy corn. Every large bag of the sugary treats in individual pouches came with an equal number of coupons for a free sample jar of "Georgia Peach." A sweet haul for every kid's trick or treat bag and something nice to take home to Mom. And just in time to spike holiday gift giving. Mags predicted "the new kid" would soon be the pick of the Choice Brand crop. Cassie shared the excitement.

It will wear well in elevators, office cubicles, and other confined spaces. Mild enough to appeal to the subconscious, assertive enough to resist comparison . . .

It had helped her recovery to keep a behind-the-scenes hand in the business. Few could understand how difficult it had been to personally recoup following the Cassandra perfume fiasco. While some had been vicious in their condemnation, a surprising amount of public sympathy had also emerged. Some friends in high places did not desert them. The governor of California called it "a freak of nature" and fashion model Elan praised the Dixons' quick actions to take responsibility and "prevent a full-scale disaster." And, in a much publicized testimony, the mother of one of the young women who died in a dog attack commended the Dixons "for doing all within their power to support our family through this unfortunate and accidental loss."

God is merciful.

For many sleepless nights, she and Nick struggled with the guilt. Sometimes just walking down the street, it slammed her with all the force of a delivery truck jumping the curb and pinning her against a building. At those times, she could do nothing but grab hold of something stable — a fence, a parking meter — and wait it out. Once a paramedic happened by and administered something like smelling salts to keep her from falling.

Thankfully, those episodes became fewer and farther between.

She knew when it sideswiped Nick by how long his daily jogs lasted. Only once had he spent an entire night in the park, but sometimes he didn't come in until after midnight.

And though King David repented of his sin, it was required that he pay in full the consequences justice demanded.

Cass! You guys okay?" Nick appeared at the bottom of the draw where the worn track passed through swampy ground. Hands on hips, face upturned in an expression of concern, he bounced lightly on a short makeshift bridge of small peeled logs laid parallel in the squelching mud by a government trail maintenance crew.

"Okay, chief," she called back. "Cody's off on another of his nature studies, if you get my drift. We'll be down directly."

Nick disappeared back the way he'd come.

That boy is taking his sweet time. She didn't want to disturb him if his constitutional was of the more involved kind, but the day was fast fading and it was their last night in the woods. She wanted to bake a cake in the Dutch oven and surprise him with thirteen candles and a rotten group rendition of the birthday song. *There's one advantage of being deaf — not hearing your happy birthday serenade butchered by well-meaning well wishers with silly grins.*

Bottom line, she wanted him to have all the fun and freedom he could absorb in one weekend. She saw — and hoped Sheila saw — how animated and happy he was to be out here. But would it make him more restless than ever back in the city? He would find out soon enough.

Cass knew she'd have to get more involved with the Fergusons, that's all there was to it. There was a fine line between friendship and butting in, she knew, but to do nothing was unacceptable.

She stood, legs protesting the short time-out. Maybe she would casually stroll back up the trail. That way if he was picking daisies, he'd see her and maybe speed things up.

When was the last time I actually saw him? He'd been just ahead of her when they'd passed that last mossy grotto. Or had he? Her water bottle was mostly full, but she knew he wouldn't pass up an opportunity to slurp water straight from the earth.

She glanced at her watch. Twenty minutes or so ago? *Closer to half an hour.* She got lost in her daydreams and never thought to look back and make certain he was coming along. He was a novice out here and needed a bit of prodding. She was a rookie too but had a good twenty years on him.

No matter how charming and vibrant and male he was, no matter how on the verge of becoming a teenager, Cody was a deaf boy on his first real trip to the wide open spaces. He bore closer watch than this. *Where* is *he?*

Cassie made her way up the slope, feeling at first a little foolish and fussy. Cody didn't need another mother checking on him, following him around, making sure he flushed. And yet, his mother had relaxed her guard this afternoon, and reassured her strained nerve endings that her son was okay, because wasn't he back there with their good friend Cassie?

Careless Cassie, more like it.

She jettisoned the pack by the side of the trail and hurried on, sore muscles protesting the uphill strain. A current of apprehension sizzled up her spine and out along her arms. She argued for loosening the reins, and inch by gradual inch Sheila did so. Then the river incident, but she was better today. The uptight mom actually walked on for a half hour or more completely out of sight of her son — not one word of caution, reprimand, or distress from lips that had been thick with all three for half a dozen years.

Cassie ran, breathing hard, darting off the trail to search in every likely clearing and around every looming boulder. She didn't care if it was for nothing or if behind the next clump of trees she barged in on him, pants down around his ankles, and embarrassed them both.

A squirrel chided her. With a squawk of protest, a jay took the squirrel's side. A four-footed rustling in the weeds, a scrambling overhead. No Cody.

There were footfalls and heavy breathing behind, and Nick appeared at her side. His gaze locked on her troubled expression.

"I — I haven't really seen him in a long while." Cassie took a swallow of water. "You know how you get in a rhythm and you lose track of time and you're so used to having him around and it doesn't dawn on you that he hasn't bugged you or checked in for too long and —"

"Cass." Nick held her arms and her focus, his handsome face blistered with beads of perspiration. "It didn't occur to me either until just now that he kept dropping back, but when we started out, he wanted to be up front, lead the way. It's probably nothing but a little touch of diarrhea or sunstroke, but it's enough to make a tough guy blush. The others have found a nice resting spot with a creek, even a little grass. Why don't you go down and join them. I'll just have a run up and grab the slacker and be down in a jiff."

She was grateful for the offer, but his eyes said something more.

"Okay."

Nick, in excellent shape from a running regimen and having scoured the world's jungles for new fragrances, bounded on with the ease of an antelope and was soon swallowed by a bend in the trail.

Cassie slowly descended, hoping for a victory shout from Nick before she had to face Sheila and Andy and dreading that it wouldn't come.

It never did.

CHAPTER 11

Andy saw Sheila wince.

"Where's Cody? He's gone, isn't he? You can't find him, can you? As God is my witness, I knew this trip was a mistake from the beginning. Why did I ever let you talk me into this?"

Andy tried to loop a comforting arm around his wife's shoulders. She shrugged it aside.

Cassie bristled. "We don't know that Cody's lost. He probably got distracted by another eagle or a scenic view. Nick's run after him, and I'm sure the two of them will come chasing each other down the trail any minute now."

The doubt in her eyes said she was anything but certain.

Sheila's face went stony. "In case it hasn't occurred to you, Cassandra, Cody is not like other boys. He bears a close watch. You saw what happened down at the river, him going all wild. Oh, I know you think I'm a horrible mother who makes her kid miserable, but it's because I've been so vigilant and particular that he's made it this far in life. He can't afford to act on whim. Children like Cody need protection, *deserve* protection. You may think that whatever doesn't kill him makes him stronger, but that's easy to say about someone else's child. What kind of mother abandons her child to the elements hoping fate will be kind?"

Andy didn't want to jump to conclusions. "We should pray. The Good Shepherd went after that one sheep. You know, Sheila, when all of heaven threw a party after the sheep came home?"

"Exactly." Cassie was adamant. Before Andy could begin, she was off again. "Honestly, Sheila, you talk about Cody as if he were some endangered species. He's as sharp as a pin and has lots to offer, but who'll ever know how much if he's kept in a box? You're a good mother, devoted in every way. But where's the room for a smart, rambunctious boy to express himself?"

Andy cringed. *God . . . give me strength.* "Excuse me, Cass. Sheila has a point. Cody can't be allowed to go off by himself. You heard the ranger. We need to stick together in bear country. An animal like that could sneak up on Cody before he knew it. We need to find him and have a serious talk with that boy."

Both women stared at him.

This time Sheila allowed his arm to encircle her shoulders. "Thank you, Andrew. For the support."

"Of course, you're right. Cody thinks he's Daniel Boone. He has to understand that we work together to stay safe or we can't go camping. Too risky. What I do think would be good for him is when we get back home, we get him into a Scout troop."

"No, Andrew, I don't think —"

"I *do* think, Sheila. He'll be a man in a few years and he needs more male role models. We each have to give a little, for Cody's sake."

Uncertainty clouded Sheila's eyes. She turned her back on Cassie and Andy, folded her arms, and walked away to stare at a small, noisy creek in its pell-mell rush to join the river farther down.

It was forty minutes before Nick returned, breathing hard and grim-faced. No trace of Cody.

This time, Sheila accepted Andy's embrace, weeping softly into his shoulder. "I don't understand." Andy looked every bit his age. "If he's wandered off and can't locate the trail, why doesn't he blow the whistle?"

There were a few theories in Sheila's head, and she didn't care for any of them. She saw the degree of apprehension painted dark in the hollows of her husband's eyes.

"He's probably gotten turned around. Most kids do their first time outdoors." Nick's reassuring tone layered wafer thin. "Let's use the remaining light to systematically search the area around and down from where he was last sighted at the mossy spring. Everyone put on your brightest clothing, and no doubt he will spot one of us."

The urgent undertone of the words made them hurry, and soon they were climbing single-file in reds and yellows back the way they'd come.

Andy, in the lead, startled them with a sudden yell. "Cody! *Cody!* You answer me right now!" He stopped dead, cupped shaking hands to his mouth, and turned in a circle. "Code-man! It's okay, come on out, buddy!"

Sheila rushed up and grabbed his arm. "What in the name of good sense do you think you're *doing?* I'm sick of being the only realist in this family. Snap out of it, Andrew, this is not helping!"

Andy met his wife's angry glare. With visible effort, he kept an even tone. "Of course I know he's deaf, Sheila. You remind me a hundred times a day. And you know what else your words remind me of? What a blessing it might be not to hear. That's right. Not to hear the pessimism, the negativity, the putdown. Do you *ever* reinforce what he *does* have? Talk about what he *can* do? Do you know who his favorite inventors are, what sports figures he admires, or where in the world he'd like to travel some day? Or is he, because he's deaf, not entitled to express those things?"

Sheila took two steps back. "I'm beginning to know those things. Up there at the rest stop when he and I went for a walk, we had a nice talk and he told me about other deaf people, accomplished people, that he admires. Don't be ridiculous, Andrew; of course he's entitled to express himself."

Andy's voice became more urgent. "Then please try to understand why I called his name. Even if he can't hear me the conventional way, I believe he can hear in ways we don't comprehend. If he can't actually hear the sound of my voice, maybe he can sense that I'm near. You know, how some animals sense danger or an impending earthquake, how some people are prompted to pray for someone at the very moment of their distress. Mysteries. I spoke his name aloud because I want to believe in what might be possible. Maybe by affirming his existence we'll find him that much quicker. Besides that, it makes me feel better."

For once, Sheila had nothing to say. She just allowed Andy to hold her.

"Dear God, we ask you to keep your eye on Cody." Andy stood in the middle of the trail, hat off, head bowed. "Have him stay put and wait for us. Protect him. Thank you, Jesus, for looking so hard for your lost sheep. We need you now to guide our search. Amen."

"Amen." Nick cleared his throat. "Okay, folks, the day is fading fast. Andy, you walk up to the spring and work both sides of the trail down to here. Sheila, you look from here down to the root ball of that big fallen cedar. Cass, you start at the root ball and work your way back to where you sounded the alarm. I'll skirt the territory at the far edges. Go at least fifty yards in on either side of the trail. Stay sharp for boot tracks, freshly broken branches, squashed blueberries, candy wrappers, anything like that.

Each of you take a length of this blue surveyor's tape and mark the trail at the spot over from which you find any trace, anything at all. We'll meet back here when only a quarter of the sun is left showing. That should leave enough twilight by which to reach camp. Be careful and don't wring Cody's neck until we can all do it together."

The Fergusons, dispirited but determined, took up their search positions, but Nick held loosely to Cassie's elbow and moved her up the slope.

"I thought you wanted me to cover from the root ball down."

Nick held a warning finger to his lips. In the trees, about fifty feet off trail, he pointed at the ground where a sizeable mound of black-brown dung held up a blanket of iridescent blue-green blowflies. "I saw it earlier when I took a break."

To Cassie, the exact significance of the excreta did not register until her husband pointed to several streaks of runny blue.

"Blueberries?" she said.

He nodded.

"Lord help us. Don't tell me it's . . ."

He nodded again. "Bear." He blew a shaky breath. "Recent." He snapped open his cell phone. "I'm calling the authorities."

■ ■ ■ ■

The shadows lengthened as the sun made a slow, fiery descent.

Another mile and he emerged from the trees onto a rocky outcrop above a little jewel of a lake, half the size of the one they had fished earlier. Cody didn't know its name. Didn't care. No one had taken him to it, shown him where it was on a map. It was just there, nameless and pristine, not a ripple in its mirrored surface. It was how Lewis and Clark had found every lake in their path. Clean and unexpected.

The pack dropped to the rock. He yanked off his T-shirt and let the sun wash his pale chest and back with the last of its glorious heat. He felt the burn at the back of his neck, and even that was fine. The sting said Cody Ferguson was alive. He kicked off the boots, pulled off the socks, and dropped the pants. He wasn't giving up the underwear. Not yet.

Sitting there in nothing but briefs and baseball cap, almost all of him gloriously exposed to air, light, wilderness, he unzipped the lower legs of the cargo pants and stowed them in the bottom of the pack.

He lay back, hands behind head, spine

shaping itself to the curve of the outcrop. Head lower than legs, he felt a rush of blood to the brain, the prickle of ancient stone against bare shoulders, calves, and feet. His eyes rolled to the top of his head and drank in the forest, upside down, sky and ground switched.

He liked calling the shots. Move or not move.

Part of him dared them to find him. He felt dizzy and irresponsible, like a kid in a clothing store who hides from his mom among the coats. The only problem there was that those kids weren't twelve.

His other part missed his mom. He enjoyed their time at the Snow Bowl. She'd listened. Really listened to him. All that cool stuff about Indians and echoes. And Charlie Tates! Too funny. When she told it, she looked younger, happier.

He shook it off. *Stay alert.* If they snuck up on him, he wouldn't hear them coming, but there was little he could do about that. For now, in this place, it was just Cody and the wilderness. He could do whatever he wanted.

A sudden wave of nausea seized him. The world swam before his eyes. Dizziness fooled him into thinking he would drop headfirst into the lake. He threw arms wide to catch himself, buttocks tensing, eyelids slammed shut against the coming plunge.

How many minutes he lay like that, he didn't know. Long enough for the nausea to subside and the earth to snap back where it belonged; long enough for the tailbone to remind the rest of him that hard stone and living bone weren't meant to spend long periods together.

Cody lifted his head and opened his eyes. A fragile butterfly the size of a half dollar and the color of a sweet potato rested on one knee, slowly lifting and lowering its wings as if preparing for takeoff. When he raised the knee, the creature took a short flight to his belly button, a move that tickled and made Cody laugh out loud. He clamped a hand over his mouth, but not before the butterfly took flight in search of a more stable resting place.

A large ant rushed onto the field of play, and Cody delighted in inflating and deflating his belly in rapid succession. The ant careened from side to side, trying to keep its footing on the crazily tilting sidewalks of the human fun house.

The rock was no longer as warm as it had been when he lay down on it. Cody was surprised to see gathering clouds in the distance. He brushed the ant aside, slapped his belly a couple of smart bongo raps, and sat up.

Get going.

What am I doing?

The two thoughts banged against the inside of his skull like angry wasps. He tried to shove them away and began to dress. He needed to remain positive, keep spirits up, put himself first for once. Freedom felt fantastic.

Now that he'd tasted it, he wanted all he could get. He didn't like that it came with a catch — a defiant edge that wasn't him. He'd been obedient, compliant, loyal, and polite for as long as he could remember. *But I don't want to end up an emotional loser.* That meant he had to get a grip on his own life. He — and others — had to see what he was made of.

He didn't need his mommy.

His stomach growled and he wolfed down two granola bars, the chocolate bar, and one of the oranges before he stopped himself. The ranger said the bears were finding plenty of food, but he needed to get a grip, conserve, run a lean machine. You never knew about tomorrow.

The bar wrappers and the peel went into a side pocket of the pack. *Leave the campsite cleaner than when you found it.*

Back in the forest, the light faded fast. Cody couldn't move as swiftly as he had. He was still alert to step carefully, cover his tracks, and walk wherever possible on hard rock.

At the next opening in the trees, he sat on his haunches and watched the sunset change from pink to purple, shot through with knife rays of liquid orange. Clouds boiled on the horizon. As far as the eye could see, there was nothing but dark forest, spiked rock, rushing rivers, and trackless canyons. His world had never been so big, so empty. He couldn't hear it. He couldn't share it.

The firsts in his life were piling up.

He would've liked some company. Beth, maybe. He was sure she wouldn't judge him. He hugged bare knees and fought the urge to scream the names of his mother and father. To summon help. To lie that he had gotten turned around and lost. Return to hot dogs, a late-night round of Speed Spell, and warm sleeping bags.

And a too-tight leash.

The panic passed. *I love my parents. But I hate being watched, treated like I'm disabled or breakable.* He wasn't stupid. He saw it coming. The day when he turned eighteen and everyone ruled *so sorry, but you can't be an adult after all.*

No! No one's keeping me under lock and key. I'm as strong and capable as any kid ever born. Give me a chance. Watch what I can do.

Stand back.

The immediate need was night shelter. Cody descended thirty yards down the south-facing side of the ridge he'd been following. As a general rule, he'd read, the south side stayed drier and received more sunlight in the mornings.

He found two fallen logs, three feet in diameter, which, despite a sixteen-inch gap between them, formed a kind of roof over a small gravel depression beneath. He left his pack behind and went in search of fresh fir boughs with which to cushion the night's rest. Though it taxed the little saw on his Swiss army knife, he netted two broad, springy branches and laid them down beneath the logs as the last of the sun drained from the ridge and dark slammed down tight as a pot lid.

At that elevation, when the light went, so did a good deal of the warmth.

Cody traded his shorts for the long johns, and buttoned his wool shirt to the neck. One pair of socks went on his feet, the other on his hands. He'd give anything for a wool hat, but settled for the Giants cap and a makeshift T-shirt turban.

If Beth could only see me now. I'm stylin'.

A half hour later, Cody had tried and rejected every position he could think of. His limbs, already sore from the day's hike, didn't agree with rocks and stiff branches. He was poked by his very bones working against him from the inside. His neck burned. He knew now just how tender his tender places were.

He'd be thirteen tomorrow, old enough to join the Boy Scouts. If he were normal. No way would his mother budge on his joining a troop. Over her dead body was her deaf boy going anywhere near all those ropes and hatchets and tourniquets. She called it "macho nonsense. Guys grunting."

A good grunt can be very satisfying. And what about the power of the Scout law, sign, salute, and those cool badges? He already knew the sixteen points of the compass, the history and composition of the US flag, how to tie four different kinds of knots — the square, fisherman's, clove hitch, and half hitch. Thanks to the Internet and a copy of the early Scout handbook, he felt reasonably sure he might even be able to stop a runaway horse.

A Scout tells the truth. He keeps his prom-

ises. Honesty is part of his code of conduct. People can depend on him. The first Scout law was "Be trustworthy," and the minute he'd begun to plot his getaway, he'd broken it. *But all I want is a chance to see what I can do.* He hoped God saw it that way.

A Scout is true to his family . . . Strike two.

He tried skipping the other laws, but he'd learned them too well. Each one accused him.

A Scout looks for the bright side of things . . . He tries to make others happy.

Strike three, never mind the other nine. No, make that eight. Nobody could take the bravery of law number ten away from him: *A Scout can face danger even if he is afraid. He has the courage to stand for what he thinks is right even if others laugh at or threaten him.*

To live off the land took guts.

With a heave and a grunt, he flopped onto his back and stared straight up through the gap between the logs into the cosmos. The Milky Way threw off a powdered sugar trail of galaxies so thick he wiped his mouth of "crumbs" just for fun.

It was stark still. Back at the family camp, he'd sensed every-one's presence and was surrounded by the familiar. Here, he was a stranger. Alone.

He thought of the bedtime story his dad used to make up back in the good times when his son could still hear. That made him smile. The continuing adventures of Grievous Mudswop.

First, though, little Cody had to climb into the tub and soak away the day's "boy grime" before getting his hair washed and rinsed followed by a vigorous toweling. He started to giggle ahead of time because he knew what was coming. Pops would roll up the towel, throw it around his back and under his armpits, and Cody would hang on for dear life. Tethered to his father, he flew naked around the family room like one of those Midway parachute rides he'd watched but never ridden.

Then it was on with the warm pj's and into bed, where he would squirm down and before good-night prayers chant, "Mudswop! Mudswop!" until his dad relented. "Once upon a time in the land of mud burps and dirt drops, there lived one Grievous P. Mudswop. Yessir, little man, Putrid was his middle name . . ."

Mudswop barely escaped one scrape after another, and always thanks to a magic potion that was two parts toe jam, one part morning breath, and held together by an extra large dollop of earwax. Dad constantly reassured Mom that had Cody been a girl, the stories would of course be all about fairy castles and handsome princes. That was when Mom had begun to perfect her skeptical scowl.

Something with wings beat against his cheek, and Cody sat straight up and banged against a very hard log. He rubbed furiously at his head and eyes. He wiped away the wetness from his cheeks with the sleeve of his long johns.

"I wish I had a hot dog." He said it aloud and instantly hated himself for it.

"Sissy! You can't even go one night without whining for your teddy bear."

He waited. "I could have had four if I'd wanted them."

"Wienie!"

He was two people who didn't like each other. Two people in one body.

Rather than dwell on what they do not have, men of the wild take stock of nature's pantry. So far, that amounted to mountain blueberries he hadn't dared eat for fear of alerting the others to his whereabouts. He bit his lip.

Exactly where am I?

"He who dwells in the secret place of the Most High shall abide under the shadow of the Almighty."

It had been his favorite psalm from childhood. *"You shall not be afraid of the terror by night . . . nor of the pestilence that walks in darkness . . . no evil shall befall you . . ."*

Sadness filled the hideaway. Because of him, his parents were hurting. Their deaf son, their only child, was lost.

Claws big as barbecue forks . . . teeth up to three inches long . . .

Without thinking, he reached for the leather thong around his neck and slid the whistle between his lips. Gently, he sucked it, feeling the little ball inside stir with life at each breath. There was comfort in it, a link to his mother.

He dug fingernails hard into the palms of his hands and fought the thoughts that threatened his plans. *"He shall cover you with His feathers, and under His wings you shall take refuge . . ."*

Forcing his breathing to slow, he tried not to think of what he'd done, of bears that could run thirty miles an hour. He tried not to think at all. No easy task. All he did these days was spend time inside his own head.

"God." He spoke aloud, felt the vibration in his throat, the slim flutter inside the whistle, and waited. "Jesus God."

As best he could, he curled his body into a ball and wrapped arms tight around himself. "Jesus, be with my parents tonight. Be with Mr. and Mrs. D. Be with me. Don't let 'em worry. Please help me know what I'm doing."

He forced himself to hum the root beer song and made it as far as bottle number sixty-three before falling asleep.

CHAPTER 12

Sheriff Dan Myers and Deputy Claire Overman of the North Snoqualmie County
Sheriff's Department met Cassie and Andy
just as the last of the day's light departed
Dodge Creek Campground.

Since Sheila adamantly refused to leave
the area of Cody's vanishing, and Nick was
in the best shape of them all, it was agreed
that Sheila and Nick should remain on the
mountain while Cass and Andy met the
sheriff at the campground.

Andy didn't look so good. Cassie watched
the officers approach. Myers was tall and
heavily built, an older man with probing,
experienced eyes, not quite skeptical, not
quite believing. His expression was professional, fleeting, the forced smile of a man
more accustomed to unpleasantries. A large,
square head sat on his shoulders like a
Rushmore carving, and hard, meaty forearms were easily imagined putting the

252

squeeze on more than one felon. His worn tan uniform was clean yet lived in and faded from much exertion and many washings. In a black holster on his belt, he carried a large revolver.

Deputy Overman was his antithesis — warm, reassuring, well put together. Short blond hair, manicured nails, uniform crisp and creased, no weapon within sight. Cassie could imagine criminals confessing all to such a woman.

"Good cop, bad cop" in the flesh.

The sheriff rapped a pen on the clipboard trapped in beefy hands. "So let's see if I got this straight. You take a deaf kid into the mountains for his first wilderness experience, he gets disoriented, and you become separated after a day hike to the ridge."

"That's it, Officer." Andy, worn and hunched, wiped a hand over his face. "We kept our eye on him all day. It was only the last couple of miles when everyone was tired and hungry that we let our guard down."

Cassie wished she could rewind time. She would hold Cody's hand no matter how much he protested. "He was doing so well. Happy. Taking everything in, wasn't he, Andy?"

"Never saw him so keen about something. He knows a lot about the outdoors, from reading books mostly. Typical teenager, he gets a bit cocky when he's full of information and can't wait to try it out. Smart as a whip . . ." Andy hesitated. "Smart, but innocent."

The deputy, armed with a clipboard of her own, nodded. "We get adults like that all the time. Problem is, they're usually not half as smart as they think they are. They get out here, maybe a few beers under their belt, and suddenly everybody's Rambo."

Cassie hugged herself against the night chill. "We're from San Francisco, and because of his disability, Cody's led a somewhat" — she avoided Andy's eyes — "sheltered life. What are our options?"

Myers glanced to the top of the ridge. "It's been a busy weekend, and our search team's shorthanded right now. Normally, I'd leave this in Deputy Overman's capable hands, but we've got some overdue backpackers down Pine Gorge and a missing rock climber east of Sand Bar. Search and Rescue's spread thin as gnat wings, but we can round up some local hunters who know the terrain real well. If needed, we can tap other counties for reinforcements. I don't think it'll come to that. Hopefully he got confused is all."

"Thank you, Sheriff, you're an answer to

prayer." Andy's words came quiet, almost apologetic. "My — our — son can be a handful. Thinks he can do more than other kids his age. Sometimes not so big on the practical side. When he's with us, he's fine, but off on his own he gets reckless."

The sheriff hiked his waistband, which slowly settled back into place beneath his girth. "It's okay, Mr. Ferguson. Puberty drives many a parent to distraction. Your son might have turned an ankle or climbed to a tight spot and can't get down. They typically don't go far in these cases."

Cassie patted Andy's arm. "I'm right here with you, friend."

"Thanks, Cass. I appreciate this, officers. Cody's never been away from us overnight even for a sleepover. I think he had a little food in his day pack, maybe some granola bars. It's his birthday tomorrow. Thirteen." He started shaking, and Cassie put an arm around him.

"Cody sounds like a good kid, folks, just a little overenthusiastic." The deputy's words helped Cassie focus. Andy's shakes subsided. "He must be turned around and is waiting under a tree for morning. We'll get what boots we can up here tonight, and a tracking dog. Let's think positive. With any luck, we'll have him back with us in time to blow out his candles.

"For now, I'll accompany you back up to your spouses. We'll keep a fire going just in case Cody might spot it."

She turned, snapped on a powerful Mag-Lite, and started up the trail with Andy at her side.

Cassie made to follow, then waited until they were out of earshot. "Sheriff?"

"Yes, ma'am."

"My husband and I saw a large mound of fresh bear scat in the vicinity of the trail."

"Yes, ma'am, lots of bear activity up here."

"Are they aggressive right now? Cody called this the fattening time."

The officer reached through the window of his cruiser and unsnapped the radio transmitter. "Unit One to Base One, over." He looked at Cassie. "He put it like that? The boy, I mean?" Cassie peered at the man. Was that a flash of grudging respect? "He's right. If you bother bears at their feeding sites, or encounter them on their way to feed, they can become aggressive. A mother with cubs is always dicey."

Hot tears stung Cassie's eyes. *Poor Cody. Wandering alone, at the mercy of who knows what. Does he have a change of warm clothes? I pressured Sheila into this. If anything bad happens to him, I'll never —*

The radio crackled to life. "Base One to Unit One, go ahead."

"Yeah, Marcia, we're interviewing the adults out at the private campground with regard to the missing deaf child report. Repeat, the child is deaf. One Cody William Ferguson, thirteen years of age, average height, slight of build, longish blond hair, last seen in red T-shirt, tan full-length cargoes, new low-top hikers, blue day pack. They lost track of him on the descent from Tight, approximately two miles down. Subject inexperienced outdoors, but fair amount of head knowledge. We're going to maintain a presence on the main trail where subject last seen. I need you to raise Wally Frey and inform to bring his buddies to the top of the Tight Grip drainage. We'll need K9 backup. Tag and Shrek are deployed already, but in much of these cases a lost kid isn't far from where they get turned around, so I prefer a ground scenter over air. See if Roscoe's available. And Marcia? We have active bear presence. Boy may have food on him. Over."

Static ruled for five seconds, then, "Roger that, Unit One. Pete's on the way back from his sister's in Grants Pass and should arrive in a few hours. She came through the operation in good shape. They got it all. Over."

"When you talk with him, tell him we're all relieved." The sheriff nodded at Cassie. "Busy summer. Folks wandering off every other day. Good news is that Pete Borders will join us. His sister had cancer surgery. Pete used to be a K9 trainer. At one time, his partner could spot a thief on Mars, as the saying goes."

"His partner?"

"Roscoe, the wonder dog." Myers's tone was hard to read but for a note of irony.

"Right." *That* Roscoe.

"Tangled with a wildcat up there last spring and was in the hospital for a month, but that mutt's like Puss 'n' Boots with the nine lives."

Cassie swallowed, but saliva was a suddenly scarce commodity. "Wildcats?"

"Yeah, we get 'em from time to time. Not as likely with bears around, though."

"Oh, that's good." Suddenly weary and weak in the knees, Cassie thought of Nick's comment by the river. Maybe sarcasm *was* her color.

Sheriff Myers reamed out an ear with a thick forefinger. "We'd best move out. Don't worry, ma'am, just keep your eyes and ears open."

Cassie gulped. *That's twice what Cody can do.*

■ ■ ■ ■

Sheila scanned the endless night for her son.

It was well past midnight. Despite the chill at five thousand feet, she stood in the middle of the trail shining a flashlight into the void. She refused to accept the warmth of the small fire, built in a rocky depression, which Nick fed with dried twigs and branches. As long as she did not know Cody's condition or location, she would be his sentinel.

Every couple of minutes, she waved the flashlight back and forth and up at the sky as if signaling another life form that might have abducted her Cody. When the batteries began to fade, she banged the light against her leg for the last ounce of juice and paced the fifty feet of trail within sight of the fire.

How odd to keep vigil with Nick Dixon. She guessed he felt sorry for her, yet was glad she was someone else's handful. Not many men could tolerate a woman as tightly wound as she. Maybe her best friend in high school had been right and she wasn't the marrying kind. Maybe if she'd listened to her . . .

Instantly, she hated herself for the thought.

She loved Andy. He was a thoughtful man, a good provider, who, in their happier days, had adored and wooed with the best of them. And Cody was the beautiful baby for which they had prayed and saved, and greeted with fanfare fit for royalty. Things had taken a bitter turn when the hearing gene clicked off and he was left unable to perceive the beat of a dragonfly's wings or the blare of a car horn. Or a mother's whispered "Give me some Cody candy" that always resulted in a shower of sweet boy kisses.

"Coffee?" Nick held out a steaming cup of thick "bush sludge" made in a pan at the edge of the fire. "I checked for floaters and managed to flick most of them out."

She took the plastic cup and held it to her nose without drinking. "Mmm. Good and strong." With quick little sips, she wet her lips with the scalding brew. "Tolerable, Nicholas, thank you."

"Sheila, I can't tell you how sorry I am that we didn't keep a closer watch on Cody. He's a great kid and seemed to be getting along so well out here. I didn't want to rain on his fun. I know Cass feels terrible."

She liked how the stiff brew scalded. "Contrary to popular opinion, I'm not really an ogre. I do think I know what is best for my son. I tried, really tried to give an inch in this God-for-saken place, and look what's happened." Her hands trembled and some of the coffee spilled. "Against my better judgment, I listened to my husband and to Cass, and now here we are."

"That's where you're wrong." Despite Nick's gentle tone, she could tell he meant every word. "God has not forsaken this place. He handmade it and knows its every contour and fissure just as he does Cody's every cell and strand of hair. I think I know a little of what you're feeling, Sheila, and I'm so sorry you have to go through it. But God knows where Cody is, and the outcome of all of this is in his hands. The question is whether or not we trust him."

Late-summer frogs grumped from some damp haven nearby. A distant coyote yipped in the restless void beyond the reach of firelight.

Sheila hugged herself. A large bright moon broke through the cloud cover.

"That's a good sign for morning." Nick watched the celestial disk, eyes glinting moonshine. "We'll get a weather report once the searchers arrive, but that does look promising. That flashlight's pretty low on juice. Come over to the fire and we'll build it up a bit."

She hesitated, then followed him back to the fire and helped feed the flames from two sides, one hand gripping the coffee cup. "I don't."

"Don't what?"

"I don't trust God. Don't trust Andy. Not even Cody, for that matter."

Her words sounded harsh, but it was the truth.

"You don't mean that."

"I do. No one could prevent what happened to him. Everyone failed me."

"So who *do* you trust?"

Sheila drained her cup, her insides hollow as a Halloween pumpkin. "Me. I'm the only one I trust to keep my son safe." The words, the first time she allowed herself to say them, reverberated in her head like the echo voices at the Snow Bowl. *What am I going to do when they find him? Take him to an undisclosed location, change our names, erase our past?* How far must one go to hide from God?

"Sometimes . . . it feels like God took a little boy who did nothing wrong and slapped him into a straitjacket for the rest of his life." *Why can't I say these things to Andy?*

"There's a sad image." Nick poked the fire. "It seems to me, though, from talking to Cody a little bit and watching him, you're the only ones beating yourselves up over his hearing loss. I don't get that from Cody. He's ready and eager to get on with his life. All I see that he resents is being held back, feeling smothered and constantly reminded of his limitations. Based on what a ball of energy I was at that age, it's normal he wants to test those limits for himself. More sludge?"

He poured and Sheila turned the cup around in her hands, swirling the contents. "I've asked God many times why he couldn't in all of his wisdom have given us a deaf daughter instead. Content to play with dolls and draw and collect movie memorabilia. Do you know what he said?"

Nick raised his eyebrows. "No, what did he say?"

" 'Never mind,' that's what he said."

Nick filled his cup and settled back against a log. "And what did you make of that answer?"

She blew on the dirty brown beverage. "That it was none of my business."

"A mystery, then?"

"Yes, good word. An enigma. Like random tornadoes and cancer. Like it matters less what happens to you; what matters more is how you handle the periods in between what happens to you. Does that make sense?"

"Yes, it does." Nick picked something off his tongue and consigned it to the flames. "How are you and Andy handling the in between?"

She groaned. "Not good. I admit Andy's doing a better job of accepting what can't be changed, and I guess I resent that." Her voice wavered. "I want to be the good mom, doing what's best for my child, but anymore, anything I do earns Cody's resentment and opposition. Both my guys are about ready to turn me in for some useful sports equipment." She waved a hand in the night. "I'm not looking for pity; it's just the way it is. I'm not ready to relinquish my hold, and, frankly, I didn't care for God's answer one bit."

"Don't give up. God says he'll neither leave you nor forsake you, and Andy made that same pledge. I think Cody going missing is God trying to tell you something."

"And what would that be?"

"Could be something like, 'Do not fear therefore; you are of more value than many sparrows.' He wants you to trust him, to trust that Cody's deafness is a blessing, not a curse."

"Did the — you know, the perfume incident — did you ever see the blessing in that?"

Nick fished a rock from under his tailbone and flung it away. "Took forever, because I was too much into being the captain of my own fate. I had to experience humility before I could hear God. I couldn't learn to yield to something bigger than myself until I was yanked from my visions of grandeur."

Sheila shook her head. "Believe me, having a deaf son is plenty humbling. But it hasn't brought God and me any closer. No way. Was I too happy before? Is a healthy child too much grace to expect? It was like he reached down and poked out one of my eyes so now I see in only one dimension. That's something a capricious Greek god would have done."

From down the trail, a powerful beam of light came toward them, bouncing off the stones and trees like a colossal, drunken firefly. Voices drifted toward them, and Sheila leapt to her feet, hurrying out to meet Andy.

He, Cassie, and a man and woman in uniform came out of the darkness, moving into the light of the fire. Breathing hard from the swift climb, Andy opened his arms to Shelia, and she settled into them, letting him hold her.

Andy raised an eyebrow at Nick, who hugged Cassie. "All's quiet." Sheila watched Nick tighten his hold. "It's looking like the weather might favor us."

"Yes." The woman deputy with Andy stepped forward. "Weather report says fair and dry overnight, a chance of some thunder shower activity toward afternoon tomorrow. That should allow us sufficient visibility to find your son and get everyone off the mountain before anybody gets wet." She looked at Sheila and Nick. "Where are my manners? Hello, folks, this is County Sheriff Dan Myers, and I'm Deputy Claire Overman."

The big man and the attractive woman shook hands with Sheila and Nick.

"Deputy Overman says that a team of search volunteers is coming up and a K9 unit will be here at first light to look for Cody. He won't forget this birthday." Sheila guessed Andy was being brave for her.

Nick offered coffee but the officers declined.

"My sense is the boy's within a mile of us, tossing and turning through the most uncomfortable night of his life." The sheriff paused. "Hopefully, we find him tonight and won't need the K9. Tell me, is this young man going through a rebellious phase?"

"Nothing all that unusual, officer." Sheila hung her head. "He and I got into it last night and it ended up with him getting slapped for mouthiness, but we made up today. He seemed happy on the trail and had a lot of milestones. First time mountain hiking. First time catching fish. First time out of my sight just hanging with the guys. He was getting a lot of what he wanted."

"Probably just excited then, not paying enough attention to his surroundings. We'll find him."

In another two hours, the clearing filled with a half dozen men in hunting gear and neon orange vests. One man, more grizzled and somber than the rest, spoke to the sheriff in a low voice. The sheriff tensed.

Sheila hurried over to the men. "What is it? Did this man bring news?"

The new arrival wore a hooded camouflage jacket of cotton twill and matching camouflage pants with leg pockets and drawstrings at the cuffs. His head was covered by a cap embroidered with "Big Rack Trading Company" on the front and "Hunt Texas" on the side. His rifle, slung over one shoulder, looked powerful enough to bring down large game.

"I'm the missing boy's mother. Do you know anything new?" The stranger looked from the sheriff to the deputy, then down at Sheila. He tipped the cap. "Wally Frey, ma'am. Sorry to meet under these conditions. We've received word of a rogue bear several miles northeast of us but moving generally in a southwesterly direction. It's unlikely that it would reach here, as its behavior is highly erratic and random."

"Rogue? What makes a bear a rogue?" Sheila stood her ground.

Deputy Overman rushed over. "Mrs. Ferguson, I wouldn't listen to unconfirmed reports."

Sheila wasn't listening to the deputy. She saw in the hunter's eyes the recognition of steely resolve in her own. "Well, ma'am, a rogue is often bigger than usual, old, injured in some way — maybe a hunter's wound — and unable to hunt or forage in typical fashion. It's often mad with pain and hunger. It's unpredictable, full of attitude, and itching to kill anything in its path, including another bear."

Sheila felt Andy's hand at her waist, but didn't flinch. "Thank you, Mr. Frey. I sense you're an honest man."

"I try, ma'am, I really do."

Sheriff Myers gave the hunter a warning frown. "You know, Wally, nothing handicaps you so much in golf as honesty."

Nick eyed the moon, then Myers. "Look, Sheriff, we need to know your gut assessment. What are we facing here?"

Myers looked from one couple to the other before speaking. "Well, folks, between you and me, I'm pretty worried. Far back as I know, we've never had a handicapped kid lost in our jurisdiction. They usually come up as part of a group home outing or special needs tour of the ranger station and the demonstration forest lab we've set up over Draper's Corner way. Mind you, typically they were blind or developmentally disabled, so how a deaf kid would fare, it's hard to say. Your Cody sounds like a strong, healthy kid, but I'd be lying if I said I wasn't concerned about the way circumstances are lining up."

Sheila grew impatient. "You mean the number of people currently lost in your jurisdiction at the same time?"

"That's only part of it." Frey buttoned his jacket to the neck. "We're shorthanded and rogue bear sightings get everyone in a froth. Black bear season's on, but some stud hunter looking for bragging rights" — here he gave his comrades a knowing look — "may take early target practice at a wounded silvertip."

But for the creek burbling in the darkness,

there was no sound.

"Silvertip?" Sheila looked from one face to the next. "What do you mean, silvertip?"

"I mean, ma'am, that our rogue bear is a grizzly."

CHAPTER 13

Cody was half asleep, half awake. He was getting his first dog, a sheepador — half sheep dog, half Labrador — named Buddy. His mother stood at the top of a mountain, foot tapping, and greeted them as they arrived from the city animal shelter. She called to them, and they loped to where she stood, a silver dog bowl in each hand. She set the bowls down, and Cody and Buddy tied into mounds of bacon and scrambled eggs. A pretty blue porcelain plate of muffin toast with sweet butter and clover honey came next, followed by two more silver dog bowls overflowing with creamy hot chocolate, the good dark Swiss kind.

He fully awoke to four alarms: a full bladder, a ravenous hunger, joints so stiff he thought they'd set like cement, and — most disturbing of all — a screaming bout of claustrophobia.

Breath coming in gasps, he wriggled from

the lair beneath the logs, threw off the hand socks and the makeshift turban, and creaked erect beneath the faint first rays of sunlight. As far as the eye could see, the treetops were bathed in the gold light of a new world. He stepped gingerly off to the side and let loose a satisfying stream. There followed a gratifying scratch in all places acceptable and rude, then a great stretch of the skeleton that unknotted some of the worst of the night's kinks.

His ears felt the morning chill. He shivered.

Sore as he was from the hike, it was sensational to be alive.

No clock. No wake-up call. No place to be. No one's to-do list to do.

No agenda.

It was enough to be alive.

Free!

He popped open the snaps on the long johns and beat his bare chest until he was coughing and chortling, then danced on a table of rock like some mad troll. Arms akimbo, knees at ten o'clock and two, he crouched and did a kind of warrior hop, complete with unintelligible chant.

The demons of the night evaporated in new light.

Except for loneliness.

And guilt.

"Happy birthday to me!" *Stay busy. Don't think about home or how much trouble you're in.*

He hauled his pack up out of the hole, quickly dispatched a granola bar, and slurped down the other orange. Who needed cake? Who needed to invite kids who never came anyway?

Cody was careful to put the peels back in the pack. *No slip-ups.*

He'd find an out-of-the-way place to collect blueberries. Fresh fruit would keep the scurvy away. *Happy birthday, dear Cody, happy birthday to me.*

He stripped off his night clothes and decided on just the shorts, yesterday's T-shirt, and the hikers. As the shirt slid down over his body, Cody breathed in the tang of his own sweat from the hike and marveled that he hadn't worn the same shirt two days in a row in probably three years. He was getting musky, just like the gold seekers of 1898 who toiled for the precious yellow metal in the frozen Yukon.

Another couple of days and he'd be gross. The thought birthed an ear-to-ear grin. What a smelly great birthday present!

In the chill dawn air, goose bumps marched a hundred abreast up and down his bare arms and legs. It felt so good, he imagined he could hear their tiny little boots stomping in unison. He giggled, then ran to a lightning-shattered tree and smeared his fingertips with charcoal black from fire.

In the mirrored surface of a small pool of snow melt shaded from the sun, he drew horizontal lines across his forehead, lightning bolts on his cheeks, and blacked his eyelids. He liked the wild man look, ran back for more charcoal, and added a rising sun to the left side of his chest and a crude eagle's head to the right. For the finishing touch, he drew an arrow shaft straight down the middle of the torso, its stone head pointing to his belly button. He was "Straight Arrow," Comanche chief of misunderstood boys. *Straight* was what his mother expected and the way she locked him in, but it also said a great deal about his determination and strength of purpose.

The name was a start.

Most important, he was alive. "Better believe it!" He lifted an arm and checked on the armpit hairs, recently acquired. *Growing nicely, if a bit pale in color.* Man hair. His friends at home thought it was funny to cup their hands and make their armpits talk, but since he couldn't hear the effect, it did nothing for him.

Half the bag of peanuts would give him protein for the day, and he sat cross-legged on the table rock cracking shells. Before he had cracked open three shells, two chipmunks joined him. They took his offered snack into tiny agile hands and neatly removed the nuts with their handy teeth. Under the "two for you, one for Cody" peanut plan, the bag was soon empty.

"Sorry, guys, that's all I can spare today. Since my food supply's a bit low, I might be coming to you to share yours. Fair?" He took their bright eyes and quick movements as a yes.

It wasn't much as breakfasts went, but he had to ration. Just three granola bars and a package of red licorice remained. Living off the land would sharpen his wits and burn away the bit of excess civilized fat he carried. Lean was good. He'd see what he was made of.

Sound. He hardly noticed the absence of it. Not with the changeable air rippling across the surface of his skin and the textures of rock and bark and running water. The smells of earth and sky and manly sweat. Did oxygen have an odor? He began to think so, to think that he could see farther, feel more deeply, and take the pulse of everything around him. Every sense was sharper, clearer, tingling in anticipation of what new thing was down in that glen or up on that rough outcrop.

He was Straight Arrow and, like his native brothers, one with nature.

A surge of joy pumped through him, like a hydrant fattening a fire hose. He lay facedown on flat stone, legs thrown wide, arms thrust straight out from his sides. The rough granite tingled, delicious as carbonation against knees and palms. The air flowed over the stone with mineral earthiness. In a TV movie once, an Indian had stretched himself facedown in a vision quest for his totem, the revered symbol in nature that spoke of his ancestry and oneness with the land.

God, make me strong. Help me know who I am, why I'm here. Please take care of me. Help me find you. Help me find me. Don't let Mom worry. Let Dad know so he can let Mom know I'm okay. I just need to do this, God, for me, Cody, 'cause I've been feeling like I'm sort of fading, you know? I don't want to lose me and I don't think you want that either. Tell me where I fit. Give me a symbol of me, just me.

He lifted his head a little, and the unmistakable fragrance of sweet rose tickled his nostrils. He looked to the side and saw a shrub thicket dotted with the reddish pink of wild rose blooms.

"Oh that's great, God. My totem is a rose. Just call me Cody Rose, king of the wild frontier flowers." He shook his head, then was struck with a thought. *That flower isn't the answer to my prayer. That eagle, day before yesterday,* that *was my answer! I saw it first. That's the real me. Strong, cool, majestic, specially equipped to fly above deaf, way above deaf.*

"I am Eagle Arrow. Sharp, accurate, and true."

Then what did the flowers mean?

He got up and went to the bush, where the many blooms enveloped him, pleasing and sweet. The pinkish-red petals formed little bowls for a profusion of yellow stamens. He remembered his woods lore. "I get it. You take care of me. Thanks."

He snapped off a couple of the rose hips, hefted the swollen seed pods, and took a bite. His taste buds slammed shut like tiny sea anemones. *Bitter. Not so bad. High in vitamin C.* He could boil them for tea if he dared a fire. *No way, can't draw attention.* He must blend with the forest, test himself a little. "Suck it up." He chewed the pods, swallowed the tolerable, and spat out the tough outer husks.

A wave of homesickness smashed against him. The colorful flowers, the thought of tea, the wafting sweetness carried him with blinding speed into the kitchen at 1357 Brinker Circle when he was seven and home from school with the sniffles. Outside was rain and wind gusts; inside was warmth and steaming chicken noodle soup in a mug and his mother smoothing his hair, feeling for fever, smelling of the rose perfume from Dad at Valentine's Day.

Cody trembled. Second thoughts. Volleys of doubt repeated fast as the thoughts could reload. Even as the air warmed to the rising sun, he felt fingers of cold grab the joy out of him. *Some Comanche chief I am.* Oh yeah, he was Eagle Arrow all right, just not the sharpest arrow in the quiver. More like the rubber-tipped variety for sale down at the joke store for a buck.

"Crackers to go with that soup, sweetheart? Your little head is so hot. Here, let me wipe your face with this cool, damp cloth. There, now, doesn't that feel better?" He could see her lips move, cooing endearments, could feel her making him feel better.

Cody turned and scrambled up the hill as fast as his legs would carry him. Just one last look to see if they were still there, waiting for him. He'd not show himself, but maybe God would give them a stronger sense that he was alive and okay and maybe they'd be comforted. *Okay, maybe I'll feel better. Whatever.*

What mattered was proving to himself he could do this. Spend time on his own, make his own way, pass a difficult test. That he was not forever doomed to be Momma's little deaf boy. *I have to know. Have to.*

One thing he knew for sure, they'd be out searching.

Suddenly he doubted his choices, raced uphill, cutting himself on sharp rock, scraping the skin from his shins. He didn't even stop to erase signs of his passing. Heart pounding, lungs aching, dust-caked cheeks streaking with tears, he dropped downhill, then up again, over and over, following the wavy geology until he had clawed his way back to Tight Grip Trail for one last look.

He almost blew it. If he wanted to go through with this, now was not the time to be spotted. Or did he want to be found after all? No! He just wanted to see with his own eyes if they cared enough to search for him.

With a last determined effort, Cody thrust his head above a knoll. Around him was a shielding copse of alders and patchy wild grass. Between the trees, down a hundred yards to his right, a knot of people stood around maps; a few pointed at distant landmarks. There were six people in camouflaged hunting gear listening to instructions from a large, stocky man in khaki uniform. A woman in uniform stood at his side. At first Cody didn't see his parents or the Dixons, then caught sight of them hovering on the periphery. Were they wearing yesterday's clothes? Even at that distance they looked disheveled and sleepless, like they were the ones who were lost.

He fought panic. *Don't shout. See this through. Forgive me, God. This is the only way to get their attention. Her attention. Only way.*

Cody ducked out of sight and flopped on his back, trying desperately to calm himself. *Think.*

Can't.

The blood was loud inside him, shot through with adrenaline. His thoughts were a scattered, shattered mess. He couldn't even take an ounce of joy in the fact that his sense of direction had been good. Dumb luck, was all. They'd called out the troops. He was — what had his dad called it? — AWOL. Big time.

What have I done?

Shut up! Wimp! You go crying back now, they'll know — you'll know — what a handi-

*capped wuss you really are. Cody's no cow-
ard. Cody's no quitter.*

He took one more look — determined to
make it his last — and almost choked. A
huge bloodhound the color of toffee had its
nose buried in Cody's fleece vest. The
saggy-faced animal became immediately
agitated, running in tight circles, vacuuming
the ground for Cody's smell. He found it.
The dog threw back its head in what Cody
imagined was an eager bay and wriggled,
ready to be off after the stupid deaf kid who
could barely find his way back from the
grocery store, let alone Tight Grip Ridge.

The dog looked plenty old and scarred.
Their noses wear out with age. I read that.

To Cody's horror, the dog lunged against
its leash, wrenching its handler forward. The
animal, nose to ground, strained a hundred
feet up the main trail to where the fern-lined
side track that he took yesterday branched
off. The dog seemed momentarily confused,
and then plunged into the brush. The
searchers followed in the animal's wake, his
parents and the Dixons tight behind. A
woman in uniform hung back, spoke into a
handheld radio, and Cody had the distinct
impression that any second now she would
look straight up to the knoll — and into his
eyes.

He dropped out of sight. *Ohmygosh!* The trouble he was in didn't come any bigger. Going back would be as bad as going forward, where at least he could prove something to himself.

He skittered downhill. While the searchers began at square one, he had to put as much distance between him and them before they found where he'd spent the night. His path had been a circuitous route, much of it over bare rock, but whereas he had done some daisy picking along the way, they would move fast.

He had to run, and run smart.

To keep focus, he treated it as a giant interactive game, not unlike what he imagined paint ball and laser tag were like. He gave an implacable, if shaky, smile. *Open your booklets and let the test begin . . .*

Twenty minutes later, reunited with his backpack, he angled downhill, going the opposite direction from the searchers. The sun was up in all its brilliance and the day rapidly warmed. Cody kept the absorbent cap on to avoid heat stroke and to keep the sweat out of his eyes.

He dropped lower into a brushy swale, where his boots struck water. A vigorous stream cascaded the length of the swale before rushing into the forest. Cody stayed to the streambed, gambling that his scent would be scrambled and submerged until he left the splashing torrent. The iciness of the water dulled the sting of his scrapes and cleansed the dirt and debris from raw places on arms and legs.

Another fifteen minutes and Cody felt better, even enjoyed the challenge of keeping his balance in the swift-moving current. The water was icy snow melt, no doubt from a small glacier higher up, but he pushed through until his feet passed from numb to partial feeling. Awhile more, and he came to a matchstick pile of fallen logs at the base of a rock slide that partially blocked his passage. Should be safe to climb from the creek and dry his feet, stretch out along a log, and soak up the sun. They wouldn't expect him to be on the run.

Eagle Arrow was not shy.

When he was naked and his clothes spread on the logs to dry, he gathered some elderberry leaves and soaked them in the water under the weight of a rock. Next, he spread the leaves over deep scratches on his arm and the worst of the raw patches on his shins, then lay back on the barkless log to rest. Many Indian tribes put elderberry leaves on bee stings. Perhaps they would soothe his wounds.

His biggest disadvantage at the moment was the context lost to deafness. Hearing people could hear a dog baying, the shouts of searchers, or other warning signs that people were near. He couldn't. The hearing could detect water in the distance and save time by going straight to it and didn't run the risk of missing it altogether. He, on the other hand, had to follow his instincts and stumble across it.

Some people developed almost a sixth sense to danger or the presence of unwanted visitors. At home, he knew from habit and sensitivity to the thud or vibration of approaching footsteps, the probability of where his mother or father were at any given moment. Of course, carpeting, an unexpected phone call, or running short of eggs for the meatloaf that required an emergency run to the store could change the equation of routine.

Early Indian tribes had been attuned to their surroundings. They knew when bison were coming while they were still miles off. They could read the weather, predict a drought, talk to horses. Cody felt a kinship to them because of having to compensate for a lack of hearing by developing the other senses. His general awareness at home or in public places was more heightened. He too learned to read the signs.

Which was the reason he almost missed the plane.

Cassie jogged behind Nick and the other searchers, each one awaiting Sheriff Myers's signal to fan out across a particular area for closer scrutiny. Nick told her that it was unusual for the chief officer to join the actual search rather than run a command post, but manpower was at its thinnest all year, and no way was he going to lose a deaf kid on his watch. Not with bear sightings on the increase.

She gritted her teeth and fought the stiffness in her joints and swollen feet. They'd spent a sleepless night on the cold ground, "resting up." What a joke. The Fergusons, stoop-shouldered and faces pained with worry and fatigue, had surely spent an endless night. Nick, too, looked drawn and somber.

The hunters scoured the immediate vicinity while the hikers recouped. The shout that Cody had been found never came.

When at last Pete and Roscoe arrived, everyone was more than ready to get going.

Today is Cody's thirteenth birthday, and he's all alone.

Worse still, the urge to add two and two

together chewed at her. Plenty of others, she knew from overheard conversations, were doing their sums like madmen with calculators:

No sound of a whistle.

No shouts for help.

No trace of litter or clothing or any other sign of Cody's passing.

No indication from Roscoe the bloodhound that they were any closer to getting their boy than when they'd first set out shortly after dawn two hours before. The dog spent a great deal of time casting about for the right scent to follow. "You folks did a good job of searching along this section of trail. Roscoe's having a tough time differentiating between Cody's scent and his mom and dad's." Sheriff Myers tugged on his nose; the man was *not* happy.

And whether Cassie actually heard it, or imagined she saw it in their looks and body language, Wally Frey and his chums didn't cotton much to city slickers losing a deaf boy in their mountains.

What was I thinking?

She guessed that Cody — even lost, hurt, and hungry — would hate knowing he was being pursued by a tracking dog like a runaway slave or escaped criminal. *Why did he go so far off the Tight Grip trail?*

They broke into a clearing of rock and scrub growth, ringed with several large trees, for the most part scarred and damaged by lightning.

The sheriff called a halt. Even at rest, the hunters shifted feet, eyes scanning the woods and the way ahead.

Cassie hated being idle. It was the down times when she thought of slashing teeth and knifelike claws. Just last week she watched a nature special on television about Canadian bears. She couldn't shake the image of a massive grizzly bear pulling its head out of the ruined belly of a moose, jaws and muzzle crimson with gore.

The rifles the men carried were cold comfort.

Roscoe, like handler Pete Borders, looked crestfallen with the lack of results and flopped on his belly to pant.

One member of the search team came over and offered them some beef jerky. Nick took a piece; Cassie and the others declined. The man was short and thin, effusive and high-strung. "You folks from Frisco, I hear." He said it around an open mouthful of jerky. "What line of work you in?"

"Andy, there, he's into health insurance, his wife's a homemaker, and we're partners in a cosmetics company called Choice

Brand Beautifiers." Nick had long ago made peace between his choice of professions and his masculine identity. "This is my wife, Cass, and I'm Nick. You don't know how much we appreciate you giving your time and effort this way, Mr., uh —"

The man wiped the jerky grease on his sweats and shook hands. "Schotzel. Just call me Schotz, everyone does."

Myers took a moment to catch his breath and mop the Rushmore face. He consulted with the hunters, heard them out, and gave a sober nod.

Nick strode over. "What is it? Why did we stop?"

Frey studied them. "We're stopping because we've all examined the evidence — or lack of it — and have come to an inescapable conclusion." He paused, his face a curious mix of finality and sustained suspicion.

"And?"

"Yes, please tell us what you know." Sheila looked to Andy, who squared his shoulders. "What does the evidence say?"

A woodpecker banged away on one of the split snags. Frey inhaled and let out the air in a single explosive gust.

"The evidence says that your boy, Cody, is not lost in the conventional sense. That's the good news. The bad news is, he doesn't want to be found."

The announcement knocked Sheila back a step. Andy's bewildered look said it all.

Nick threw his hands in the air. "Oh, for the love of — What are you talking about? That's just nuts!"

Cassie looked from face to somber face. The searchers were in agreement. "What makes you come to that conclusion?"

Frey removed the Big Rack cap and wiped sweat from his forehead with a beefy forearm. "Well, ma'am, it's quite simple, really. The boy kept to rocky terrain wherever he could and avoided the easier walking on the beaten path. When he did venture onto the forest floor, he obliterated his tracks with fir boughs. It appears he may have entered more than one body of water, and thereby disrupted the scent. Hard to pick it back up again without walking both banks of a creek, and then you gotta get lucky."

Schotzel put both hands on his hips. "No garbage anywhere, not so much as a gum wrapper. Pretty tidy for a teenager. He's not blown the whistle you say he carries, nothing. You can bet your Aunt Matilda he's running from us, all right!"

Cassie didn't like the matter-of-fact way he said it. The nasal twang, so friendly a moment ago, now bordered on the accusatory, as if the San Franciscans had dreamed up the whole thing to give the locals a jolly run for their money.

Sheila and Andy spoke at once. "He's been this way? Cody's okay? How do you know?"

The sheriff gave his chin a pull. "One at a time, folks. I've seen it before. A kid gets ticked at his situation and on impulse changes the situation. Not a lot of thought goes into it. More hormones than anything. Eventually they come to their senses and find a hole somewhere to wait in until we can find them."

Andy's eyes widened. "Now just a minute, Sheriff. He's just a boy. Are you saying that Cody . . . that our son . . . that he —"

"Cody ran away?" Sheila gaped. "Why would he *do* that? He said he wanted to go camping, and we gave him what he wanted."

The sheriff shrugged. "Why do carrots grow down and trees grow up? Kids do what they do."

Deputy Overman nodded. "The good news is that Cody is in the area and we'll find him. Let's move out."

In another half-mile, Schotzel dropped back and walked close to Cassie, as if not wanting the others to hear his words. "You don't mind my saying, you people seem out of your element, maybe the kind who get their jollies attracting attention in unusual ways. I hear Frisco's full of folks like that."

At first she thought she must have misheard him. "Excuse me?"

Schotzel ran a long-fingered hand over a two-day stubble. His sharp, narrow features reminded Cassie of a dachshund. "You see it on the tube all the time. Say you need to dispose of a child for whatever reason. You take the kid off the beaten path, shove him into a ravine or bury him up some forgotten draw, then cry wolf, something about him being deaf and lost and all. You get the big search, nothing turns up, case closed, insurance collected, problem solved."

Cassie's throat tightened. She wished Nick weren't so far ahead. She walked faster. "Problem? What are you talking about?"

"Like the Lindbergh baby 'n' all. Enormous public sympathy. Maybe even enough to cover up that bad perfume stink of yours. Tragic figures gettin' more tragic, all like that. You don't think the past is goin' away without a little help, do you? No way. You write the book, sell the film rights, and watch the sales of new products go ballistic."

Cassie stopped and backed away from the man. She looked at him, mouth open. "You think this is some publicity stunt for financial gain? You're nuts. I think Sheriff Myers might be interested in your theories." *Why do they trust this guy with a rifle?*

"Nah. I'm just blowin' smoke, pretty lady. Dan knows what a kidder I can be. Conspiracy theories. UFO abductions. Unsolved mysteries. All like that. I call it 'what iffing.' What if the Feds already have cold fusion or a perpetual motion machine? What if Adam was a Neanderthal? What if someone went from California to Washington to bury the past? You know, how would they go about it?"

What if she smacked this idiot right on his too-prominent schnoz?

"Nick! Could you wait up, please?" She left Schotzel mired in "what ifs."

Andy was a swirl of emotions. He couldn't believe Cody had it in him to do this, not the way they said.

Deputy Overman tucked a damp strand of blonde hair behind an ear. "Weather report says we're in for some stormy conditions this evening, and I don't like the thought of your boy stuck in that. Even if he's doing the rebellious teen thing, I don't wish a Cascades thunderstorm on anyone. Our guy in the sky will stay up until conditions say otherwise. That little Cessna of his has brought home more than one wanderer."

She pointed skyward, and necks craned to see a small white plane fly directly overhead. The shiny fuselage flashed sunlight before disappearing behind the trees.

Andy's heart beat faster. "Sheila, did you hear that? It can't be long now."

"Can't it?" Sheila wiped the dampness from her neck. "Maybe our son's more savvy than we'd like to believe." She scooped a branch up from the ground and snapped it like a wishbone. "I'm so angry, so disappointed!"

She stumbled off to the side of the trail and Andy followed. The rest of the searchers continued on.

She stopped, planted her hands on her thighs, bent and trembling.

Andy gripped her upper arms. "Don't be too hard on him, honey. The sheriff's right. Kids do things spur of the moment, and suddenly it's harder to go back and face the music than it is to go forward and tough it out. He loves you and wants you to be proud of him."

She whirled, face streaming tears, and beat against Andy's chest with clenched fists. "I'm not angry and disappointed at *him!* I'm angry at *me,* and disappointed in God for letting things get to this place!"

Andy tried to hug her but she slapped away his arms. "No! I'm afraid, Andrew! I've been terrified of this day ever coming, and now it's here. Our baby is too strong, too big for me. He's capable of his own decisions. I thought he needed me, that I was the only person who could protect him. Now I know I can't. *I can't!*"

Andy ached to hold her but held back. "I know, sweetheart, I know. But this is where we need to believe God has his eye on Cody. It's faith, Sheila. Faith. We lose that and we've lost everything."

He held out his arms and Sheila folded into them. Slow and halting, her arms encircled his waist. "That's what has me most scared. What if that bear takes everything we have?"

He stroked her hair and kissed her. "We need to pray that doesn't happen. Pray for a miracle, Sheila. Even a grizzly has its master."

CHAPTER 14

Cody spotted the plane as it banked around for another look. He rolled off the log and landed with a squish on his side in the soft gravel three feet below. He wriggled under a log held off the ground by a second log at right angles. *Must not be spotted.*

He'd gotten careless. Of course they would send up a plane. He'd known that, which was why, at first, he was good about checking the sky every few minutes. But under the warm sun, he turned lazy.

Stupid, stupid!

The gravel raked his tender parts, and the frigid backwater of the stream was shocking cold against his nakedness. *Brilliant, Eagle Arrow. Expose yourself to the world and pay for it in one easy lesson. Maybe Rosebud is a better name for you.*

My clothes! A red shirt, tan shorts, white socks, and brown boots, not to mention a blue backpack, lay spread across the top of the log. Before that search plane returned for a closer look, he needed to grab the telltale laundry.

Biting his lip against the cold, the wet, and the grit, Cody wriggled out from under the log, snatched down the clothing, tossed it into the hiding place, and grimaced as it soaked up with water again. The pack was too high off the ground to reach. He scanned the sky. No plane. Taking a deep breath, he scrambled to the end of the log buried in the gravel, crawled out along its length on all fours, kicked the pack to the ground, and crawled back.

He just had time to scramble down the bank, grab the pack, and wriggle back under the log before the plane reappeared, lower this time — the pilot probably double-checking what he thought he spotted.

Under normal conditions, Cody would have loved watching the plane, maybe even waved at it. Today he thought of all the clues he'd given the pilot. Wet patches on the log where the clothing had been. Skid tracks from where he had made his hasty moves up and down the bank. *Please, God, no trace. Make the pilot miss it all. Please.*

The guilt, never far from the surface, bubbled up again. He shouldn't talk to God at all if he was going to ask for wrong things.

God didn't play games. How could you ask God to look the other way, even *help* you, when you sinned?

"Sorry, God." Cody didn't like the feel of ice water in his nether regions. He liked even less the feeling that he was a sneak. Best not to think at all — except that was all he did, every waking moment. He *lived* in his head. Just once, why couldn't he shut off his brain long enough to enjoy things? His new world was as cluttered as the old one.

If anything had given him away, it had probably been the glare off his pasty white body. He smacked his stomach with the flat of a hand. It growled back. He needed food. He thought of the package of licorice in his pack, then shoved it from his mind. The cheese was starting to smell too. *No, those are emergency rations. Nature must come through.*

He waited a good twenty minutes, almost moved, then decided on ten more before poking his head into the hot, saving sunlight. When he did, he was so cold, his top teeth danced against the bottoms. His numb fingers ached.

Once again, he wormed his way from beneath the log, snatched up the soggy clothes, and wrung them out. Despite the torture of doing so, he'd have to put them on wet. They'd dry just as fast in the afternoon heat if he went in search of blueberries. He'd feel safer and less vulnerable fully clothed and under the cover of dense forest.

After only a few minutes of discomfort, he began to warm as the clothes dried. He moved faster, was strengthened by the renewed exertion.

And with renewed strength, came renewed thoughts.

How do I tell Mom that not hearing sound is not the worst thing that can happen to a person? Shoot, he read enough to know that, sometimes, the chatter of politics and technology and scandal kept some people from hearing the voice inside them. He was no philosopher, but he did wonder if his deafness was not a disability but a blessing in disguise. If it eliminated the outside noise and he could concentrate on his school subjects, or think about Jesus and eternity, NASCAR and snowboarding, God and girls — especially God and girls — wasn't that a good thing?

He grinned. What kind of geek takes the name Eagle Arrow, runs around the woods in his birthday suit, then dodges a rescue plane only to debate the pros and cons of deafness? All he was saying was, if forced to choose between a full-ride scholarship to Cal State or the return of his hearing, there were days when he might need time to think about it.

Sometimes the five senses were all but useless. How well could the first transatlantic explorers see where *they* were going? They traveled blind, except for steering by the stars. Westward expansion happened only by learning to speak with nature and Native Americans. Those who didn't learn, died. Everything known in medicine, science, and invention came to those willing to "see" with their minds and to "hear" with their instincts. His history teacher had it right. "Only by faith in the unseen and the unheard were great discoveries made." According to Father B, it was even spelled out in the Bible. *"He who has ears to hear, let him hear"* was more about spiritual understanding than extra sharp ears.

It was why Cody wanted to earn a pilot's license with an IFR rating — Instrument Flight Rules. With that, he could fly in all weather conditions and at any time of the day or night. It meant trusting the instruments to tell you which way was up and if you would clear that snow-capped mountaintop in front of you without taking further action. Instruments were your eyes and ears when the human senses were of no use.

One day he might be the rescue pilot searching for the lost hiker. Searching for someone just like Cody.

Which reminded him of all the people looking for him, including the police. A bloodhound. A search plane.

I am in the way biggest trouble ever.

So there were these three hard-of-hearing dudes standing on a street corner.

First hard-of-hearing dude says, "Brrr, it's windy!"

Second dude says, "No . . . it's Thursday."

Third dude says, "Me too, let's go get a soda."

Though he'd heard it a million times, Cody took comfort in the familiar joke. Deaf people had their dark humor same as surgeons, same as soldiers in combat. It helped you get through the tough stuff.

Cody maneuvered along the top of a steep slope thick with Douglas fir and hemlock. He soaked in the sight of forest without end. He marveled at a nurse log in the way, fallen and rotted and sprouting a miniature fairy landscape of little trees, ferns, mosses, and toadstools. He crouched beside it, waved away a trio of pesky mosquitoes, and studied the riot of life growing from the death of the tree. He was Gulliver in the land of Lilliput.

His dad's favorite was the one about the deaf couple in the library who were having a heated argument in sign language. Judging from the large signs his wife was using, her husband could see she was getting more and more upset. Finally, he grabbed both her hands in his and signed, "Honey, you don't have to yell — I'm not blind!"

Cody laughed out loud, thought how funny it was that he had, and laughed again. He thought a minute until he had it as right as he could make it: "If there is a laugh in the forest and no one is there who can hear it, does it make a sound?"

The centipede to which he addressed the question made its way across the log without comment. Cody grinned and wondered how much noise that many legs made at centipede level. Could the little yellow spider at the base of the brown toadstool hear its neighbor coming?

He breathed in the rich, loamy fragrance of damp soil, rotted wood, and luxuriant plant growth, closed his eyes, and tried to prevent it from happening. He couldn't. The Argument, his name for it, came at him like those persistent mosquitoes. He knew the buzz all too well.

To sign or not to sign, that was The Argument. He was told that not learning sign language made him uncooperative, fearful, and standoffish. Worse, it meant that he got at best only seventy-five percent of what was said or taught. Lip movements just weren't that reliable. One research psychologist discovered that only seven percent of what people said regarding their feelings and attitudes came from the words used. Fifty-five percent came from body language. Cody was good at body language.

It was the other thirty-eight percent where the trouble was. That understanding, closed off from the deaf, came from the voice and all its variations of inflection. Because he refused to use sign language, his parents and most doctors felt he was stubborn and shortsighted. Too quick to slam the door on one of the most useful tools a deaf person had to gain full understanding of the world around him. It was like a hearing person insisting on wearing ear plugs all the time.

And the longer he waited, the more difficult it would be for him to master sign language. Children, with their quick minds, were wired to learn languages.

Then there was the other side of The

Argument.

Cody's side.

He didn't need someone else to tell him how to understand people. You didn't need words to know you were unhappy. Or sick. Or in love. Or that someone else was those things. Sure, it was cool to watch people sign well. Beautiful, even. They were like artists, painting in the air. The drawbacks, though, were huge. Subtlety and shades of meaning could be lost. So much of sign language was paint by number. It seemed like what the average person would settle for.

But Cody? Nah. Signing wasn't for him. It was like poetry readings. Some people enjoyed them; others got more out of spending the same two hours at a hockey game. Cody was smack in the hockey camp. The poetry was in the action, in the team dynamics and intricate stick work, and ultimately, in the goals scored.

Even, much to his mother's horror, in a fist fight or two.

He would not settle for average, not when exceptional was possible.

Besides, signing drew attention. Hearing people might admire a signer's work, but did anyone really see or admire the people? No way. People who had to use sign language were different. Signing just proved the deaf were disabled and needed help.

Well, to heck with special services. Fine. He was deaf. He'd overcome it. No one was going to label him! Being deaf didn't define him, not by a long shot. From what he saw, it would only get worse when he got older. Better to find coping mechanisms that proved he was not just as good as, but *better* than the average hearing guy.

Deficient? Him? Not hardly. Not in life, not in work . . . not in any way.

A movement down the slope to the right in a pretty sunlit patch of vine maple caught his attention. Cody tensed, ready to bolt. He prayed it wasn't one of the searchers hunting for him — or a bear.

A deer's head poked from the foliage. A supple tan body followed, as if spilling from the brush of a master illustrator. The doe paused, tested the air with its nose, big ears rotating for the slightest sound. Cody was statue-still, heart racing at the deer's beauty and grace. It bent to lick a foreleg, then snapped to attention when Cody shifted his weight. After half a minute, the doe moved downhill, dainty tail the last to disappear from sight.

Cody stood, shook off the stiffness, and walked around the fallen log. He looked back often to see if the magical apparition would reappear. It was comforting to know the doe was there, its sharp senses on the alert. He wondered how long a deaf deer would last in the wild.

Not long.

The Argument flared two or three times a week or more. His mind was made up. So he polished his defense. *It's possible to learn to pitch without ever throwing a ball.* Harder, maybe, but possible. "Many prisoners of war came home with abilities they never had had before the war." His history teacher, Miss Barclay, was smart. "In captivity, their cellmates demonstrated how to play musical instruments or use sports equipment that existed only in their minds. The POWs made great students. They had hundreds of idle hours to invest in mental practice and eventually came home good at any number of things."

Rounding a granite bulge above a racing torrent, he leaned into the rock face and drew a long cold drink from the splash and spray that tumbled down the hillside. It joined the main stream, sparkling in sunlight far down the steep embankment.

A year after going deaf, he threw a fit when his parents suggested he enroll in an American Sign Language class. The old family cocker spaniel had entered the room and started barking. "See, Code?" His dad was always trying to lighten the mood. "Chester agrees you should learn to sign."

Cody swiped at tears. "Nice try, Dad, but you misunderstood. Chester says you shouldn't make me. You forgot that I can read dog lips too."

His wit had been rewarded with a month of nothing more said about the language class. But then The Argument returned. It'd been with them off and on ever since.

"What do pigs speak?" Cody watched a pair of squirrels play tag around a tree trunk. From their blank looks, he guessed they were stumped. "Swine language."

Without a chitter of approval, the squirrels returned to the chase.

"Tough crowd."

He made one last attempt. "How do lighthouse keepers communicate?"

This time, the squirrels didn't even stop to consider the punch line, but tore up the trunk of one tree, out along a springy limb, and through the air to the next tree.

"Shine language." Cody pitched a stick at their retreating backsides. He watched until the battling rodents were out of sight and dropped his pack.

Hot and sweaty again, he washed his face

in the stinging cold water bursting from the rock. He held his Giants cap under the flow and dumped the refreshing contents over his heated skull. Hands on hips, hat soaked, chin dripping, he studied a spot where the stream below formed an inviting pool of deep, slow water at the base of a series of foaming riffles. Resistance, as he'd read in his *Star Trek* novels, was futile.

He looked for a way down. A cautious descent would take him along the edge of the maple grove from which the deer had emerged. No way would the deer have taken its sweet time — ears twitching for sound, nose testing for danger — if the bloodhound and its handlers were anywhere near.

Cody calculated he could grab hold of the maple branches and use them to swing past the steepest part of the descent. Calf and thigh muscles acting as brakes, he kept arms outstretched and skidded down the decline. Just as he reached for a maple limb, his feet shot out from under him and he sledded down the slope flat on his back.

With a helpless yelp, he flew off the bank where it dropped away, took a stinging slap across the forehead from an overhanging branch, and dropped like a rock into the deep pool he'd spotted from above.

Icy cold shock snatched his breath away.

He kicked for the surface and broke into an even brighter world than the sunlit one left behind. Despite raw skid rashes on bare thighs and a sore forehead, he whooped out his delight, then thought better of making so much noise.

Just in case.

He stroked over to the shallows, got out on the shore, and shed boots and shorts with abandon. *No way can that plane spot me back in these dense trees.*

He laid out the contents of the pack on a rock to dry. He swam, dove, floated on his back, and spouted water from his mouth like a whale. He cupped hands, made waves, and splashed like a wounded seal. A half dozen times, he hauled out of the stream, climbed a mound of dirt pushed up by the root ball of a downed tree, and cannon-balled back into the pool. He wished his friend Blake were there to share in the coolest, most awesome swimming hole on planet Earth, but if God wanted him to have it all to himself, then he would gladly accept God's will.

"First thing I do on the other side is find the head angel and tell him, 'Gabriel, sir, Cody W. Ferguson reporting for lifeguard duty on the Crystal Seashore!' "

He laughed despite the trouble he was in.

If they found him in the altogether talking to angels, he might have trouble explaining his way out of a rubber room.

They couldn't find him. He wasn't done tasting independence. Eagle Arrow wasn't finished flying free.

In his favorite fantasy, Cody was Thomas Alva Edison. And present at the creation of his 1,093 American patented inventions — including the phonograph, one of the earliest motion picture projectors, and the incandescent lightbulb — all of which made Edison a hero in Cody's eyes.

That and the fact that Edison was hard of hearing, almost deaf. As were his father, and son, Charles. Genetics, pure and simple, and not about to slow him down.

One of Cody's prized photos was a print of Henry Ford shouting straight into Edison's ear. It was Edison, the greatest inventive genius in the world, who convinced Ford to follow his dream of manufacturing a gas-powered car.

"To invent, you need a good imagination and a pile of junk."

There he was, a twelve-year-old Al Edison, the newsboy on the train that ran between Port Huron and Detroit. "John Brown hung! Lincoln elected! Civil war declared! Paper, mister? Paper, miss?" There he was in the baggage car, where he set up a laboratory to continue experiments with electrical and mechanical things. There he was setting off a small explosion that started a fire on the floor of that car that cost him his first job. Nor was it Al's first fire. By the time he was six, he had accidentally burned down the family barn.

But what most endeared Edison to Cody was that he was largely self-taught. Teachers thought Edison was slow — one called him stupid — so he was home-schooled by his mother and read constantly.

He was cooped up with his mother every day, and look how he turned out.

Cody often struck an inventor pose in front of the mirror in his room, as if he were Edison, being interviewed by reporters.

"Mr. Edison, sir! Why, if you are near deaf, have you not invented a hearing aid?"

"I'm working on one — for others. As for me, I find there are distinct advantages to being deaf."

"And those would be?"

"For one, it forces me to read, and reading beats the babble of ordinary conversation. For another, it helps me concentrate on my work and spend less time answering darn fool questions from individuals such as yourself. Next question."

"Mr. Edison, it is said that you spent only a few months in a traditional school. If true, why sir?" This time the question came from a pretty young lady in lace and gloves who was easier on the eyes. In fact, she bore an uncanny resemblance to Beth Dixon.

"Most conventional schools teach children the rote memorization of facts, when they ought to have students observe nature and to make things with their hands. I favor the Montessori method, education through play. It is then that learning becomes a pleasure."

The young female reporter batted her sparkling eyes. "Why, is that so?"

"Indeed, my dear. It follows the natural instincts of the human being rather than the artificial present system which casts the brain into a mold. Discovery comes not from conformity but by the encouragement of original thought or reasoning. I feel certain that there were those who must have tried to discourage you from taking up the life of a journalist. 'How improper for the fairer sex! How against femininity to exercise an aggressive, investigative mind in a man's world!' Am I right?"

The young lady could but nod before so striking an intellect.

311

Cody was there in 1879, at the birth of the incandescent lightbulb that brought the light of day indoors. And while he was at it, Edison invented the electric power system that provided the dynamos to generate the power, the wires and fuses to control the flow, and the switches to turn the lights on and off.

"Genius is ninety-nine percent perspiration and one percent inspiration!"

Cody even pretended he watched much of Edison's life's work go up in flames one December night in 1914 when his laboratory burned to the ground.

When Edison's deaf son found him, he was calmly watching the dreadful scene. "Charles, where is your mother?"

"I don't know, Father."

"Find her. Bring her here. She'll never see anything like this as long as she lives."

The following morning, the inventor stared at the ruins. "There is great value in disaster. All our mistakes are burned up. Thank God we can start anew!" Three weeks later, he managed to deliver the first phonograph.

Now that was Cody's idea of Deaf Power!

He looked around his forested world and wondered if his imagination was up to it. To making something more of his life. To turning his mother into an encourager like Edison's. To making a name for himself.

To being more than just Cody the runaway.

The climb back was difficult. Soggy shorts constricted his ability to stretch for handholds. Rocks on the damp hillside dislodged easily. After a couple of slips and painful slides, mud and scratches turned his chest and belly dirty red. He put his shirt back on and took his boots off, flinging them to the top of the slope. Instantly he found better purchase by digging bare toes into the softened earth. Fifteen minutes of carefully picking his way along a diagonal route brought him ten feet from where he'd first spotted the refreshing pool below.

Cody was hot, dirty, and sticky. The scrapes hurt, and he'd been jabbed below the belt by a stob of wood he'd tried to brace against. While he rested for the final ascent, a low-lying fir branch poked him in the face. Worse, the occasional mosquitoes of an hour before had recruited a squadron of needle-nosed air aces to join them. He took futile swings with his cap, which they dodged like tiny insect matadors.

Next time, grab the bug spray.

He couldn't slap his tormentors *and* keep

his footing. Growling, Cody grabbed hold of the branch in his face and, with a mighty grunt, pulled hard to haul himself up.

The branch snapped and Cody somersaulted backward. Halfway down, he slammed to a halt against a tree trunk. The last thing he knew was the back of his head ramming a hard, immovable object.

And black. Lots of bottomless black.

It was muggy.

A faceful of dead tree needles — and the incessant poking of blood-sucking insects — brought him back. His vision swam, cleared, and swam again. The first word that formed in his addled mind was *arboreal*. A Speed Spell exclusive. *Must use in a sentence.* He looked around. *I'm wedged against a lone spindly hemlock, a determined arboreal refugee.*

The guy who fell from up there was a dummy; the guy who woke up here was a genius.

He grinned, aware of three persistent aches: a knot at the back of the skull, a bruised groin, and a throbbing left kneecap.

The knee alarmed him most. The left leg was bent back, the foot wedged in a pile of forest debris caught in the bottom twisted branches of the scraggly tree.

With difficulty, he dislodged his foot. Bloody crimson scratches ran down his leg and across the top of his toes. As if someone had stuck an airhose in it, the knee swelled. *How do I climb out of here now?*

Nothing could stop him. He was the Evel Knievel of roof jumpers.

He hand-walked himself upright, pressed against the tree trunk, then, bracing himself with the good right leg, tested the left. Though it hurt like mad, he could still put weight on it. Nothing broken. *Thank you, God.*

Walk it off.

That was a joke. He was on a thirty-degree slope. Another false move and he'd be up a creek. Or in it.

Keep that sense of humor, Code-man.

His stomach growled again. Food was the next order of business. He was a mess, but everything seemed to be working. Even the injuries reminded him he was alive. Alive and taking risks.

Taking risks with nobody to get him out of trouble but the Code-ster himself.

It was a new feeling — one followed by a flood of apprehension so strong it nearly knocked him down again. *What if I can't get out of here? What if I die and my body isn't found until spring? Or ever?* He didn't even

315

want to think of his parents, how worried they must be. Or what his death would do to them.

Stop it. If you let yourself think those things, you'll quit. Start a signal fire and just surrender.

In the end, the mighty Eagle Arrow would be nothing more than a wounded parakeet, ready to return to its cage.

He couldn't quit. No way would he prove to everyone that the poor deaf kid was an idiot and needed help all his life to stay safe.

No. *No!* No way. He had to prove he was capable. Could use his wits. Had guts.

Biting his lip, ignoring the pain, he slowly worked himself over to the hillside. He opened a pocket on the pack and ate one of his precious licorice whips for an energy boost. The smell of wet, unrefrigerated cheese made him sick. He'd have to decide whether to eat it or discard it. As he chewed the delicious licorice sweetness, he scouted out a longer but more gradual ascent.

It was tough, teeth-gritting work. Step by careful step, Cody worked his way up. A half hour later, sore but jubilant, he flopped onto flatter ground, where his boot prints were still visible in the rich soil.

"You da man!" He panted and spit dirt. "You da macho man!" He sat up and flexed his biceps. Good thing he'd been working out. "Oh yeah!"

He retrieved socks and boots and put them on, wincing when he tied the left one. He stood, brushed himself off, tested the leg. Not bad. He washed his face in the stream and took another long drink before saluting farewell to the pool below. *Our hero came, he saw, he left limping only a little.*

Softly whistling what he remembered of the theme to *Star Wars,* he waved away the mosquitoes and fought the tears stinging the corners of his eyes. He'd find a meadow or clearing with some kind of food. Eat his fill. Look for the night's shelter. Think how impressed Beth would be when he wowed her with his adventures.

How do two people in love communicate? Sighin' language.

He could do this. He could.

CHAPTER 15

Cody shrugged off the doubts. He didn't feel lost, not really, just a strange sense of having entered a 3-D movie. Whenever he chanced to look back, the audience in the weird cardboard glasses was made up of his family, friends, doctors, and therapists watching his every move, wondering how this episode in *Cody, the Movie* would end.

Deep in a dark stand of hemlock, he remembered reading that hemlocks loved moist areas. He followed no discernible trail through the woods, but rather natural passages and openings that took him across a narrow opening in the evergreens thick with willows, alder, and bracken fern.

A hundred yards beyond the open area, Cody struck pay dirt — a small catch basin of rainwater overshadowed by hemlocks and fed by a couple of tiny streams, now late summer trickles. At the far end of the basin, where the mountainside took a steep plunge into the thickly wooded ravine and his friendly creek tumbled on, a neatly constructed beaver dam zipped everything tight. Around the pond's perimeter was marsh grass as bright green as the fronds in the fish tank at home. A dozen pointy stumps of cut trees ringed the pond, gnawed to earth by sturdy incisors. Wood chips old and new encircled the base of the stumps. The beavers were at home.

He watched one of them execute a sharp slap on the surface of the pond, and spreading ripples greeted Cody. He caught a glimpse of rich brown fur, webbed feet, and a smooth, scaly paddle of a tail. The caretaker of the dam submerged near a large hump of a lodge fashioned from sticks, leaves, and mud. A pretty branch of creek dogwood, recently added and still sporting clusters of white flowers, poked from the top of the lodge.

"Nice touch." Cody was surprised to see beaver at this elevation. "I'll recommend you to my mom."

Sadness crept in. Quick with purpose, he fought it, turning his attention to a thicket of bulrushes growing in the shallows of the pond.

The way there was strewn with mushrooms. There were white ones with golden brown tops, brown ones with white under-sides, and a patch of pale purple-tan, funnel-shaped ones that faintly resembled ragged pigs' ears. Cody didn't know their names, or which, if any, were edible, but he knew enough to leave them right where they grew.

The bulrushes were another matter. They were good for food, fiber, and quenching thirst. Again Cody removed his boots and socks and waded in. The cool soothed his knee and would bring down the swelling.

He pushed a hand into the mud and felt along the rootstock until he found a pro-truding bulb from which a new shoot grew. Just like the book said. He snapped it off, rinsed away the mud, and took a tentative nibble. It tasted mild, almost bland, a cross between onion and celery. The Indians peeled, dried, and pounded the tough bulbs into flour that resulted in bread. The shoots were also woven into baskets and sandals, but Cody was grateful for his sturdy, store-bought boots.

He forced himself to eat two more bulbs, and harvested half a dozen to carry in the pack. When a water source couldn't be trusted, he wanted to have nature's water bottle in stock. He was surprised to find how filling the bulbs were. Now all he needed was dessert.

A flash of yellow on a branch revealed what he thought might be a yellow warbler. He thought of it as the common chickadee in a party dress. "Take me to your berries." He used his best Martian voice.

He felt suddenly, inexplicably, lighthearted and giddy. *Am I cracking up? Is it lack of food?* Maybe it was that he could find his way, feed himself, so far stay one step ahead of bloodhound, trackers, and aerial surveillance. Would newspaper accounts of his disappearance mention how capable, knowledgeable, and resourceful he proved to be? He hoped they wouldn't add "for a deaf kid."

More important, would his mother read those accounts and clip them? When this episode ended, would anything change?

Easy there, Eagle Arrow. You've been on your own just shy of twenty-four hours. Hardly the stuff of legend. But you know, if we were keeping score, you'd be ahead — for the moment.

Dang straight.

Instead of grinning, he frowned. Suddenly freedom on these terms didn't feel right. A far cry from lighthearted and safe. It would be dark again in a few hours, this time far from camp and family. *God, why can't I be a*

Joshua? A strong, brave leader who obeys you? I can't ask you to be with me everywhere I go if I don't listen to you.

He shoved the thoughts away. There was plenty else to think about.

He thought about promising medical breakthroughs, like the Michigan researchers who restored hearing in deaf guinea pigs with a gene and a virus. Cody looked up everything he could find on the research. The procedure formed new cochlear hair cells, the ones that converted sound waves into electrical impulses. The deaf guinea pigs could hear again. And the best part: The neuroscientist at the National Institute on Deafness said a lot of the techniques would "fairly easily" translate into a clinical setting for use in humans.

Fairly easily. He took a lot of comfort from those two words. *Fairly easily.* Maybe he could be a volunteer in the human clinical trial.

Back in his boots, he climbed down from the beaver pond into a gently sloping meadow of blueberries. Before long his fingers were blue, his tongue was blue, two new streaks of blue ran down either side of his ribcage, and rings of blue circled his eyes.

"Bye, bye, Clark Kent Cody, it will be a

blue Christmas without you."

The pile of bear scat was a surprise. He almost stepped in it, so absorbed was he with cramming himself full of the bountiful blue-black fruit. He grabbed a stout stick and eased into a crouch to investigate.

The scat didn't stink, so it was safe to assume the bear was eating mostly vegetation and berries. Cody did encounter one small patch of fine brown and white fur, most likely a deer mouse appetizer. The droppings appeared fresh, and when he lifted them with a stick, his hunch was confirmed. The grass beneath was a healthy green, not yellow with age, and there was no insect larvae present as there would be in scat that was several days old. *Probably went through here this morning.*

He cast about, saw only two other piles, and breathed a little easier. Numerous piles in a concentrated space would indicate a bedding area. On a low, broken branch of a nearby fir, dark chocolate brown hairs suggested that the same bear had stopped for a back scratch.

The argument in his head reached a fever pitch. Should he pull the blasted whistle from the pack and wear it, or would that be an admission that Eagle Arrow was really Chicken Arrow? Mentally, he pushed the whistle away. Young Indians learned to go hungry until they won. No fears would be conquered if he wore the whistle. He couldn't even look at it without thinking that it was somehow attached to a cord that ran a thousand miles south into his mother's bedroom in San Francisco.

I'm thirteen. In some societies, in some religions, that's a man.

A hungry rumble bubbled in his belly. *I would love some fish to eat.* The dark waters of the pond were glassy smooth and there were no signs of feeding on the bank where a bear might have dined. Fur traders had eaten beaver, but the thought of devouring an herbivorous rodent made his stomach lurch, even if he could think of a way to trap one. Besides, they were his neighbors. *You don't eat your neighbors.*

The day darkened in the glen beneath the hemlocks. A familiar loneliness crept over Cody. *Nights are the worst. Why can't I be a Joshua and command the sun to stand still?*

"You shall not be afraid of the terror by night, nor of the arrow that flies by day . . ."

Wasn't that part of the test? Get through the night to dance in the day? Every human struggled with the dark — the dark side, the dark force, the dark night of the soul. He wrestled with those, the terrible slamming force of lips forming the awful words: "Your son will never hear again." Could the coming of the night ever be as bad as that?

At a run, he angled uphill, fled the lower places. He ignored the pain in his knee, punished his joints and tendons, strained for higher ground. Muscles spasmed; lungs protested; the very breath tore in and out of his throat with hot fury. The loose granite stones that winked and sparked with royal feldspar and mica at noonday, were crystalless and dead in the approaching murk.

Up there where the sun still shone, where the blind saw, the lame walked, and the deaf heard, was where he wanted to be. That, he believed, was heaven.

A strangeness tinged the air. A periodic oscillation in the atmosphere that vibrated even his bones.

Lightning.

The higher he climbed, the stranger the world became. Everything went motionless. Not a leaf stirred, not a bird moved. The remaining heat of the day, radiating from sun and rock, formed a thick blanket of humidity where it should have surrendered to cold. He smelled ozone in air that felt electrically charged. When he held a hand, palm down, just above his scalp, the hair of his head leapt to meet it.

325

He slowed, tormented legs burning and barely able to support his weight.

The forest stayed close and airless to the hilltop, three rounded knobs rocky and barren, scoured bald by winter winds and weather. Cody plodded to the summit and crouched over, sick with exertion. He stooped, hands on thighs, sucking stagnant air, then straightened with a gasp.

The view of the valley and the ridge beyond was gridlocked with monstrous thunderheads, piled one atop another in a mass of eruptions. They were so close, it was as if he stared into the face of God. Great, jagged lightning bolts rent the sky and lit the clouds a sickly yellow-green. Cody's mouth went dry with the taste of metal, and he staggered back the way he came.

A lightning bolt struck the knoll and the force of it knocked him sprawling. He crawled on his belly trying to catch breath that would not come. It was as if a valve on his lungs had been screwed all but closed. *God, oh God, please don't let me die!*

He stumbled and crawled from the deadly summit. Cannons of noise exploded in every direction. He was slammed by a second thought, almost as stupefying as the first. *I* heard *that!* Did *I hear it? Is that sound or only vibration?*

A second spectacular strike illuminated the gloom, the brightness so intense that Cody and everything around him were bleached ghost white. Thunder exploded against him with such force that every tooth and bone reverberated and his heart echoed the menacing sound from every chamber. His whole body was one giant ear.

Stabbing icicles fell in heavy, stinging rain. At first a drizzle, it turned to downpour accompanied by a cold wind that whipped without mercy.

Take shelter! Lightning tends to hit the highest point in an area. Stay away from pinnacles. Descend from mountain summits on the leeward side. Ground currents may run through fissures in rocks, down wet cracks, along the surface of the earth. Beware.

The Scout handbook was quite clear. Cody had fallen asleep at the switch. Down in the secluded ravine, like the novice he was, he didn't monitor the weather. Another Speed Spell word taunted him. *Derelict.* That's what he'd been, and derelict could get you killed. Now he could just suffer the wild ride of "electrical discharge, rapid expansion of gases, numbing crash."

And repeat.

Lightning strike. Teeth-jarring reverberation. All the world a skeleton. A naked snag burst into flame, igniting with graveyard fingers of white orange.

Cold, oily dread replaced the blood in his veins the way it had the first time he saw stuntman Freddy Largo stagger toward the camera, a writhing pyre of fire.

Another crash. Cody screamed, fought the fear, rose to his knees, and was knocked flat again by concussion and illumination. *Is that ringing in my ears real?*

He lay there, exhausted and terrified, mud welling into mouth and nose, blinded by the light, wondering if he would die . . .

And if that would be such a terrible thing . . .

CHAPTER 16

"Take cover!" Sheriff Myers shouted above the shake and blow of the storm. The search team quickly reassembled under the semi-shelter provided by close ranks of Douglas fir.

Cassie knew enough to know the woods was a risky place in an electrical storm. In the open, you risked being hit yourself. Under a tree, you risked the tree being hit and taking you out too.

Some of the searchers donned plastic rain ponchos. Roscoe woofed dispiritedly, eyes half closed, as if contemplating a kennel resort for retired K9s. The dog's handler looked disgusted and a little embarrassed that in his dotage Roscoe was unable to track down a deaf kid from the city.

Cassie felt sorry for them.

Myers hiked his pants higher as if the cold wind now blowing had found a way in, buttoned the top button of his sweat-stained shirt, and yanked on a large rain poncho with the words "County Sheriff" stenciled across the back in yellow capitals. "Our pilot's sure he saw signs of human disturbance in Little Wash basin, maybe an hour from us to the southwest. We'll have a look soon as this light show passes.

"Sorry, folks. I was confident we'd have found him by now."

They'd all hoped Roscoe could do the job and do it quickly. His long ears and floppy facial folds trapped the scent right up around his nose. But, as Pete explained, there were things that worked against them. First, it was hard for a trailing hound to discern between the scent of the missing and their family members. Then factor in that the boy's skin cells would decompose faster in the hotter temperatures of that afternoon. Plus Cody covered a lot of ground fast and worked at not being an easy find.

Sheriff Myers brightened. "No matter. Hopefully we can get more personnel up here and come at it from two different positions, this one here and up from Fire Crossing where this trail comes out. I'm still trying to get us an air scent dog. They catch human scent in the air and work off-lead. And we can always bring in heat-sensing equipment if it comes to that. We'll get him."

"He's going to catch pneumonia in this weather . . ." If the rain hadn't drenched her spirits, Sheila's mother misery would have more than done the job. Cassie put an arm through hers.

Schotzel snorted. "Give the kid another night out here in this — what they call tough love, where I'm from — and he'll likely tire of the game. Come out at first light bawlin' for his momma."

"Schotz, enough!" The sheriff looked mad enough to give the man a good thrashing. "Keep your child-rearing tips to yourself. Soon as this thunder cell moves on, we head for Little Wash. There's a fairly flat meadow near there where we can brew a little tea and fry up some bread."

Cassie shivered in the cold. The others stomped their feet and blew drippy noses.

"Got me a headstrong kid." Wally Frey offered the Dixons and the Fergusons chewing gum. "Never seen the like of it. He gets awarded a full-ride scholarship to Oregon State University and the very next day enlists in the Navy. Don't that beat all?" He gave a short, wheezy laugh. "But I was no different. My old man give me the exact amount for a little Ford pickup to haul my landscaping supplies in and I go right down to the Speed Barn and buy me a motorcycle, helmet, and flight suit and haul hiney for Utah. There's a reason why the words *young* and *crazy* go together."

That started a round of stories among the hunters about their wild and wasted youth.

They started out again and the rain fell. The moaning wind battered Cassie's hopes. *That Schotzel's a strange one. His eyes never stop moving and his manner is about as smooth as broken glass.* She could tell he was nobody's dad. Hoped not, anyway, then felt bad for thinking it.

The strange, surreal light didn't help matters. It only added to a sense of battling the elements. Each flash of light and roll of thunder made her wince. She prayed Cody found shelter. She figured he began the day in high spirits, all vinegar and full of himself, glad to be somewhere, anywhere, out from under his mother's thumb. But just how far could an academic knowledge of bear behavior and outdoor survival carry him? Even the most experienced woodsman could stumble off a cliff or suffer a bear attack. Every summer came news reports of wilderness encounters gone bad.

And he can't hear danger any better than he can hear us call his name. All she could think of was a coiled rattlesnake, its warning rattle unheeded by deaf ears. Or a monster grizzly stalking the boy from behind.

She trembled. That they'd found little trace of Cody was the worst. *Did he fall or meet a . . . Is Cody hurt — or dead?*

Cassie tightened her grip against Sheila's trembling and hoped her own wasn't that noticeable.

She could only imagine what not knowing was doing for Andrew's blood pressure.

To the east of Little Wash, Harvey Comfrey cursed the cold and the trickle of icy water that found its way inside the wool bush jacket. He shouldn't be hunting alone, but the business trip to Chicago next week would eat up the rest of bear season. Moving up from Seattle had been great for Cathy and the kids. Now if he could just bag a trophy and fill the freezer with bear steaks, he'd be king of the castle for sure.

He blew on the hands encased in wool gloves without fingers and tightened his grip on the .30–06. The special lens on the high-powered rifle scope was top-of-the-line high definition — waterproof, fogproof, shockproof. But it was no night scope, and night was upon him.

Something moved. He wiped his eyes and

looked again. There, through the glaucoma of dark and drizzle, an immense silvery shape filled his field of vision.

Maybe two hundred yards upslope, big as a steamroller, a boar grizzly struggled for higher ground. The bruin threw its head from side to side in an arc of pain. Even at that distance, the ragged wound in its skull was as visible through the scope as the pronounced limp from what must be a festering hole in its right forepaw. Both significant injuries. Harvey knew they must send blinding jolts of distress along the enormous spine.

All the easier to bring this bear down.

Still, in its prime, a six-hundred-pound adult male could pursue a bighorn sheep uphill, downhill, and sidehill. It could bring down a bull elk in full rack and could pick up a matched male in its teeth and throw it down a riverbank. It could hear the bleat of a calf a ravine away and charge faster than a running cougar a fourth its size.

But number one among its abilities was an acute sense of smell, seventy-five times more powerful than a human's.

Holy Moses, what a monster!

Now a sudden switch in the direction of the wind sent it blowing straight uphill and with it, Harvey's fear scent. Like something out of a horror show, the bear stopped, tested the wind, and turned to look full-face into the scope.

A twisted, jagged snarl filled the entire frame. Harvey jumped, slipped, the rifle rattling out of his grip. Panic flooded his chest, set his skin afire with needles of fear. *It looked at me. Into me.*

He snatched up the rifle and again snugged his eye tight against the scope. He froze.

The grizzly had vanished.

Harvey scanned the upper slope with the lens. *Nothing.*

Soon as he heard the rumors of a rogue bear, without telling Cathy, he chased the thrill. She thought he was deer hunting. Instead, he was in a hole, nobody had his back, and he was lucky if a few hundred feet separated him from the killing machine.

A suffocating horror took over. He imagined the visceral hatred that the bear's wounds and the smell of a human body triggered in the creature's primitive brain. He imagined being downwind of it, secure, master of the situation.

A human left it maimed and filled its nasal cavity with the scent of brutal man. Deeply wounded, the bear had probably lain low in brush for days and nights before it could move again. Leaving behind a trail of crimson red, it would instinctively hobble to a river to cleanse the raw places and to numb the agony.

When the wounds closed and the bear was at last able to cover longer distances, it began a confused and tormented wandering south until it reached this watershed, far from its northern ancestral range. Sheer physical strength and deranged drive enabled the beast to cover considerable distances despite the disabilities.

But its size also demanded food, and the waning of summer meant fewer roots, grass, and remains of dead animals. In diminished capacity, the grizzly lost weight at a time when it should have been fattening for winter dormancy. The paw wound became infected; the tender pad pounded excruciating torment at the beast's every step.

It was ravenous. It was insane.

It was coming for him.

God is my rock, my strength, and my deliverer, he'll rescue me in time. God is my rock . . .

The Sunday school chorus filled Cody's head, a slender slingshot against the mighty thunder of Goliath overhead. The cannonades were farther apart now. With each one, he felt like one of those mechanical ducks in an amusement park shooting gallery.

He was soaked to the skin, sick and half blinded by lightning, when he saw the opening in the rock. Not much of a cave, it was a bare slit in the rock at the top of a long gash filled with stony debris that tumbled down the mountainside out of sight in the last light. He was scared by the storm and the huge scale of the terrain farther on, but the beavers had left enough fallen saplings strewn near for him to drag them over and lean poles against the outside. He could cover the poles with fir boughs as a windbreak.

Running and stumbling, he sought cover.

He threw the pack inside the cave, which went in about ten feet. From what Cody could see, the ceiling slanted upward from back to front until it was probably eight feet off the floor at the cave mouth. He hurried to gather the poles the beaver had neatly limbed, the smaller branches no doubt going for their own lodge. His legs were lead weights. He wanted to fall down and sleep for a week. The sudden cold and wet further drained his strength. The storm had moved farther down the canyon so that he no longer was the target of lightning bolts, but he felt unsteady on his feet and feared hypothermia.

When he had a dozen poles arranged side by side in lean-to fashion, the world went dark and he could do no more. In the morning, he would interweave smaller branches to bind the whole, then cover the makeshift wall with thick boughs.

He planned to stay put for a day, rest up, keep out of sight. What did the cop shows call it? *Lay low.*

Lay low, sweet chariot, coming for to bury me in Rome . . .

Head fuzzy, it was all Cody could do to peel off wet clothes and pull on dry longjohns. His fingers wouldn't work and the nausea increased. *Bacteria in the beaver water?* He slipped icy hands inside his shirt and under armpits to warm them. He sat on bare feet. What he needed was fire. As soon as he felt better, he would seek dry needles and twigs from beneath the trees and see what he could get going. Put on more layers.

His mother entered the cave and sat across from him. Why didn't she speak or offer him a sip from her thermos of hot chocolate? She didn't stay long, said she had to get back, and before he could get his package of licorice open to offer her one, she was gone.

Sucking a length of sweet red candy, he dreamed. Dreamed that his mother came back with a tray of hot baked cookies. Hot casseroles. Hot tamales. Hot sauce. Hot bratwurst. Hot pots of hot brats, lots and lots. Dreamed that he could hear, and hear not only the regular sounds most people could, but the sound of fingernails growing, eyeballs gliding in their sockets, skin cells hitting the ground, another person's thoughts. For this dream, he had the ears of God.

Miners' lamps shining from their heads, the search party halted.

Deputy Overman motioned for quiet.

A shriek of terror sounded in the night.

Sheila's hands flew to her mouth. "Cody!"

"All due respect, ma'am, that was a man's voice. Wally, you and the boys come with me. The rest of you keep moving."

Nick stepped forward. "I'm coming too, Deputy. Please. I've trekked every jungle and rainforest between here and Madagascar. The families will feel better if one of us goes along."

Sheriff Myers nodded.

Swift and without hesitation, the hunters led the way down a slender side track, their rifles a comfort in the disorienting night.

Nick was behind them. The deputy brought up the rear.

"Don't let Darren Schotzel get under your skin." It was as if the deputy spoke of a barmy old uncle. "He can be as popular as a skunk at a christening, but he buys his share of rounds at Mossy's Tavern, so the guys put up with him. A few of these mountain boys are pretty rough around the edges but would be the first to cook your grits, as the saying goes."

The storm stalled right above them. A brilliant flash of lightning turned the dripping forest fish-belly white, and the deafening boom of thunder echoed through the canyons and draws, clumsy and loud as a drunken giant.

From out of the flash, running straight at them, came a member of the undead.

Eyes sunken hollows, face drained of color by another flash, the man stumbled toward them as if not in control of his own movements. Jerky, dazed, and covered in blood.

Schotzel shouted, "It's Harv Comfrey. He's missin' half his scalp!"

CHAPTER 17

Sheila shifted again, back against the un-yielding bark of a Douglas fir, and pulled her jacket tight around her, trying not to think of what the grizzly had done to Harvey Comfrey. Tried to remember all she'd learned from Cody about courage and optimism. Tried to will him safe.

It was so cold. Cody had to be so cold.

"God." She whispered the word. It felt strange. "God, I'm no match for this. I need you. Cody needs you. Please, God."

When it came, bright spotlight pinpointing the landing site, the Mercy-Flight helicopter settled onto the open meadow where the search team now regrouped. The medics stabilized the traumatized hunter and administered a tranquilizer that finally ended the man's constant babbling. "Came on . . . so fast . . . had my head . . . raked the hide right off me . . . ." He was unable to give them an accurate fix on where he encountered the bear. He thought he'd run a long way, and severe blood loss confirmed it.

Sheriff Myers wasn't surprised the man was little help. "He's addled and plenty lucky his brains are still in his head."

Sheila held Comfrey's hand and stroked the pale, furry knuckles. Then she was left standing in the open field beside a small pile of bloody gauze watching the copter shrink into the night. She prayed that six rifles would be enough.

Cody had none.

Of course she knew Cody could ride a bike with no hands, and his heart was the heart of a Scottish warrior. Mothers knew these things.

What she didn't know was if she would ever see him again.

Stop it, Sheila! Remember the good times. Remember the summer of the Bay Days Parade, when you learned that Cody could teach a college seminar on empathy.

It was one of those sparkling hot June days when the Dixons and the Fergusons enjoyed not only each other's company, but that of about fifty thousand other central Californians. Popcorn and cherry snow cones flowed. Beth and Cody had a cotton-candy-eating race and by the end had blue sugar coating their lips, noses, eyebrows, and hands.

Cody marched with the Deaf Power kids and distributed pamphlets to the spectators, urging them to support the organization that sponsored educational and fun field trips for the hearing challenged.

When it had been time to pack up and head home, Cody was in an animated conversation with a little girl who spent the entire parade with her back to her parents and all the fun, looking sad and unhappy.

"Let's go, Code-man." Andy went closer and gestured for his son that it was time to go. He smiled at the little girl.

"Just five minutes, Dad, okay?" Cody hoisted the child onto his shoulders and spent the extra time parading her around the scattering crowd. He used his allowance to buy her a balloon and a snow cone of her own. By the time he set her down and put her hand in her mother's, the little girl was hugging everyone, beaming, and waving goodbye to "Captain Cody."

Sheila teased. "So, Captain, who's the lovely lady? One of the Deaf Power kids?"

"Nah, Mom. Julie's not deaf, she's friends-impaired. Her best friend couldn't come and she missed out on most of the parade, so we did our own Julie Days Parade right here. Nice kid."

Friends-impaired. If only more kids would take the time to know her son and appreciate what a friend he could be.

One of his friends was Flossie Larose, the elderly former star of stage and vaudeville. Cody met her when he and his classmates took holiday treats to a nursing home.

Flossie told Cody he could do better. "Don't be talking to an old has-been like me or you'll soon be washed up too. My son thinks I'm senile, but I'm only a little hard of hearing. Nothing wrong with my hearing when I was Lady Larose, singer and dancer extraordinaire!" Whereupon she would belt out a warbling rendition of "Lady L the Memphis Belle."

Cody asked to visit Flossie once a week, listened to her songs and her regrets, and was there when she died of heart failure six weeks later. Cody cried. "Her son was wrong, Mom. She was only as old and weak as he told her she was."

"Sheila, you awake? Sheila?" Andy bent over her at the edge of the meadow. "You holding up?"

"Holding up, Andrew. Worried sick for Cody. What do we do?"

"Keep looking. Keep believing." He held

her and offered a swift prayer.

She needed his strength.

He took her cold hands in his warm ones. "What were you thinking about just now?"

"Anything but that poor man's injuries." She looked away at the spot where the helicopter had been. "Thinking that Flossie Larose died of a broken heart just like Dr. Cody said."

Surprise dawned on his features at her train of thought. "Yeah, the Memphis Belle. He was so considerate of her."

"So how come he went off like this? To get back at us?"

"No, honey, I don't think he's got a mean, vindictive bone in his body. He's confused, held back, frightened. His brain's not firing on all cylinders, and he doesn't know what that means. He wants to get on with life, but others keep looking for solutions to his 'problem.' He's past that. He wants options."

Sheila nodded. "I know. I've — I've held him back."

Andy knelt beside her. "Oh, Sheila, we all have."

"No, Andrew. I mean it. You tried to tell me, but I wasn't ready to give up the reins. I'm sorry. I want another chance and I'm so afraid God won't give me one!" She burst

345

into tears.

Andy held her. "He's not like that. He loves Cody and isn't about to let him out of his sight."

"I want to believe that, Andrew, I do. I'm just not quite there yet."

"What can I do to help?"

She reached into her bush hat and pulled out a tissue. "Let me work it out on my own."

"You sure?"

"This letting go and relying on God is new to me. I need to work it out for myself."

Andy hugged her. "Sure. I can do that. But, honey?"

"Yes?"

"I'm praying for you."

She leaned her forehead against his chest. "Thanks."

Cody jerked awake. The wind howled through the little cave like a lost soul. The doorway of poles had collapsed in a jumbled pile of pickup sticks. He couldn't feel his feet and barely his hands. *Forget discovery. Need fire.*

He struggled to sit up, then looked around the cave, but no suitable fuel presented itself. The cold made brittle rods of his joints, and like a crone, he fumbled, bent over to the cave entrance. The rain had slacked off, and he felt beneath a rotted log for dry bark and tinder. Wood chips left by the helpful beaver produced more dry starter. He added some short, thumb-sized branches to the mix and stumbled, shivering, back to the center of the cave.

He pulled the box of wooden matches from the waterproof pouch in his pack, and with trembling hands and a third match, managed to coax a wisp of flame into catching the surrounding duff. It blazed into life. Just that small flash of orange sent a surge of hope into Cody's limbs and helped steady him until a decent fire made the shadows dance.

Hugging his legs, he sat as close as he dared, regular gusts of wind whipping smoke and sparks into his eyes and lungs. It mattered little. It was enough to feel the warmth creep back into flesh and bone.

I heard that thunder. I did. Why didn't my ears hurt? Wouldn't thunder that close, that loud, hurt my ears?

Not if they were useless and didn't work.

But it went through me, all through me, inside me. I heard it. I did. I still do.

FORGET IT! You can't hear now.

"Anymore, you mean." Was he two people? He felt strange and defiant and confused. It was as though the boys who had once taunted him were with him, phantom tormentors rubbing his nose in the awful truth.

Beth's face smiled up at him, her pretty hair fashioned from tongues of fire. Warm, perfect Beth. How much happier he would be if she were here . . .

Her image floated into his mind. He could see her there, sitting beside him . . .

That funny feeling grabbed him in the stomach again, but he didn't blink the image away.

"So, Code-man, let's hug for warmth." They started to when he decided he should go back to the dream. He sucked on a stiff licorice whip and let his mind wander back.

He fed another stick into the fire. He felt sick, all buzzy and weird.

A pair of yellow eyes peered from the dark, then blinked off.

Cody went rigid. Had he really seen them? Would those eyes return? It was not so much that there were eyes in the night — it was the wilderness; he expected other creatures to be out there — but the height at which those eyes had peered down. How many wild things were *that* tall? Perhaps it was a trick of wind-blown embers and a weary mind.

Or a bear.

He waited, every nerve ending alert.

He knew; he just knew in his knower. A beast waited for him out there. He'd watched about lions on Animal Planet. He knew how they could wait. Until that exact moment when he bent his head down to drink from the stream.

Cody's heart raced full throttle. Try as he might, he could not think of the words to "Jesus Loves Me." The song he could think of, he didn't want to sing. *What good are ninety-nine bottles of root beer anyway?*

He needed wood. Big wood. The fire was dying. Wild animals didn't like fire.

After what seemed an ice age, Cody sat up and removed a glowing stick from the ashes. He crept toward the cave mouth. Wind whipped the firebrand brighter, then nearly blew it out. The storm moaned past the cave, the darkness filled with the snappings and creakings of unseen bones.

Those eyes. Those were bear eyes.

Grizzlies could run as fast as a horse could run and this time of year — the fattening time — ate one hundred pounds of food a day.

Cody weighed eighty pounds.

He blanched. He read too much. Knew too much. *A grizzly in black-bear country? Canada, yeah, but rare this far south. Most grizzly attacks are over in less than two minutes. A grown male grizzly can crush a man's chest or snap his neck like a twig. The stomach contents of some grizzlies contain the partially consumed remains of —*

He hurled the flaming stick into the night.

It smells me, the fear in my sweat. It knows I'm scared.

Wasn't there a story in the Bible about a bear eating some bad kids? Or was that the Brothers Grimm? *Lord Jesus, I've been bad. After all my parents have done for me . . . Don't let me be eaten!*

He ran to the pack and fumbled inside. *Where is it? Where?* Clothing. The remaining food. Matchbox. An interesting rock from High Bay Lake.

It's not here! He patted down the outside pockets. *Flashlight. Knife.*

Shaking, fingers roamed again over the pack. *There!* He felt the contour of the hated thing and dragged it from the pack.

He turned to face the cave entrance, knife with main blade extended in his right hand, the flashlight in his left — and the security whistle clamped between his teeth. Drawing in a deep breath, Cody inched toward the mouth of the cave.

At the entrance, he gripped the knife, snapped on the light, squeezed eyes shut, and blew like there was no tomorrow.

Before long, he felt lightheaded, lay down again next to the fire, and curled into a ball. "Mama?" His thin frame shook. "Mama!"

A strong, foul smell entered the cave. Like rotten fish and old wet carpet.

And death.

CHAPTER 18

Cassie watched the hopeful lightness of dawn pink the darkness like the first stroke a painter makes on a blackened canvas. All she had to show for three hours of interrupted sleep was a nagging headache and a lower back in revolt. Everyone else looked as rugged as she felt. The hunters and the officers split into two smaller units, trading off a search of the surrounding areas with an hour and a half of fitful rest.

The searchers came to the junction with the trail to Snowball Lake. Roscoe seemed eager to head down slope to the lake rather than up the steep grade of the main trail.

Light rain came and went.

"Roscoe says down."

Sheriff Myers scanned the way ahead. "Cody likely went that way for water. Visibility's increasing, so those who can pick up the pace, let's do so."

"Anybody seen Schotz?" Frey looked from

face to face and met with a rash of head shaking.

"He's probably answering nature's call. The guy's got a teacup for a bladder."

"Or he got into some bad guacamole. He lives for his nachos and beer."

"I don't think I've actually seen him since just after we left the meadow."

Roscoe strained at the lead. "Take off, Pete, we're right behind you. Darren's got a weapon. He knows the area and can take care of himself. Let's go!" The sheriff led the way down the muddy decline.

Ahead, they heard a shout.

Nick and Andy rushed on, then heard a distant, "Nah. Too old. A discarded bootlace, is all."

"Keep looking."

Sheila stood apart, craning her neck up the main trail.

"Come on, friend, I'll walk with you." Cassie held out a hand.

"No, Cass. You go along with the others. I just need a moment alone."

"Sheila, I can't leave you by yourself. We've got to stay together with that bear out there. C'mon, girl, what do you want to bet we find that rascal son of yours trying to drink the lake dry? But if not, the plan is to come back and continue along the first trail."

"All right, Cass, but give me a moment to catch my breath and think things through. Thanks."

"I guess. I'll just visit the bushes a minute. Must be all the water I've been chugging."

"Okay, you go ahead. Stay close."

"Don't worry."

Cassie ducked behind a tree while the men slid down the muddy slope to the lake.

Sheila waited, heart banging, until Cassie was occupied before continuing on the trail they'd been following. She labored to the top of a steep incline. There the trail flattened out, and she picked up the pace.

My child needs me. I've got to do something.

Call it a sixth sense or a mother's intuition, either way she knew in her core that her son lay in that direction. She had to reach him before the bear did.

Don't tell Andy or Cassie. Seek forgiveness later. Don't hesitate. I let him get into this situation and I've got to get him out!

It was taking too long. Her child was in danger. This was no time for niceties, not if she ever hoped to have a new start with Cody. It wouldn't be the first time a mother had defied everything and everyone to get back what she was in danger of losing.

Jaw set, shoulders squared, she broke into a trot in the direction of the rising sun.

Okay, Sheila, let's get down to that lake." Cassie emerged from the bushes. "Sheila?"

Maybe she visited a bush herself.

"Sheila! Give me a shout."

Nothing.

A sneaking suspicion crackled along Cassie's spine. "Sheila!"

Not again.

Cassie ran along the beaten trail and up a steep fifty-foot grade. At the top, she searched the terrain ahead and could just make out Sheila's slight figure and bobbing light in the distance before it vanished into a field of jumbled boulders.

What is she doing? Did she see something?

Cassie raced after her.

The sound of the distant whistle brought a smile to his scruffy face. He ran a hand over the week's whiskers and wondered if Marl would like them. He'd been out trying to get a deer for her. For them. Now they might end up with something sweeter than venison. Maybe five or ten thousand buckaroos!

Things were looking up. He fingered the

355

outline of the referee's whistle he carried in his pocket. *Me and the kid have the same "scare the bear" equipment.*

He didn't like Californians. Those rich sons-a-guns thought they owned the planet. Once they built enough freeways and bought up all the beaches and paved over the earth in their own backyard, they just up and moved and repeated their destruction in somebody else's backyard.

They should go back to their own kind. Not, however, before I help 'em find their kid. His rescue should put his parents in an especially generous mood. He's a smart little brat, I'll give him that, but green as grass.

Nobody had spent the kind of time he had in these woods. Nobody knew them as well as he did. From a long line of moonshiners, who routinely conducted their business on forest land, he had a nose for these things. Schotzy had done a little side search of his own and found a red licorice whip dropped along the rock outcrop that slanted away from Bald Knob. Had to be the boy. Dumb deaf kid wasn't so smart and careful after all, was he? No sense in telling the others until he was ready to turn the kid over to the authorities. He'd catch some flack for doing his own thing, but that would all be in the past soon enough.

He bet the kid would follow the natural curvature of the topography toward the snow chute. There was the smell of smoke and metal to the air — electrical discharge and a couple of lightning-struck snags still smoldered. Gusts of icy wind whipped everything into a froth like an unseen whisk. Everything, he imagined, including the lost boy's skin cells, scattering them and their scent far and wide. Roscoe should have been retired long ago. He was old and confused and unreliable. Still, nobody wanted to offend Pete by suggesting his precious hound was a has-been.

By the time the others came back to search this knoll, Schotz would have his quarry.

The sound of the whistle proved him dead-on.

The burning question was whether the boy had actually seen a bear or was just through playing wilderness commando and ready to be found. *More 'n likely, the storm scared him silly. He wants out.*

One thing was sure. Marlene didn't give a flying fig for his excuses, and she could be more ferocious than any bear he'd ever met. North Bend was dead-ends-ville, far as she went. The mountain view was spectacular, but who could eat scenery? But there was no escape on what little he brought in. He always kept an eye out for supplemental income.

"Get off your duff, Schotzy, or I dump you like yesterday's coffee grounds." She liked plain talk. "A part-time fella is a part-time provider, and one thing I ain't puttin' up with for forever. You think I like livin' in this rinky-dink camper day in and day out? Gerbils don't live this tight. You say you love me, but you can't get me some space a woman can call her own? That ain't love, Schotzy boy, that's low ambition."

Nobody said Darren Schotzel settled for low ambition. Nobody.

And there was another thing that was going exactly nowhere. Either him or Marl couldn't have kids, apparently, because did you see any kids? And where would they put a kid in that camper? They might make some room on the top shelf of the medicine cabinet, but that was about it.

Schotzy had a hard time saying no. To Marl. To alcohol. To penny slots. The only thing he'd managed to say no to in thirteen years was moving back to Seattle. Schotz and the Emerald City were like milk and beer — they did not mix. Every time he went near the place, he woke up in jail or detox.

He'd get Marl that space of hers. They just had to get out of here and then could figure out this baby thing when the pressure was off and they had some elbow room. He wouldn't ask much in the way of a reward. A few thousand would cover first and last months' rent, and what parents didn't think their kid was worth that?

Schotz thought of his own parents and decided not to go there.

The shrill whistle in the creeping dawn went on and on. Schotz got a good fix on its location. His smile widened. The kid was whupped. He'd run into the arms of any rescuer, no questions asked.

Schotz was only too glad to oblige.

CHAPTER 19

Cody's head pounded. Throat brittle dry, jaws aching, he blew against death. *Can't stop. Mustn't stop. Please, God, make the bear go away.*

Dawn's feeble light didn't help. He could sense the thing, out there, waiting, a hunting machine, claws and teeth stained bloody red from past kills.

Mom. Dad. I'm so sorry for the awful way I've . . . for being so . . . You were only trying to protect me from . . . from . . .

It was half a minute before he understood what he was doing with his thumbs. Why he was pressing them hard into clenched hands. He wasn't making fists to ward off the evil beyond the cave. He was pressing the imaginary button connected to the lamp at his mother's bedside.

He flung his hands out and shook them, as if, could he only get them to detach, they'd take the memory of the loathsome button with them. But they remained in place. He felt sad, but glad too, because he wanted to summon his mom to save him from the big bad bogey bear.

Everything wrong I could do wrong, I've done.

I came alone.

I told no one where I was going.

I covered my tracks so I wouldn't be found.

I saw bear sign and wrote it off.

I walked right into their feeding territory.

I've backed myself into a cave and the only exit is guarded by a bear.

It can smell me. Stinkin' me!

Genius!

He tore open the pack and rifled for the plastic bag of ripe cheese. At the mouth of the cave, he flung the fetid lump into the gloom.

"Smell *this!*" Maybe stinky cheese would cover the scent of his fear and sweat.

Fat chance.

Even the strong smell of wet socks can attract bears.

He fell to his knees and was punished by the hard granite floor. He didn't care. The sore knee shouted and he shouted back. "Stop hurting, please stop hurting!"

Cody massaged the knee and swiped at the tears. His guts churned. The only things going for him were the fire and the whistle his mother forced him to carry, both of which wild animals didn't like. Except that now the fire was dying and the only available fuel was out there.

"You shall not be afraid of the terror by night . . ."

A sob tore from his chest. He spit the whistle out and was consumed by a violent shaking. How much was fear, how much a falling core temperature? He could see his breath. *Hypothermia.*

I need wood. Fire was life-saving warmth. A shield from the bear.

Cody fumbled with the buttons of the thermal shirt and fastened them to the neck. He tied his boots tight, clamped the small flashlight between his teeth, and with a last shuddering breath, limped into the first real stab of dawn.

Where are your wives?" Sheriff Myers looked at Nick and Andy in disbelief. "First the boy, then Darren, now those two? This isn't funny!"

"Nobody's laughing, Sheriff." Nick grabbed Andy's arm. They'd lost an hour getting to and from the lake and spending too much time poking around the shore. They'd gotten nowhere. "C'mon, buddy, let's check the main trail. Knowing those two, they've taken matters into their own hands."

Sheriff Myers shot out an arm to stop them. "Hold it right there! You two aren't going anywhere. I'll radio it in and have our guy in the sky keep an eye out."

"Those are our wives, sir, and you can't stop us!" Andy glared, the muscles of his jaw working a wad of gum.

"You're wrong, Mr. Ferguson. This is my jurisdiction, and I'm not having five tourists off on their separate wild goose chases."

Nick cupped hands to mouth. "Cassie! Sheila!" He started to storm away when Wally Frey and two of his fellow hunters stepped across his path, rifles slung at the ready.

Nick turned to glare at the sheriff. "Am I under arrest?"

"No, but you will be if you keep this up. Let us do our jobs."

"So far, that's produced nothing!" Andy paced. "You saw that hunter's condition last night. With a crazed bear out there, we don't have time to hunt and peck like this. You've got to *do* something!"

"And I'm doing it. I radioed for more manpower from two adjoining districts, and I'm glad to say that the rock climber has been found safe and only a fractured arm to show for it. The people from that search will join us. We're all frustrated, but if we keep it together, we can have the best outcome, and you'll all be reunited by nightfall. Deputy?"

Deputy Overman hurried over. "Yes, Sheriff?"

"I'm going over there to place a radio call to have our sky guy keep a watch for the wives and let us know their position. Please keep an eye on these two. They try to go anywhere on their own, arrest them."

"Roger that."

The radio crackled to life. "Base One to Unit One. Unit One, do you read, over?"

Sheriff Myers snatched the microphone to his mouth. "Base One, Unit One. Talk to me, Marcia, over."

"Air Rescue has sighting at Harlequin, one person moving north up the chute past Outcrop Cave, another moving west of the chute, possibly a third just at the southeast corner of the mouth of the cave. West acknowledged the plane; North did not, nor did the third person, over."

Nick and Andy slapped each other's back. "That's gotta be them!"

Sheriff Myers held up a hand for quiet. "Don't jump to conclusions." He spoke into the handset. "Roger that, Base One. Is gender apparent, over?"

The radio snapped and fuzzed. "Negative, Unit One. Air Rescue reports a faulty gauge, unable to do thorough reconnaissance, must return to base. Difficult to distinguish detail in light and shadow conditions, over."

"Roger that, Base. We can reach the site within the hour. We'll radio Life Flight if needed. Unit One to Base, clear."

The clamor resumed and again, Sheriff Myers raised a hand. "Please, gentlemen, I don't have the answers. What I do know is that there are some steep drop-offs west of the cave and with that bear still on the loose . . . well, suffice it to say someone new to the area could get into serious trouble."

"Then we'd best make tracks." Nick raised his eyebrows.

The sheriff nodded. "Let's move out. And you two stay where I can see you."

The wind started to die in the growing light. The air was tangy cold and smelled like the charcoal from a Roman candle — a smoldering, lightning-struck tree. Darren Schotzel smoked a cigarette and watched the firelight grow small and dim in the hollow of the granite rock face below him. The sky in the east high over Tight Grip lightened. Here, lower down at the beginning of the subalpine declension known as the Harlequin Snow Chute, dark was reluctant to leave.

He zipped his jacket to the throat and raised the collar against the chill. He tried not to think of the flesh hanging off Harv Comfrey's head.

Ironic how this party of greenhorns was from California, once home to thousands of grizzlies. Old Ephraim, an infamous California cattle killer, had outsmarted posses for a dozen years. When they finally shot him, he tipped the scales at more than a thousand pounds.

The kid suddenly bolted from the cave, guided by a small flashlight. In less than a minute, he dragged dead wood into the cave and immediately the small hole in the rock blazed orange. Back out went the kid, quickly returning with an armload of fuel for the fire.

Schotzel removed the cigarette and picked a stray bit of tobacco from his tongue. The dying storm winds gusted in fits and starts. He shivered.

Nice of the kid to make the cave all cozy for company.

A third trip, and the kid hauled in wet wood, judging from the smoke that poured from the cave mouth. The shrilling of the whistle resumed, and he could just make out the profile of the kid on the cave floor, trying to avoid the smoke and find some warmth.

Heartbreaking.

Schotzel stood, rifle nearby, cigarette pinched between the thumb and forefinger of his left hand, a sweat-stained kerchief around his neck. A coil of rope in his right hand came from a hidden equipment stash he kept near where he liked to hunt. In case the kid in his distress put up a struggle.

They'd make their way down the Chute, the straightest line between Tight Grip and the highway. He'd call from the truck stop, and Marl would be there for him with the Ford 4X from the garage. She'd get over her annoyance that he brought a guest and do it in a hurry or he'd give her a thump to straighten her out. Take the kid to town and start spreading the news of how he had risked his life to find the missing and the disabled. Why, he'd be halfway to hero before the sheriff could resume command and arrange the medal ceremony.

Finish the cigarette. Enjoy being in the driver's seat for a change. Some might think it wasn't much as plans went. But his daddy's favorite saying 'bout covered it: "It sure beats shootin' hoops with a bowling ball." It was the only wise thing Schotzy could remember his daddy saying, and it made him feel luck was finally on his side.

On another trip for wood, he saw the grizzly.

Smelled it. Like dead fish.

As if turned to stone, Cody's limbs locked in fear.

Avoid hiking at dusk or dawn.

It stood fifty yards away, blinking, tossing its great head from side to side, testing the air. The right forepaw hung free above the ground. The wind ruffled its long, matted coat. The creature swayed.

It had to be eight feet tall. Claws like meat hooks.

Avoid eye contact. Back off. Increase the distance between you.

The bear dropped its head, ears flattened, clicked its teeth, and exhaled a hissing stream of condensed breath. The tongue flicked out and around the muzzle.

Cody screamed silently at unresponsive limbs. *Move! Dear God, help me move!* He did. One agonizing step backward at a time.

Don't turn. Don't run.

The great head swung side to side.

Don't look like fleeing prey.

Slobber poured from its jaws.

"The Lord is my shepherd."

Cody's chest hurt. He tripped over a small boulder, tried to recover, and fell hard onto his back.

The bear charged.

A rifle shot exploded in front of the bear, spraying its face with granite shrapnel. The animal changed course and disappeared into the trees.

Darren Schotzel still had it in him, even if his aim was a little off.

CHAPTER 20

Sheila prayed nonstop. She refused to think what the rifle shot meant.

The wind diminished, moaned, and darted between the trees in fits and starts. It no longer rained. Instead a damp frostiness dug for her bones the minute she stopped. So she didn't stop.

Cody was near, the feeling as real as the throbbing in her head. His external world was smaller than a hearing person's. He wouldn't keep going indefinitely. Whether he would admit it or not, he liked the familiar. Needed it. So much big, strange territory, though fun at first, would soon begin to frighten him. That's when fatal mistakes happened.

She switched off the flashlight and listened to the rapid beating of her heart. Morning's creamy pink glow highlighted the ragged remnants of storm clouds tossed recklessly about the sky. She hesitated only for a moment, then fished the cell phone from the pocket of her fleece and prayed for a signal.

Amazed when she got through, Sheila half hoped she would have the answering machine message upon which to collect her thoughts. She was not prepared for Father B himself to pick up on the second ring.

"Father Byron Wills, St. John's Cathedral." The line suffered only a little static. Even at this early hour, he sounded alert, vigilant, on guard for the church. The familiar rich baritone made her throat tighten.

Her voice, on the other hand, rang like a small lost child's. "Father B, this is Sheila Ferguson."

"Sheila? Is that you? Thank God! I tried calling but couldn't get a connection. Is everything all right? How's Andy? And the Dixons? How's Cody taken to frontier life?"

A reply caught in her throat. She stood silent, shivering, afraid, and alone. Her silence spoke volumes.

"Take my hand, dear." Father B was calm, resolute. "In your heart, reach out now, and I'll grab hold."

In her mind, she felt the grip of that kindly hand and saw before her the caramel brown complexion, the clear luminous eyes, the slightly rakish goatee, and the blue brocade vest finely stitched with ancient Christian

371

symbols.

Sheila took a long breath. "He's missing, Father B. Cody got separated from us and has already spent a couple of nights on his own. We thought he was adapting, having a good experience. The police and a search party are helping look — there'll be a rescue plane up again today — but no sign of him yet." Her voice caught. "A badly injured hunter had to be airlifted to the hospital. Bear attack. I can't stand the thought of Cody out here alone. He needs me, Father, and I'm not there for him."

"Nonsense, Sheila." The voice at the other end of the line was gentle, yet firm. "There's not a mother alive who could completely corral a healthy, inquisitive boy like Cody. Nor would you want to. He's closing in on manhood and needs to take responsibility. Go easy now. Don't dwell on past choices, but on finding Cody. What do the police say?"

She took a deep, shuddering breath. "I'm on the side of a mountain ridge near where we think Cody may have hiked to. I have the strongest sense he's close by but it — it's all so big."

"Can you put Andy on? I'd like to hear his take on things."

Sheila held her breath. "He's not here."

"Sheila, it's but six in the morning. Where could he be?"

She wanted to cry. "He's with the other searchers a mile or more from here. He — I left without telling him, Father B. I know that's awful, but please don't call anyone. Not yet. Give me a chance to work this out on my own."

Father B did a slow exhale. But if she expected to be chastised, it didn't happen. "What can I do, Sheila? How should I pray?"

She loved him for that. No speculation. No harangue. No judgment. "Just be there. And would you call the Midnight Church? Cassie says when they get with God, things get done." Cassie told her that whenever the homeless and the street people gathered at St. John's for "after hours" intercession, answers came in juicy clusters. All Father B had to do was hang his little homemade wooden sign by the back door to the fellowship hall. In simple block letters, it read, "Midnight Tonight." It was as unauthorized as it was unorthodox.

"I will. And before my morning cornflakes, I'll pray a covering over you all."

"Thank you."

"Indeed. I'm still praying this trip of yours turns out to be a gift."

"A strange gift." Suddenly she could not stand the thought of him hanging up.

"That's what they said about the Christ child, and you know how well that turned out."

She smiled. "I hear you, Father B."

She kept the phone to her ear long after the connection had been broken.

Cassie didn't know when she got off the beaten track. But here she was, trail petered out, nothing but a jumble of brush and fallen logs ahead. An unpleasant dampness crawled down her back like the night she had driven into inner-city LA and gotten lost. The street came to an abrupt stop at weeds, a rusted metal barricade, and a chain-link fence. Somewhere in the black distance was the concrete expanse of the Los Angeles River. At her back was a half block of busted streetlamps and condemned housing. Unseen dangers held a feeding frenzy in her mind. Never had she been so glad to find a well-lit convenience store despite its barred windows and the wary Asian man behind an equally fortified cashier's cage inside. Armed with his directions, she sped away in one piece from an imagination at full howl.

Now the howlers were back. As she

trudged along the way she'd come, she felt beast eyes upon her and rising anxiety. *Help me, God. Help me.*

Schotzel angled down the slope, far enough above and behind the boy's rocky retreat to remain undetected.

Why'd the little goof run back into the cave? You don't run from your savior.

He wore the coil of rope like a bandolier. He wanted his hands free. It wasn't inconceivable that the kid had a weapon. *Or is mentally unstable.* Or would panic, run off, and fall down the snow chute. Maybe this wasn't such a good idea. It wasn't much, but no sense in losing what little he had.

And Marl? If he botched this, she'd drop him like an empty soda can.

Cut the crud, Schotzy. It's a kid, for crying out loud. Walk in there, throw him over your shoulder, and tell him to shut his pie hole or you'll shut it for him. Except he can't hear you say it, so you use a little back-of-the-hand sign language.

You're in the driver's seat, Schotz. You.

Sheila followed the trail downhill. On the Forest Service map from her Swiss army hat, it said the country opened up near something called Harlequin Snow Chute,

375

five hundred feet lower in elevation and maybe a mile southeast of the spot where Father B's voice had renewed her hope. The topography contours showed sharp, steep terrain all around the Chute. While he had no map, the natural tilt of the terrain, a boy's thirst for open spaces, and the contour of the rocky trail might guide Cody to gravitate there.

The forest smelled new. She couldn't remember air this fresh. It kept her mind from fearful thoughts and spurred her to cover ground. Next stop, Harlequin Snow Chute.

Never had he been so scared of dying. Was there a more horrible death than being eaten alive?

Cody's eyes locked on the world framed by the cave entrance. Where was the bear? Where were the angels of God that stopped its charge and sent it crashing into the woods?

"Cripes, that was close!" Had he been holding his breath the whole time?

His head ached outside and in, his muscles sore, his limbs unyielding as if they'd been soldered stiff. Eyes puffed and vision blurred; skin and flesh nicked, scratched, scraped, and otherwise abraded. And a general tingling of the skeleton that came and went, source and destination unknown.

So fast had the bear vanished that for a few minutes he actually thought it might not have been a bear at all, but a mirage cooked up by the cold and an overworked mind. Then he remembered the paralysis and the animal's charge and knowing he would die. Hollywood couldn't come up with a special effect that real.

He got the smoldering fire under control by subtracting the wet wood, tossing it down the shale slope in front of the cave, and grabbing a couple of dry sticks now that he could see. He wore all the clothes he had and the nausea passed.

He finished off the now-slimy bulbs he'd harvested from the mud at the beaver dam and one more of the red licorice whips. There should be one more whip, but he probably ate it sometime in the confusing night.

The meal didn't satisfy, and with the awakening of his appetite, he was hungrier than before he'd eaten. It was the same with water. He licked up the moisture clinging to the leaves of an alder bush just outside the cave door, which only further reminded him how thirsty he was. He needed to move on, find a stream and more fern and berries.

How did bears do it?

It's all they do.

Still, he was not quite hungry enough to eat the fat white grubs squirming in the rotten wood of a thick branch, too punky with moisture to burn. He set it aside. The insects would live to squirm another day, and that thought brought him some comfort. Good company was hard to find.

He repacked the contents of his pack, but the knife he placed in his vest pocket and the whistle he kept around his neck. At the mouth of the cave, he watched the world awaken. Sadness gripped him. He didn't want to be out here anymore. He didn't know where he wanted to be.

God bless Mom and Dad . . .

Whistle in his teeth, lungs filled with air, he blew hard and angry.

I'm Cody and I'm still alive!

The sudden blast of the whistle directly below startled the bear-tense Darren Schotzel. He lurched to one side, feet flying from beneath him, fell, hit the sharp slope, and tumbled off the edge, legs and arms flailing.

Sheila stopped. First the rifle shot so near, and now the shrill bleat of a whistle, plain as day! Her heart soared. *Cody?*

Is that a cave down there? Tumbled boulders and loose rock, rugged cliffs. A gash in the earth that could only be the Chute. In another three months, the place would be wild with ice and avalanches. All that loose rock and the steep drop said stay away.

Perfect boy country. She almost yelled for Cody, then caught herself. Instead she turned toward the sound, picked her way slowly along the rough geography, gradually worked her way down, joy almost trumping caution half a dozen times.

He's alive. Alive! "Thank you, God, thank you!"

A rain of dirt and stone gave the man away just before his body hurtled past the mouth of the cave, struck the ground, and rolled down the shale slope.

Cody yelled and jumped backward as if burned. It took a moment for the situation to register, but he soon shrugged off the pack and ran-slid down the slope to help.

The man, a coil of rope around his body, dug heels in the loose earth, and stopped his fall. He just lay there, palms clamped to forehead, torso rocking slowly side to side.

Cody bent over the man — there was blood in his hair — and put a hand on his shoulder. "Mister, hey, mister! You okay?"

In a flash, the man wrapped Cody in a clumsy headlock. Shocked, but on his feet, Cody had the advantage and instinctively dropped a knee into the man's middle. The arms fell away long enough for Cody to scramble away uphill.

Why'd he grab me? Is he loony? What's he want? Instinct said run.

A man's boot toe hooked Cody's ankle, and he fell flat against the hillside. The man twisted onto his stomach and grabbed Cody's left ankle in both hands. Cody kicked back with the free foot and connected with bone.

Free!

Without another look, Cody crab-crawled up the slope. He half sprinted, half fell into the cave.

Dead end.

Cody jerked back around. Too late. The man, face streaked with blood, reached up and grabbed onto a jagged ledge of rock to steady himself and step up the last rise into the cave.

Cody reached into his vest pocket, slid out the Swiss army knife, snapped open the large blade, and with a lunge forward stabbed the back of the man's hand. The bloody face contorted into a scream of pain.

The man staggered, again lost his footing, fell backward — and tumbled out of sight.

Cody dropped to his knees, trembling and blood-smeared. He puked. His mind wouldn't process what had happened.

Wouldn't. Couldn't.

When Sheila heard the scream, she almost missed the narrow defile leading to the mouth of the cave. The whistle was silent, but she had at least a general fix on its location. It looked as if there was a hole in the rock where a young boy, *her* boy, vinegar and adventure at low ebb, might spend a cold and stormy night.

Her heart pounded. Who else was down there? That wasn't Cody's voice. *Slow and easy. No sense in getting ahead of yourself.*

She planted one careful foot in front of the other on the damp rocks, not wanting to add herself to the flotsam down the snow chute.

Moving as quickly as she dared, Sheila stepped down into a thin gap between two stone formations. The cave entrance should be right around the corner. *Hang on, baby, hang on!*

Cody backed away from the mouth of the cave until shoulders scraped the sloping stone ceiling and he could back no farther without getting on hands and knees. Bent double, elbows on knees, he fought rising panic, struggled to catch his breath.

Who is that man? What does he want? Everything he'd read said outdoorsmen were generally trustworthy, helpful, only too eager to have you enjoy the wilderness as much as they did. But this maniac . . .

All he has on him is a rope. For rock climbing?

The next thought made him lose his breath again.

For tying someone up?

It had to be. He had no other visible gear for a longer stay in the woods.

His parents had told him to watch out for nut jobs.

Cody had to make sure of the man's location. He threw on his pack, then hefted the spongy branch alive with grubs. It was surprisingly heavy.

He started forward, every muscle tense.

A shower of rocks to the left.

A hand slid around the edge of the cave entrance.

Without a second's thought, Cody shot forward and swung the branch around the corner hard as he could against the place where he judged the side of the person's head to be.

The sodden branch exploded in a hail of wet wood, dirt, and grubs.

Cody didn't hesitate. He bolted for the right side of the cave, scrambled out and up.

That's when he saw the plane.

Elation so intense it threatened to burst through his chest filled him, then doubled when he saw the pilot waggle the wings in recognition. He flapped his arms like a wounded mallard, received one more waggle from the sky, and the plane disappeared.

Save me! Now! Please!

Cody couldn't stay there and wait. The deranged man would have him long before rescuers ever arrived.

He scrambled to the top of the slope. A faint animal trail skirted the snow chute away from the cave. He raced ahead and tried not to look back.

CHAPTER 21

Cody ran across granite and low, flat alpine scrub. He topped a prominent rise in the terrain and dashed down the other side. *If I stay in the open, I'm too exposed. Got to find cover.*

A movement to his right. No. Seeing things.

He ran low to the ground to relieve the pressure from the sore knee.

Pungent smells were everywhere. His own BO reminded him that he'd never sweat so much in his life. He felt better in the open air, away from the smoky cave. A patch of pale yellow wildflowers gave off a sweet, honey-like aroma. Though the day began to warm, bracing hints of the recent storm remained in the sharp air and damp earth.

So did rotten fish.

Pray with me, buddy." Nick's long strides were matched by Andy's. In the lead, Pete and the hunters set a mile-eating pace, and this time it was the beefy Sheriff Myers who fell behind, with Deputy Overman ferrying the radio.

"Thanks, Nick. My mind's a mess. You go."

Nick slapped him on the back. "Father God, we're afraid, but we're counting on your love to save Cody and Sheila and Cassie from harm. Help us, weak as we are, to find them soon. Protect us from danger. Bless Harvey and help him recover from his injuries. Thank you for the officers and the hunters and everyone out searching. We bless you for the best outcome and will give you the glory in Jesus' name."

"Amen!" The benediction came from the deputy, who had nearly caught up. "The Proverbs say to trust in the Lord with all your heart. They don't tell you that in police academy, but it ought to be on page one!"

Cody froze.

The bear emerged from the treeline far to his right, and Cody imagined its lungs whooshing with exertion.

Heart in his throat, he forced his gait to remain steady. He smelled what the bear could without a doubt — a sour mix of sweat and terror. The animal moved with purpose, despite its hobbling injury. But Cody knew . . . hunger would overcome physical limitations. In no animal was there a stronger will to survive.

The bear disappeared behind a rocky shelf.

Jesus loves me this I know.

When he again saw the bear, the bear saw him. It stopped, rose to its full height, pawed the air with one agile limb, and opened its jaws wide. Cody couldn't hear the roar, but on the inside it rattled every cell he owned.

He lost it. Yelled. Hurled a rock in the bear's direction. Blew on the whistle like a madman.

Enraged, the grizzly hit the ground on all fours and charged.

Sheila moaned. She touched the side of her head and instantly yanked the hand back. A knot the size of a large egg lodged between her left ear and what she hoped was still the top of her head. Dirt and bits of rotted wood clung to her hair. She felt a small, soft blob and pulled it away between her fingers.

The thick white larvae squirmed; a tiny head thrashed side to side. Sheila flung the wormy creature away, pawed at her head, and cringed until shudders of revulsion subsided. She found the Swiss army hat and gingerly put it back on.

She didn't want to, but forced her eyes open again. Pain throbbed and ugly purple blotches bobbed in her vision. Her fingers came away from her scalp, wet and sticky with red.

What did I run into? All she could remember was reaching around to steady herself, and the next second a blinding flash sent her to the outer reaches.

"Ow!" The effort it took to stand was considerable. She swayed on unsteady feet and squinted into the cave.

Empty but for a smoldering fire.

She looked around at the shattered remnants of the rotten log and wrinkled her nose at the fat, dislodged grubs wriggling at her feet.

She stumbled back out into the spreading sunlight and carefully removed her pack. Out came a water bottle and T-shirt. She soaked one with the other and applied a moist compress to the swelling. Slowly, her strength and her senses returned.

Did my son just clobber me? Why? He's deaf, not blind. Didn't he know it was me? Or is he that desperate to be free?

Her head couldn't take too many questions.

All she knew for sure was she had to find Cody and convince him to stop this — this — *whatever* it was he was doing. He had everyone's attention. He didn't need to keep on running. Out here, that could get you killed.

Gritting her teeth against the pain in her head, Sheila found her way back to the top of the snow chute. It was breathtaking how it started here where tons of snow accumulated each winter, then swept downward for thousands of feet to the valley floor. Over time the weight of snow had ground the rocks fine and scoured the chute of all vegetation. The unobstructed view from five thousand feet to ground zero gave her vertigo. She hastened to the top where the high country topography leveled off and forced herself to stay focused on the ground around her feet.

Which way did he go?

Every five minutes, she enlarged the circle, looking and praying for some clue. Nothing. The hard granite was unyielding, the scrub as coarse and unrevealing as steel wool.

It's taking too long.

"Lord, help me. You are the God of that which is lost. Cody's lost. I'm lost. We're all lost without you."

■ ■ ■ ■

Cassie was about to turn in the opposite direction when she saw it — a shiny red object, four feet upslope in the brush. It was caught by a ring of metal at one end and held off the ground by a dead twig sticking up above the scrub. Had it not caught there, the object would have fallen out of sight into the leaves at the heart of the bush.

A Swiss army knife. A father's gift to a son.

What on earth? Cody would never have parted with the prized possession. Either he had dropped it without knowing or — or what?

In the distance, she heard the faint blasts of a whistle. It was a pattern. Three short blasts, three long, three short. Repeat. A half dozen times.

Unless she was mistaken, and it had been a while since her Girl Scout days, that was Morse Code. SOS. The international distress signal.

The whistle stopped but its message hung in the air. *Dear God, it's Cody! Hang on, buddy, hang on!*

He couldn't believe it. His mind screamed one fact over and over: *Grizzlies are scarce around here. I read that!*

With a quick glance over one shoulder, Cody danced out along the top of the boulders that formed a narrow rampart jutting into the dizzying space between earth and sky. The earth fell away and the sky was the biggest he'd ever seen.

His chest constricted; boots fumbled for a foothold. The massive grizzly, with its pronounced hump and silver-tipped fur, filled the space where rampart parted with earth. It roared its fury and paced where the scrub brush ended and the thin fingers of stone began. Its great head and massive shoulders bobbed like a compass needle thrown off by minerals in the surrounding rock. It placed its good paw, large as a dinner plate, onto the jutting stone, then snatched it back.

Cody felt top-heavy, flat-footed, uncoordinated. He told himself not to look down and when he did, it was as if the mountain suddenly shifted and he was Superman stripped of all super powers.

A wave of nausea made legs wobble and

head spin. He could not hold on.

He slipped, started to pitch forward, wind-milled his arms, twisted his body around, and fell back into the chasm.

CHAPTER 22

Cody couldn't move. Small rocks and dirt dislodged in the fall rained down, pelting him in the face. Mosquitoes attacked the Giants cap on his sweat-drenched head.

He'd landed hard, but thankfully the pack had absorbed much of the impact. He could wiggle fingers and toes, but his left leg felt as if a giant had clapped two rocks together with his knee in the middle. Sore, but he could move it. What he could *not* do was catch his breath. It felt like someone had duct-taped his chest so tight that the lungs had nowhere to go and were folded small as a deck of playing cards.

He struggled to sit up but was wedged, feet up, head down, into the armpit formed by two slender prongs of gray-black rock a dozen feet below the lip of the Chute. He lifted his head and saw that the pack straps were what constricted breathing. They were pulled taut in the fall, caught fast by the forked limbs of a fallen tree.

He panicked. *I don't want to suffocate!*

Wrenching his torso first one way, then the other, he snapped one limb. Sweet oxygen entered his lungs.

He slid out of the freed strap and twisted onto his right side, gritting his teeth against the pain in his knee.

After a third hard yank, the remaining limb cracked in half and spun into the abyss. He slid.

Cody jarred to a stop against the pack, his head deep between the twin prongs of rock.

He stared straight down the throat of the snow slide and shrieked.

Sheila's heart clenched at a sound both familiar and foreign.

Her son's voice. That she knew well. But the sound it made was one she'd never heard before.

Screaming. In sheer terror.

Cody!

She stumbled, tripped, ran on. "Being blind separates you from things, but being deaf separates you from people." Helen Keller, who had long been Cody's inspiration, inspired Sheila now. He was *not* alone. She would not let him be. Mother and son could connect. *Would* connect. *Hang on, Cody!*

Suddenly, she was caught by the arm and whirled around.

Cassie! Out of breath, hair wild, eyes wilder, she jerked Sheila into a mighty hug.

"Cody needs me."

"I know. I heard. Let's go!"

The two mothers ran like the wind.

The blood rushed to his head. Cody closed his eyes, squeezed out the terrifying sight of the hundred-foot drop onto bare rocks. He prayed, lifted his head, and squinted for sight of the bear. The sun blinded. Good. Had the beast still been there, its bulk would have blocked the sun. The animal had moved off.

He felt for the whistle and fished it from where it had come to rest above and behind his head, still attached to the twine.

It had nearly slipped off. He didn't know why he was so glad it hadn't. What good had it done him? It hadn't scared off the bear. No one had answered his distress signal.

Sweating in the increasing heat of the day, Cody carefully lowered his legs, sat up, removed the cap, astonished that it was still there, and brushed the dirt from his hair.

By pressing back against the cliff face with the good leg and focusing straight out at the expanse of the Cascade Range, he avoided looking down.

He regarded the surroundings. He was caught in a cup formed by the twin fingers of rock jutting from the cliff face, and a couple of scraggly, but good-sized fir trees clinging for life in the crevices. There were wide gaps between the rocks and trees, and the "bottom" of the cup was a loose platform of fallen stones and forest debris precariously trapped by a web of exposed roots and shale.

Every time Cody moved, the web trembled. Every time the web shifted, shale and loose soil slipped between the roots and fingers of rock and plunged down the throat of the slide zone.

Think of something else. He grabbed his ears and squeezed to quiet the pounding in his head, willing the blood away from his brain. He felt hot and disoriented, the sweat and dirt and fear coating him in desperation.

The ears he clutched were useless for anything but appearances. In his nightmares, he sometimes cut them off, threw them in a dumpster, and went to live in a bell tower like the Hunchback of Notre

Dame. Unable to hear the pealing of the bells, he "rang" with their vibration like a human tuning fork.

They aren't coming. No one's coming. Nobody comes for deaf kids.

"God!" He yelled it, even though there was no one there who could hear it.

"I am with you."

Oh! At the reply ringing within him, tears cleaned a path through the desperation.

"I will answer you. I will be with you in trouble. I will deliver you and honor you."

Cody sobbed. He was tired of being deaf. Of being Eagle Arrow. Of playing Indians in the woods. Of being alone with his thoughts. Of people assuming he was stupid. Of people disapproving because he didn't want to be forced to learn a foreign language that was spoken with the hands. Of being the one who had to change.

He was missing a sense. He couldn't hear. Wasn't that change enough?

"God!"

"He shall give his angels charge over you . . . in their hands they shall bear you up, lest you dash your foot against a stone."

He looked up at the blue and heated sky just as an enormous bald eagle floated to a landing in the top of a three-pronged snag. Its back to him, it perched on the edge of a giant, tightly woven construction of dead branches, fir boughs, and twigs, and fanned its mighty wings. Clearly visible between the bird's impressive shoulders was a distinctive splash of white.

It was the same magnificent bird that had left his dad and him awestruck on the trail.

A shower of gravel rained down and a football-sized rock crashed past, nearly striking his left leg. A distinctive stench filled his senses . . . Cody went sweaty cold all over.

The grizzly was back.

Wait, Sheila, wait!"

They were in a strange world of wild vistas and gut-wrench-ing vertigo. Massive steel transmission towers cut a swath up forested slopes and over raw, barren granite. A loud hum and sizzle attested to the electrical mega-wattage surging through the lines overhead. On the ground near them and behind the metal gridwork of one of the tower footings was a utility box, its thick, plastic-insulated wires exposed. The box's protective plastic covering lay in the brush.

Cassie didn't want to think about what had torn the box apart.

"I'm sure Cody's screams came from that direction."

Sheila made to go on but Cassie held fast. "Don't, Cass. Don't try to stop me."

"I won't. I want to help. There are a million places to fall around here. Let's be careful. And what happened to you? You look like you were in a fight."

Sheila's lip trembled. "I think Cody was scared and mistook me for something — or someone — else. He whacked me a good one. Oh, Cass, what if I lose him? I couldn't live with myself. My stomach's in knots."

"Let's trust God to not let that happen."

Sheila, eyes glistening, looked at the ground. "I'm glad you came after me, Cass. I couldn't do this alone. I'm beginning to see I can't do any of it alone."

Cody could guess what made the bear so relentless. Survival. The need to feed. It was shabby and straggly, obviously hurt. The bruin had probably retreated to the dark shelter of the trees to lie down rather than risk the precipice where its prey had fallen. Feeling old and near death, its resolve came and went. But Cody, caught like a moth in a web, could mean easy prey.

More gravel rained down. The bear couldn't figure out how to reach him, but it wasn't giving up.

God, make it go away.

The eagle watched from the tree. It aired its wings, extending the feathered marvels six feet from wing tip to wing tip.

The eagle flexed its legs back toward its body to rest on the edge of the nest. Cody knew three toes pointed forward, and one toe pointed back, gripping the perch and staying locked until the bird awoke and straightened its legs, releasing the lock. It had to be that way, otherwise sleeping birds would fall out of trees all the time.

He tried to take comfort in the presence of the eagle.

But he shivered and fought not to think of what lay below. No one could survive that fall to the rocks. And above . . .

The adventure had gone wrong. Very wrong. He wanted no more of it.

Maybe this is what I get for being a bad kid. How am I ever going to get out of here?

"He will call upon me, and I will answer him . . ."

"God, Jesus, help me, please!"

It was a full five minutes before it struck him that no gravel had rained down in all that time. He leaned out far as he dared and looked up.

No sign of the bear. *Where is it? Did something else distract it away?*

That's when he saw them. His mother and

Cassie picking their way cautiously along the escarpment, peering down into cracks and fissures looking for him. He almost cried out, then bit his tongue. He couldn't shout out to them and have them come running, not with —

His stomach dropped. Now he knew what had distracted the bear and why it no longer waited for him above.

It stalked the two women.

Frantic, Cody snapped his head back and forth, scanning the rock face for a way up. Too far. Too crumbly. Too steep.

Too late.

He was going to freak. He fought for air. Fought to stay conscious. Fought to hear the voice of God.

"No harm will befall you . . . angels . . . to guard you . . . cover you with . . . feathers . . ."

There. An exposed root, a narrow channel up — if he was Houdini. More easily, it was a channel from which he could fall like a weighted stunt dummy, only it would be his broken body in the stone graveyard below. Perhaps they wouldn't find him and he would spend the winter locked in ice and snow, every avalanche taking him lower and deeper and colder —

Shut up!

Something snapped under his weight. The

loose network of root, soil, and rock tipped, dropped, and jerked to a halt. Cody leapt for the thick, exposed taproot and for one sickening moment he guessed it was not enough. Then he slammed into the unforgiving rock and grabbed hold of the tough, fibrous network with both hands.

Eyes and teeth clenched, he hung there, knowing it was that split second before the elevator cable snapped and he plunged to the basement of the world. He forced his eyes open to watch the Giants baseball cap sail away, shrinking to the size of a doily, and flip twice before it was swallowed whole between the ancient lips of two time-encrusted boulders.

The terrible jagged throat of the snow chute raced at him. Dizzy, confused, he fought the urge to let go. *Idiot! This isn't jumping off the roof at home. Hang on! God, help me . . .*

Eyes again squeezed shut against the horror, he prayed not to fall. He was light-headed, wobbly, voted most likely to wimp out. *No! Mom needs me!*

His arms and legs were made of jelly. Panic hit him so hard, he hyperventilated and couldn't get enough air. It passed.

"And under his wings you will find refuge."

Seconds later, boots braced against the

rock, he prayed for the strength of Samson and climbed.

CHAPTER 23

"Why doesn't he blow the whistle again?" From the look on Sheila's pale features, her mind was not short on questions. "Is he hurt? Is he alive —"

"Don't, hon. Don't speculate worst-case scenarios." Cassie put an arm around her friend's waist, willing calm into her. "Come on now. We're trusting. Hoping. Believing. Remember?"

She turned back to the path — and almost passed out.

A grizzly rose on hind feet, not thirty feet away. It threw its head from side to side, and let loose a ferocious bellow that echoed in her bones. The great gaping maw bristled with teeth, glistening like ivory daggers.

All feeling fled Cassie's legs; she sagged to her knees. She tried to shield her friend, but both women stumbled over each other as the grizzly pawed the air, then dropped to all fours and charged.

With a savage cry, Cody sprang from behind a Volkswagensized boulder and ran straight at the bear, a dead branch hefted in his grasp like a vaulting pole. Before Cassie could form the words to scream at the boy, he rammed the branch into the bear broadside.

The spear sheared off, three feet from the tip. Cody tripped and went down. The grizzly veered sideways with a loud *whuff* and contorted the front half of its body to bend toward its injury. Clamping powerful jaws over the remainder of the pole, it snapped the wood in two.

Cody stared into the huge furry face and saw murder in the creature's eyes. The grizzly loosed a primal bellow and came at him like a runaway semi. Cody jumped up and bolted for the concrete footing of the transmission tower, followed by the stench of rotting fish.

He swore hot breath seared his neck.

Exposed utility box wires. Thick as vacuum cords. He dashed behind them, putting them between him and the unobstructed opening in the steel-lattice pylon. Grabbing up the plastic-covered wires, Cody bent them like a horseshoe, braced, and turned.

The bear, roaring and whuffing, closed

the final twenty yards and threw itself at the gap in which Cody stood framed. In reflex, Cody cringed and thrust the wires forward. The bear crashed into the steel girding and snapped its slavering jaws shut on the live wires.

Just an instant after Cody let go.

Even so, he was close enough that the power surge knocked him on his fanny. The crackle and spark of thousands of volts surged into the bear's body. It thrashed once, stiffened, face frozen in dumb shock. Then the beast quivered and stilled.

The electrocution was final.

The smell of scorched flesh covered even that of rotting fish.

Arms grabbed Cody, lifting him. He looked up into his mother's face and wrapped his arms around her quaking body. Together they rocked, transfixed at the sight of the dead giant, its expired body wedged tight in the pylon opening, mouth, tongue, and teeth a blackened hole.

Tears streaked Cody's cheeks. He looked at his mother. "I thought it would kill you, Mom."

She stroked his head and kissed him. "Me? Oh, sweetie, we thought it had taken you. We prayed so hard —"

"Me too." Cody sobbed. "I was so scared,

Mama . . ."

"Me too." Cassie knelt and put an arm around them both. "God is here."

"And our hero. God's hero." Sheila looked at Cody, and he saw wonder in her wide eyes. "Crazy, amazing kid! You were braver than brave. Most *men* wouldn't have reacted that fast." She bathed him in kisses until he squirmed from her grip.

"Good thing I didn't give it a whole lot of thought!" He shook his head at the bear and started to cry again.

Sheila pulled him close, looking down into his face, her smile proud and warm. "You and that Internet."

"Mama, how come the side of your face is all scraped and swollen?" Cody gently picked bits of wood from her forehead. Then his eyes widened. "Was that — Were you — ?"

She kissed the top of his head, then looked into his face. "Shush, it's nothing Cody. Just nature's way of correcting a stubborn woman's blindness."

He hugged her neck. "Mom, I'm really sorry. There was this guy who grabbed me. I freaked. I thought you were him." He just finished filling them in on the bear's earlier visit and the weird attack by the man at the cave when Sheila pulled him to his feet and pointed. "Cody, Dad's here."

He spun, and when he saw his father running toward them, Cody flew across the uneven ground. "Dad! *Dad!*"

He threw himself at his father, oblivious to Nick, the hunters, the sheriff's officers, and an excitable bloodhound dancing and straining against its leash.

His father, tears streaming down his cheeks, lifted Cody high off the ground and swung him around, before setting him on his feet. "Code! Oh, Code!"

Cody hugged his dad's neck. "I'm sorry I made you worry, Dad. Sorry I hurt you. It was a crummy thing I did." He sobbed.

His dad held his shoulders. "You mean the world to us, Code-man. Thank you, God. We'll work this out." He held an arm out for Sheila. "Are you and Cassie okay, honey? What happened to the side of your face?" He gently wiped her tears, then looked past her, eyes widening. "Good heavens, is that a bear? Is that *the* bear?"

Nick drew Cassie close. "What a way to go."

One of the men in camouflage was already at the carcass, poking it with the barrel of his rifle.

Sheila brushed dirt from Cody's back, then turned him around and brushed the front. "You won't believe what your son did."

His father kissed them both. "I'm beginning to think I might."

Cody swiped his runny nose with the back of a hand. "I needed to prove something to myself. To you guys. See what I could do."

"Did you?"

Cody swallowed hard. "Yes, sir. I proved that I can get myself into a whole lot of trouble, without any help at all."

His father hugged Cody again.

Sheila's eyes shone. "You're not the only one, Son. Stubborn, impulsive behavior runs in the family. Sheriff, I'm sorry we just took off like that. Mother bears want to protect their cubs. We don't always think it through. And, Andrew, I owe you an apology for a lot of things."

The large man in the police uniform mopped his brow. "There'll be time for those discussions later, Mrs. Ferguson. Right now I want to ask Cody a few questions, including what happened to Darren Schotzel. We found him back a ways in the snow chute with a broken leg and a bruised ego."

"You know that guy?" Cody shook his head. "He tried to grab me and he had a rope like he was gonna tie me up!"

The female officer smiled. "Easy now, Cody, we'll sort it out. For now, this is Sheriff Dan Myers, over there is Pete Borders and Roscoe his tracking dog. I'm Deputy Claire Overman, and these here are some local hunters who pitched in to help find you. Wally, Ted, Clifton, George Bates, and George Sorrelli. They all deserve our thanks."

Cody shuffled his feet and looked at the ground. "Thank you, everybody. Is any of my birthday cake left?"

Nick laughed. "We decided to wait until we could all enjoy it together."

Cody regarded his dad. "Don't suppose there's any hot dogs left?"

His dad grinned. "I'm sure we can find an old shoe for you to chew on back at camp. Here, put on this sweatshirt and eat this energy bar."

Cody struggled into the shirt and wolfed down the bar. "Can I invite everyone who searched for me to my party?"

His mother frowned, but her eyes gave her away. "*Party?* You'll be lucky to escape the rock pile. You can invite them to your chewing out."

Most of the men laughed.

Frey pointed at his mom and dad. "You're lucky to have parents like that, kid. If mine had been half as concerned about me, I wouldn't have wasted so much of my life."

Overhead, two eagles circled their interrupted world.

"Look at that." Andrew pointed skyward. "The bigger one has the same markings we saw on the eagle in the woods, Cody. That's a good sign."

"Yeah, it is."

The eagles spiraled lower, craning their necks.

Cody's words came between sniffles. "Bet you they're good parents too."

CHAPTER 24

The Dixons, the Fergusons, and the officers were airlifted back to Dodge Creek Campground while the hunters minus one returned to the hunt. The bear's remains were flown in harness to the Fish and Wildlife field station at Draper's Corner for autopsy.

After Cody answered the sheriff's questions and Darren Schotzel was confronted with the testimony, the sharp-faced hunter confessed his plot to extort money from the Dixons. He was clapped in the county jail to await trial, bail set at $250,000.

The next day they shared belated birthday cake at the Dodge Creek campsite. Cassie played photographer and made Sheila relight the candles three times before she got the shot she wanted.

Cassie watched Cody think long and hard about his wish and hoped it came true, in spades.

Deputy Overman stopped by the campsite, then Joanie arrived to collect them for the return to SeaTac Airport and the flight home.

". . . and man-y more!"

Those gathered finished the birthday song with an exaggerated flourish. A subdued Cody, sporting several fresh Band-Aids, sat cross-legged in the middle of the picnic table, knee reeking of deep muscle rub. He held a hot dog slathered in mustard and relish in one hand, and a fat slice of Dutch oven cake with melted chocolate bar frosting in the other. On his head perched a cardboard crown fashioned from a soda pop box. His mother sat behind him, arm around his chest, eyes aglow with his safe return.

Something's troubling him. Cassie wondered what it could be.

She had cornered Sheila that morning in the tent. "It's going to work out, you know. You've seen how much he's learned and he's seen how much he's loved. Each of us loses sight of those things at one time or another."

Sheila's answer surprised her. "You're right. In my mind, Cody was still a little six-year-old who sometimes needed help getting dressed. But he moved way beyond that. I've discovered a young man who is bright and capable and full of plans. I hope he'll discover a mother who can change and not be a roadblock."

At the picnic table, Andy Ferguson cleared his throat and hoisted a can of root beer. The others followed suit with their beverages. "To God, for answering our prayers and giving his angels charge over our son. To everyone who worked hard to get our boy back. To Cody, for his safe return, sharp instincts, and lessons learned. To Sheila, my loving wife and devoted mom, for putting up with the guys in her life. And to all of you, for your friendship and devotion to duty, for sticking by us and keeping us sane in our hour of need."

His voice caught, and when it looked as if he could not go on, Nick started singing "Amazing Grace." The others chimed in as they were able, including Deputy Overman. All grins, Nick added an original verse of his own:

"When we found Cody safe and sound,
His body in one piece,
We gave God thanks, his eagles too,
For all our fears did cease!"

Andy waved his arms to get Cody's attention. "So, Son, when we get back to civilization, what else would you like for your birthday?"

Cody glanced at his mom. "Do you think I'll ever go camping again?"

She smiled. "Well, your dad and I talked, and he's going to look into a backpacking trip in the Grand Tetons for next summer, just the two of you."

Cody whooped. "Then my wish just came true! Thanks, Mom and Dad, that is too cool! In that case, I'd like a new whistle. Mine got lost, and I think they come in handy, yes?"

That got a laugh. "And one other thing. The rest of the money to pay off the Buck hunting knife I've been saving for."

Sheila walked over, removed his crown, and plopped her Swiss army hat on him instead. "Then you might need this!" Another laugh, and then a giant watermelon that had been cooling in the stream was hauled dripping cold to the table for slicing.

"Mom?"

Cody looked at the ground, shifting his weight from one foot to the other. "Could I tell you something?"

Sheila looked up from the watermelon.

Cody opened his mouth to speak, squeezed his eyes shut, closed his mouth, took a deep breath, and exhaled. He took a firmer stance, both feet solid beneath him.

Cassie saw that Nick, Andy, and Joanie had stopped eating and sat silent, watching. It felt like a scene from a movie, where in freeze-frame, everyone and everything stopped while the camera swept the perimeter, emphasizing the breathlessness of the moment.

And then a single leaf would move, breaking the spell.

Cody's hands were that leaf.

He touched his lips with the fingertips of both hands flat, then moved the hands down and forward from his chest until their palms faced up. "Thank you." He made the motion again. "Thank you."

Sheila's hand flew to her mouth and trembled there.

Cody dropped one hand, but held the other up, fingers curled in a loose fist. His pinkie finger rose straight up — "I . . ."

Down with the pinkie, up with the forefinger, and out with the thumb — "love . . ."

Down with the forefinger, thumb and pinkie out — "you!" He smiled and repeated the motions. "I love you!"

Cody pointed to himself again. "I am" — one hand, fingertips to palm, thumb up, circled his heart — "sorry."

An open hand encircled his heart, then he placed hands together in a washing motion, and finally pointed to himself. "Please forgive me."

Sheila started to rise, to go to him, but an upraised hand stopped her. Cody pointed to himself. An open hand, fingers together, moved forward from the side of his head in a downward thrust. "I will" — a hand out, fingertips to palm, thumb up, pushed forward and slightly upward — "try. I will try."

Andy stepped from the assembling shadows. "Sheila, honey, all aboard . . ."

She took his hand and kissed it, then looked at their son. "Cody, show us again how to say, 'I love you.' "

He did, and then the three embraced as if they might never let go.

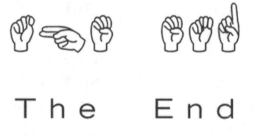

The End

ABOUT THE AUTHOR

C. L. Kelly is a communications specialist for Seattle Pacific University and the author of *Scent,* the first book in the Sensations series, as well as novels for both children and adults. As a journalist and freelance writer, he has written on a wide variety of topics from dinosaurs to child rearing. Clint and his family live in the Seattle area.

The employees of Thorndike Press hope you have enjoyed this Large Print book. All our Thorndike and Wheeler Large Print titles are designed for easy reading, and all our books are made to last. Other Thorndike Press Large Print books are available at your library, through selected bookstores, or directly from us.

For information about titles, please call:
(800) 223-1244

or visit our Web site at:
http://gale.cengage.com/thorndike

To share your comments, please write:
Publisher
Thorndike Press
295 Kennedy Memorial Drive
Waterville, ME 04901

419